Nobody who lived in Provincetown would ever forget that summer.

Not the wet summer, when the rains wouldn't leave, and the tourists wouldn't stay.

It was the weird, angering, frightening summer when we were allegedly invaded by an alligator and definitely invaded by a vicious-tempered journalist. Most of us thought the alligator less threatening.

Not the hot, dry summer, when the rains *wouldn't* come . . .

. . . it was that crazy, funny, fearsome summer when the actors came to town and brought laughter and romance and murder with them . . . murder that would seem to have been committed by one of our most beloved citizens.

As innocently as *that* summer began, and bizarrely as it ended, Provincetown was her usual early-season self . . . charming, sparkling, breezy, energized and just a *tiny* bit greedy. We watched the parade of cars and buses come over the hill like an invasion of benign and colorful insects; we watched the excursion and ferry boats sail into the harbor with self-satisfied oom-pah pahs. We heard the whine of airplanes approaching our runway. Provincetown—we thought—was ready.

The world was our codfish.

Other Bella Books by Jessica Thomas

Caught in the Net *A winner of the Golden Crown Literary Award*
Turning the Tables *A Golden Crown Literary Award Nominee*
The Weekend Visitor

MURDER
CAME SECOND

Jessica Thomas

Bella
BOOKS

2007

First Edition

Editor: Cindy Cresap
Cover designer: KIARO Creative Ltd

ISBN-10: 1-59493-081-3
ISBN-13: 978-1-59493-081-2

To Bunny with special love, and a toast to our future meeting on that little village green near the cozy little pub!

And thanks to my editor, Cindy Cresap, who almost makes it all seem easy.

About the Author

Jessica Thomas is a native of Chattanooga, Tennessee, where she attended Girls' Preparatory School. She later graduated cum laude from Bard College, Annandale-on-Hudson, New York, with a bachelor's degree in literature.

After an early retirement, Miss Thomas spend a bit of time doing some rather dull freelance assignments and ghostwriting two totally depressing self-help books, always swearing someday that she would write something that was just plain fun. When her friend, Marian Pressler "gave" her Alex and Fargo, Jessica took them immediately to heart and ran to her keyboard.

Miss Thomas makes her home in Connecticut with her almost-cocker spaniel, Woofer. Her hobbies include gardening, reading, and animal protection activities.

Chapter 1

Nobody who lived in Provincetown would ever forget that
summer.

That summer. The weird, angering, frightening summer when
we were allegedly invaded by an alligator and definitely invaded by
a vicious-tempered journalist. Most of us thought the alligator less
threatening.

Not the wet summer when the rains wouldn't leave, and the
tourists wouldn't stay.

It didn't take visitors long that year to figure out they could sit
around, damp and chilly, watching little stop-and-go rivers on
their windowpanes at home . . . a lot cheaper than they could do it
at a motel in Ptown.

That summer. The crazy, fearsome summer when the actors
came to town and brought laughter and romance and murder with
them—murder that would seem to have been committed by one of
our most beloved citizens.

Not the hot, dry summer when the rains *wouldn't* come. When

1

the air was so sticky you felt you could wipe it off your skin, and the rain teased us every afternoon, sending in the high, rolling cumulus clouds, dark and heavy with unspilled water, heat lightning signaling from inside them like a candle flickering behind a curtain. But without a drop of rainfall. The summer when wafts of hot air sent small dust devils cantering slowly up Bradford Street, gritty and weary, as if they'd just ridden in from Laredo.

Neither overly wet nor dry, *that* summer came to us with a disarming smile and wearing spring's clothing. The tulips and daffodils and hyacinths gave us just the right sugary look, and we were almost ready. We touched up the paint and starched the curtains. We washed the windows and spread our wares. Owners of shops and restaurants rubbed their hands in anticipation. Most old ring-up cash registers had been replaced with quiet, computerized models, but to those who punched in the sales figures, the carillons of tourist expenditures still rang in their ears with a resonance equal to the bells of Notre Dame.

The tourists were here. They had come to us again. All hail.

Almost everyone who lived in Provincetown was in some way dependent on the tourist. The restaurateurs, of course, plus those who provided lodging, sold souvenirs or sold clothing. I think there must be factories all over China whose workers produce nothing but T-shirts for Ptown. But there were other dependents. There were the grocery stores and the art galleries, the nightclubs and the whale-watching boats, the clinic doctors and the vets who patched up the unlucky and the pharmacists who filled their prescriptions.

The dependents included, to a degree, my Aunt Mae, with her own little "season" every year. When my Uncle Frank died, Aunt Mae got interested in raising herbs, mainly as a time filler. But she became an expert at her hobby and had now converted her garage into a small shop where she sold live herbs in little pots and dried ones in little jars to an amazing number of people. She had actually published two small books on the subject and sold enough to keep them in print.

Even the bank, where my lover Cindy was the in-house certified financial advisor, processed millions in travelers' checks and enjoyed a great volume increase in their commercial accounts. Unfortunately, they also had the wearisome job of trying to help those feckless few who always managed to lose their wallets and/or checkbooks and came into the bank crying *help!*

And of course, there's me. I'm Alexandra Peres. I was named after my great-grandmother, who was herself named after the strikingly beautiful, doomed Tsarina of All the Russias. Aware that I don't fit the first part of the Tsarina's description and hopeful I don't fit the second, I prefer to be called Alex. My work, too, picks up between April and October.

Why? Because tourist spots are like candy stores to children for those who like to make money while posing as vacationers. Most of them are typical accidents—real or imagined—that could actually happen: like slipping on wet tile. Some are more creative, and sometimes not too smart. One man sued the B&B where he was staying because the porch steps collapsed under him. Indeed they did, and when he fell, he was still holding the saw he had used to cut through the supports. Of course, genuine accidents do happen, and several insurance companies keep me on retainer to sort out the possible from the simply frivolous.

Sometimes I also check out other types of insurance fraud. And I do background investigations on potential employees for local businesses. I look for runaway kids thought to be in the area. And, God help me, I am occasionally broke enough to check out a spouse whose other half believes "Something is going on and I damn well want to know what it is!"

Fortunately, following errant spouses is becoming a less frequent endeavor thanks to my learning how to use a camera because of it. I now take a lot of nature photos just for fun and am told I have a good eye for it. Certainly I have a love of it. Of late, my photos have been selling well at several galleries in Ptown and Wellfleet, at very good prices and in surprising quantity. So my finances are considerably more stable than they were a couple of years ago.

This greatly pleases my partner, who has a penchant for expensive rawhides. My partner is Fargo, and to clarify the above sentence, Fargo is a ninety-pound Lab with a lustrous black coat, a personality all his own and a heart beyond measure. He's my pal, my clown, my protector, my confessor, and I'm happy to talk about him and his many attributes at any time.

There's one small character defect I may lightly skip over. When Fargo is faced with, shall we say, a stressful situation, like a firecracker going off nearby, or someone approaching us threateningly, he has felt since puppyhood that he can best protect me if he is in my arms. When he was a puppy it was adorable. Since he is grown, ninety pounds of Fargo flying through the air and landing on my chest is much more likely to render *me* more *hors de combat* than my presumed assailant and leads to embarrassment all around.

So now, when I think this protective move is imminent, I do a little dance step to the side and grab his collar to let him know I am all right. I say sternly, "Easy, Fargo, not now, not now!" He has no idea what it means, but I hope it sounds to humans as if I am commanding him not to attack, and we take it from there. Look, he has never complained about the cold nights we have spent shivering in the car surveilling a house. He doesn't mention that my omelets have been known to defy a steak knife, and he has *never* told me that a particular blouse makes my face look green. He loves me. All right, he's a creampuff. I don't sweat the small stuff.

So, as innocently as *that* summer began, and bizarrely as it ended, Provincetown was her usual early-season self: charming, sparkling, breezy, energized and just a *tiny* bit greedy. We watched the parade of cars and buses come over the hill like an invasion of benign and colorful insects. We watched the excursion and ferry boats sail into the harbor with their self-satisfied oom-pah pahs. We heard the whine of airplanes approaching our runway. Provincetown was ready.

The world was our codfish.

Chapter 2

We were about to have that conversation again.

You see, when Cindy first took the job with Fishermen's Bank, she rented a great little cottage from my Aunt Mae. Four rooms, two of them pretty good sized, plus a small deck overlooking a small pond. She loved it.

I already lived in my house that I'd owned for several years. Five rooms, all good sized, bath and a half and a detached garage, plus a large—for Ptown—backyard.

I loved it.

Shortly after her arrival, Cindy and I began *dating*. Before long we began *dating exclusively*, then next we were *dating seriously*. Subsequently we started using words and phrases like *relationship*, which we both disliked, and *we must have something going here*. Finally, we gave up, declared ourselves in love and wanting a lasting, monogamous *affiliation*.

We breathed a sigh of relief and were very happy. Then slowly, we began to realize that we were one couple with two abodes only a mile apart. Occasionally, I had an overnight business trip, and Cindy would stay at the cottage. Or Cindy would have a seminar somewhere or a weekend parental visit down to Connecticut, and I would be alone at the house. Sporadically, when we were both in town, we simply spent the night apart for no special reason. Usually, we spent weekends at the cottage. Somehow it seemed like a relaxing, faraway break. As time went on, however, the maintenance of the two places began to seem somewhat extravagant, and our friends began making veiled comments, and we began to talk of living together.

In the words of the immortal poet, this scared me to death. I'd been badly burned in some past relationships, and had been leery of becoming involved again at all. I was glad I had. I loved Cindy. I liked her and, as far as I knew, wanted to be with her forever. But *living together* was something else.

There was, of course, the question of where to put things. Like Cindy's computer. The logical place was my office, but my computer was already there, along with a desk and file cabinet and a large table where I matted and put simple wood frames around my photographs. It was not a neat room. Cindy was neat. There were other spatial problems, although most of them could be worked out with a little ingenuity. Actually, "things" were not my real problem, anyway.

My problem was I was afraid I would slowly disappear, that we would become one amorphous mass, no longer each a clear individual structure. I was afraid I would look in my psyche's mirror one morning and see a foggy, shapeless blob. Oh, my head or a foot might poke out once in a while, but basically, Cindy and I would be one colorless splotch. I would be, I was certain, sexually happy, intellectually challenged, entertained, loved and cared for, perhaps even healthier. But slowly I would no longer be Alex as I knew me. I would be *alexandcindy*. And then I would have to run away. Even though I loved her very much.

Now this may not make sense to you. In a way, I hope it doesn't.

But it was a real and present fear for me, and I am sure Cindy must have sensed it. So when we spoke of living together, we verbally trod successfully on eggshells that never broke, because neither of us ever said anything heavy.

Tonight, I guess I felt singularly close to her, and perhaps very safe, for I was just beginning to find the courage to let these little terrors of mine be articulated, when the phone rang.

I wanted to scream, "How dare you ring now?" and rip it from the wall, but of course one never does. One picks it up and says politely, "Hello . . . this is she . . . oh, yes, Bill . . ."

Bill Meyer of the Chambered Nautilus Bed and Breakfast Inn. He and his wife Martha owned and ran it. It was a lovely old building in the Victorian style, with six or seven rentable rooms and baths, all nicely decorated. The downstairs sitting room was filled with genuine antiques plus a baby grand piano which Bill often played in the early evening, alternating light classics, show tunes, a little understated jazz, while the guests enjoyed tea or sherry if they wished. Both owners were thoroughly charming, and not just to their guests.

Their liability insurance was held by Plymouth Rock Security, which retained me to investigate claims in the Provincetown area. Naturally, I had nothing to do with the settlement procedures of serious injuries or serious frauds. Sometimes, however, troubled waters could be quickly calmed by a few well-spent dollars, or frivolous claims could die aborning with the delicate mention of the penalties of fraud.

I figured Bill had one or the other of these problems at hand.

"What can I do for you, William?"

"Alex, we've got the craziest thing I've ever heard of here. One of our female guests—lovely lady, known her for years, a real treasure—climbed up a tree in the front yard and fell out of it, stark naked, screaming there was a six-foot alligator chasing her. There were two other guests coming up the walkway at the time, and they—"

"Bill, did you say she was naked and being chased by an alligator?" I looked at Cindy and entertained a moment's concern that her eyebrows had disappeared forever into her hairline.

"That's what she said . . . still says. But I can't find the damn thing! I've since gone over every inch of the house and shined a flashlight around the yard. They all ran for the house, when she tumbled out of the tree. Mr. Joyner fell up the steps and sprained his ankle. Alex, can you get over here *now?*"

"On my way. And, Bill, stay in the house. Just to make sure." I hung up. Cindy and I looked at each other, then smiled, giggled and finally roared. I ran for the office where I took four crisp one-hundred dollar bills out of the safe where I keep ten of them, for insurance business only. Then I hit the bedroom, peeling off my T-shirt and replacing it with a clean sleeveless mock turtleneck top and light cotton blazer. I figured the jeans would do. I kicked off the sneakers and slipped into my boat shoes. "I'm off!" I gave Cindy a hug, then held her away from me and stopped laughing. "Hold this thought: I love you."

"I love you, too," she answered softly, and then smiled. "Be careful of that gator."

As I backed quickly out of the driveway, I was guiltily grateful that Bill and Martha had an alligator on the loose. A certain conversation would have to wait until another time. Again.

After parking on the street, I walked slowly up the path toward the inn and shined my big flashlight into the limbs of the mimosa tree. To the best of my knowledge alligators didn't climb trees, but something else might have. I saw nothing but a drooping broken branch, the delicate leaves already folding in prayerful farewell. I flicked the light around the flowers and shrubs, again with no result, and climbed to the porch. Bill came out to meet me.

"Thank God you're here! What an unbelievable mess! Gale Withers still swears it was a great big alligator! By the way, she's got a nasty looking scrape from the tree on one thigh. Can she sue? Nobody told her to climb the damn tree."

I wondered if he preferred she had lost a leg to the alligator. "Stay out here a minute, Bill, and give me a little background. Take

8

a deep breath. Nobody needs immediate medical attention, do they?"

"No." He flashed a ghost of a grin. "Unless you count Martha and me. Okay. Gale Withers and her husband have been customers for a number of years. Always pleasant, no trouble, no noisiness, some drinks, but no problem. When Gale got here today and Martha was getting her settled in her room, they were chatting, and Martha found out Gale's husband has left her for a newer model. He served divorce papers on her a few days back, on their wedding anniversary, if you can believe such sensitivity. Her two kids—in their early twenties, I think—insisted she get away for a few days and get her head together before she tries to deal with any of this. I guess she was really shocked and broken up."

I tried to guess who wouldn't be shocked and distressed, and had no luck.

Bill held his hands out, palm up, in explanation. "Of course, the Chambered Nautilus, all of Ptown, for that matter, holds a great many memories for her. I could almost wish she had picked another spot, if that doesn't sound too unkind. Oh, by the way, according to Martha, Gale was knocking back the sherry pretty hard earlier." He shrugged. "That's about it."

I nodded. The poor woman was probably reliving happier days and wondering what kind of truck had hit her. "Do you know if she went out for dinner or just settled for the sherry?" I asked.

"Yes, she did go for dinner. She asked me to book a table for her at the Speedwell." It was an upscale restaurant in town, named for the second ship in the Puritans' little armada, which failed to live up to its name by arriving several weeks behind the Mayflower. "Unfortunately, if I recall correctly, the restaurant was a favorite of Gale's and Tom's in the past. That choice can't have cheered her up, either." He managed a wry smile.

"Okay," I said. "Let's go in."

We entered the sitting room, which at that moment held four people. Bill's wife, Martha, sat a little apart in a wingback chair. A stocky forty-ish man lay on the couch with his left ankle on a pillow and sporting an icepack. A woman about the same age sat in a chair next to him, and a nice looking female in her late forties—Mrs. Withers, I presumed—now quite primly covered in a high necked robe and bedroom slippers, was half reclined on a settee. In addition to whatever damage she'd done to her thigh, I noted a couple of scratches on her arms and one on her face.

Martha jumped up and came to me to bestow a tight hug, which I found not the least unpleasant. "Alex. Are we glad to see you!" she whispered. "This is unreal."

"Have no fear," I breathed back. "The cavalry is here."

I went into my act. "Mrs. Withers, Mr. and Mrs. Joyner, sorry to meet you at such an upsetting time. I'm Alex Peres. I represent Plymouth Rock Security insurance. Martha and Bill are clients of ours, and we want to get you all settled down and comfortable as soon as possible."

I looked at Mrs. Withers and Mr. Joyner. "Do either of you need a doctor this minute, or can you give me just a little time to go over the evening's events?"

Both nodded and gave what I took to be affirmative grunts, so I continued. If there really *had* been some kind of animal, we needed to get the thing off the streets.

"Now, Mrs. Withers, could you please start at the beginning for me?"

"Yes. It's all very simple. My room is in back on this floor, around the corner of the front porch, where the side porch turns back. I returned from dinner. My room was, uh, warm, so I turned on the fan. I made myself a highball and decided to go on the porch and have it and wait for the room to cool. Uh, well, you see, I had, uh, disrobed in order to cool off more quickly, so I, well, I climbed out the window onto the little side porch, where I knew no one could see me. I was sitting in one of the chairs, having my drink, enjoying the breeze, when I heard this kind of scratching noise. I looked up, and this *giant* alligator—at least six feet—was coming toward me on the porch! It was terrifying. He was grunting, and his mouth kept opening. I vaulted the rail, ran across the yard and climbed the tree."

With gargantuan effort, I kept my face completely neutral. "And then what happened?"

"I heard him scratching around the base of the tree and was sure he was climbing it. But there was nothing more I could do, so I just hung on. Then I heard the Joyners coming up the walk and was afraid he would get them, too. I screamed something at them. At that point, I was too far out on the limb. I heard it crack. I fell and then we all ran inside."

"I see. That all seems straightforward." I hoped my eyes weren't as round as I thought they were. I turned to the Joyners. "Is the last part of that account basically what you recall also?"

Mrs. Joyner nodded. Mr. Joyner added, "Yeah, that about covers it. I managed to trip, running up the stairs, and as I was trying to get up, I may have heard a noise over by the fence, but I'm not sure."

"Well," I said cheerfully, "That's all quite clear." Sure it was.

"Here's what we'll do. Right now, Bill and Martha will get you over to the clinic. We'll get that ankle X-rayed and taped and get something to soothe those scratches. Make sure neither of you is in any pain. Of course, this is all taken care of by Plymouth Rock. Mrs. Joyner, feel free to come along if you wish. Now, while Bill helps Mr. Joyner to the car, perhaps, Martha, you'll give me a minute."

When the sitting room cleared I turned to Martha Meyer. "Well, luv, we may have dodged a bullet. Nobody is screaming lawsuit. Nor should they. I assume you did not stock the front yard with alligators. Nobody told Withers to climb naked out a window or up a tree, and the front steps have no loose boards. So I really don't see liability suits for you unless we find alligator scales on the back steps. Of course, the night is young."

She took my hands. "You're a good friend, Alex. Maybe I can finally stop thinking I'm going to throw up. Joyner did say something about your being remarkably prompt. I think he was impressed." She still looked worried but no longer verging on frantic. She looked younger than her years, and quite desirable, and once again I wondered if she were absolutely *sure* she was straight.

I brought myself back to why I was there and freed my hands.

"Good. The faster we work, the better. Get them in and out of the clinic. Ask the doctor privately if he can think of some reason to get some blood out of Withers and quietly run an alcohol level, but don't push it. Then I suggest the following menu."

I lit a cigarette and saw Martha cringe. "Come in the kitchen. We can't smell up this room."

"Okay," I continued in the large kitchen. "Offer to put them all up in a motel or one of your second story rooms tonight if they're uneasy."

"The Joyners are already on the second floor, but he may not want the climb. We do have one empty room upstairs that Gale could have."

"Got you. Well, see what they say. Then tell them however many nights they have been here are no charge. It really is important they don't feel like they paid anything to get hurt and scared. Tell them of course you would love to have them stay their full reservation as your guest, but the Joyners may not want to limp around, and Withers may be dicey. So you offer them a long weekend free in late October. You may have empty rooms by then anyway."

I flicked ashes in the sink, and Martha tried not to look pained. She nodded slowly as she turned on the tap. "Yes, it's a good idea and a lot cheaper than a lawsuit. We'll do it that way."

"Good. I'm going over to the Speedwell and see if I can find out how much La Withers had to drink, just in case we need that information later if she gets difficult. I'll meet you all back here, and you can tell me what they've decided. Then I will flash a couple of large bills and say how sorry I am their evening was ruined, and tomorrow why don't they all have a nice dinner, courtesy of Plymouth Rock. Then I get them to sign the release. That's the tricky part."

Outside, Martha walked over to their station wagon, and I began the four-block walk to the Speedwell. It was faster than trying to drive it. I felt strangely relieved to be in a brightly lit area, even though I really didn't think Ptown boasted any alligators, not the four-legged type, anyway. Arriving at the Speedwell, I asked for the manager and was routed to a very important-looking woman, who showed some teeth and asked if she could help me with something, and really didn't seem to mean any of it.

I smiled insincerely back, introduced myself and explained there had been a minor accident at the Chambered Nautilus, and I wondered if she would check her credit card dupes, just to confirm that a Gale Withers had indeed dined there tonight. She sighed at the enormity of it all, but finally turned and walked toward the waitresses' station.

When she pulled out the slip, I took it gently but quickly from her hand and looked at the order stapled to it. From what I could make out, Gale Withers had had three martinis, scrod and something, a glass of Pinot Blanc, followed by what looked liked a Cointreau and coffee. Well, *of course* Gale had seen an alligator! Who the hell wouldn't, after two or three sherries, three martinis, a glass of wine and a liqueur, plus a highball? I was only surprised she didn't invite him in for a nightcap.

I asked the manager if she could make me a copy of the credit card slip. Her answer was about what I expected. "Oh, I'm sorry, but, no. In a restaurant of this caliber, our customers do expect privacy, you know."

"Yes, ma'am, and I have no intention of making this public. I am a private insurance investigator, investigating an accident. While you make me a copy of that and I speak briefly to Mrs. Withers's waitress, not a soul will know what's going on. Or in twenty minutes there will be two uniformed police officers here, and they will not speak quietly, and they may even wonder loudly and officially why your establishment continued selling liquor to an obviously intoxicated woman who later injured herself and caused injury to another person. Your call."

She grabbed the paper from my hand and turned toward a door marked "Private." Over her shoulder she snapped, "Her waitress was Shelley, the blond girl who's now serving the front table."

I waylaid Shelley en route to the kitchen. She did remember Mrs. Withers, not by name but as the lady who had "really put it away." She recalled that the lady had, "Looked so sad, you know? She didn't eat hardly any of her meal. I asked her was anything wrong with it, and she said no, she just wasn't hungry, and then she wiped her eyes with the napkin, you know? I felt sort of sorry for her, but I didn't think I should say anything. I hope she's all right. She seemed pretty sloshed."

"Why didn't you have the bartender cut her off?" I asked.

"What? And have her get mad and cause a scene and I'm the one who gets fired? I didn't feel that sorry for her."

I could see her point. The manager returned with my photocopy. I thanked her sweetly and left. I didn't bother to tell her that the cops would probably be there tomorrow anyway, asking if anyone had seen an alligator.

Back at the inn, while I waited for the wounded to return, I gave the area a more detailed look. There were some scratches on the porch floor, which could, I supposed, have come from an alligator. Or luggage, or golf shoes, or a toy. The plants where Gale had made her leap were crushed, as they would be. The lawn at the foot of the tree was not disturbed any more than normal from someone trying to climb the tree and then falling out of it. At the back of the property was a hogwire fence, with a short length broken and pushed up, as if something had crawled under it. Big dog? Small kid? Big coon? Small alligator? Tonight? Two months ago?

Off to my left, I heard a plant rustle. I quickly aimed the light in that direction and saw a hydrangea bush move slightly. My mouth went dry. Could I make it to the house before *whatever* made it to me? I took a careful step back. The last thing I wanted to do was fall. Out of the bush popped Martha and Bill's sleek black ex-tom cat . . . come to say hello.

"Mew."

"Hello, Lexus, you scared me to death." Lexus sat on my foot, in case I hadn't realized I was supposed to pet him. I complied and then scooped him up. "I don't think you better be outside tonight, chubby. You might have more company than you bargained for."

As I carried him up the steps, his weight was making me pant. "I dunno, maybe I ought to let the gator chase you around the block a few times. It's that or join a health club, fella."

I set the cat down in the kitchen and closed the various doors. I gave him some water and me a cigarette. Surely I wasn't over five for the day, my daily allowance. If I exceeded that allowance, I gave myself a harsh scolding.

The group arrived home, casualties bandaged and salved, all ready for bed. Mrs. Withers opted for the upstairs room, the Joyners took her vacated one on the ground floor. Apparently alligators weren't an issue for them. Everybody would leave tomorrow morning and return for a weekend in the fall. Not as a threesome, I judged. I dispensed Plymouth Rock's largess, got my releases and the three guests toddled off to rest and recover.

Bill made us a very welcome drink, and I broke the news that while I waited for them I had also called police headquarters with news of the event. "I felt there wasn't a choice, guys. There is one chance in a million Withers is right. There is one chance in a thousand she is wrong about the alligator, but saw something else. We can't take the risk that something lethal is wandering about."

"You can't believe her!" Martha exclaimed.

"I believe she thinks she is telling the truth." I took a sip of my drink and yearned for a cigarette. "But she was certainly drunk and had very little dinner. Add that to her mental stress at the moment, probably little sleep the last few nights, plus a tiring drive from her home to here. She probably thinks everything in her life is an alligator right now. I think she fell asleep and had one of those terribly realistic dreams you can't seem to get out of, and she thinks it really happened."

"Oh, God, and now the cops will come at midnight and wake everybody up," Bill moaned, mustache aquiver.

"I don't think they'll be on your property tonight unless something else happens," I reassured him. "I spoke with Sonny."

Detective Lieutenant Edward J. "Sonny" Peres is my brother, and sometimes he gives me credit for having a brain. I told him I'd covered the inn property and what I had seen, and not seen. He agreed that anything that might have been there was now gone. But he would have his minions on the alert overnight and speak with Withers and the Joyners in the morning.

"Thanks again, Alex." Martha patted my hand. "I'm sorry all this had to happen."

"Oh, don't be. Cindy and I were about to be reduced to watching the Red Sox stomp all over Texas," I lied happily. "Anyway, it'll give everybody in town something to do. I anticipate three hundred and six alligator sightings by the weekend."

"Oh, God," Bill groaned again. Humor was not always his strong point.

I downed my drink. "Go to bed. You have to feed people in the morning."

As I drove home, I admit my head was on a swivel, looking for an alligator.

But alas, I saw none.

I closed the car door quietly and met a silent Fargo at the back door. We went out for last patrol, and Fargo didn't flush anything, either. Inside, most of the lights were off and Cindy had fallen asleep, eyebrows back in place. As I climbed into bed, she stirred and asked, "Did you catch it?"

"Yes," I replied. "It's sleeping overnight in your car."

"Oh, isn't that sweet!" Cindy smiled. She turned over and snuggled down and I turned out the light.

Chapter 3

The Joyners and Gale Withers all got an early start for home Wednesday morning, which was fortunate, as the media arrived around nine. There were a couple of cable TV stations with nothing better to cover, plus some radio and press reporters, all looking for the naked lady who had fallen from a tree, escaping ravishment by a giant alligator.

Martha and Bill Meyer appeared on their porch, tight-lipped and unhappy, trying not to accuse Gale Withers of being either a lunatic, a liar or a drunk, and so managing to sound rather lunatic themselves. Bill wrapped it up nicely, I thought. "We've known Mrs. Withers for years, and if she says she saw an alligator, I'm sure she did, although, of course, we know there wasn't one. Naked? Yes, she was naked. Haven't you ever gotten hot and taken off your clothes?"

Police Chief Franks was also unfortunately uneasy around cameras and microphones, and stubbornly refused to use a typed statement. His ad lib remarks did little to confirm the very real intelligence and common sense he had. "Yes, we are investigating the uh, possibility there was an uh, alligator, although we don't have alligators in Provincetown. They don't like our uh, cold climate, although of course it is warm now. We are looking into every uh, pond and making sure everyone there is uh, safe. And we are certainly taking the sighting of Mrs. Withers seriously. No further comment."

Various passersby squealed their delighted fear into the cameras and mikes or laughed it off or announced with tough NRA grins that they were ready with loaded guns to take care of the scaly bastard, which must have thrilled my brother. A bunch of trigger-happy fools, heavily armed in a town crowded with tourists was the perfect recipe for acid reflux.

I clicked off the noon news and turned my mind to the deck attached to the cottage my Aunt Mae rented to Cindy. A couple of floorboards were rotting out, and one of the railings was wobbly. If anyone had accidentally leaned hard against it, it could have been dangerous. Although slightly beyond my own carpentering expertise, I did not think the job was a large or complicated one.

The complications were with Cindy and Aunt Mae. As soon as Aunt Mae noticed it, she would have it repaired. This would upset Cindy, who would feel that since she was paying quite a low rent for a year-round cottage, and since she was the one who most often enjoyed the use of the deck, she should pay for the repair. If Cindy noticed it first and had it repaired, Aunt Mae would be upset that Cindy had paid for repairs on property Aunt Mae owned. In either event, each would take it as a serious failure in their stewardship.

They were quite fond of each other, and I wanted no rift, however small, to come between them. The simple answer would be for *me* to have it repaired and present it to them as a *fait accompli*. They could both unite in being upset with me, but probably not for long.

I knew that Aunt Mae would be away Thursday and Friday at an herb growers' show and convention down in Stonington,

Connecticut. Cindy would be gone those same two days to a financial advisors' seminar in Boston. So-o-o, all that remained was to find a handyman who could complete the repairs during that period. I thought I knew the person.

I saddled up Fargo and we went in search of Harmon. Harmon is a town character who beachcombs and sells driftwood and other artistic detritus that washes ashore—lobster pot markers, shell-encrusted old bottles, broken oars, etc.—to gift shops and arts and crafts stores.

But if he'd been looking for odds and ends, he would have been on the beach at or before dawn, not at this hour. Harmon also sometimes fills in as an extra hand on a fishing boat to bring in an additional bit of income. If that were so, you could easily spot his old rattletrap pickup, once red and now a delicate faded pink, parked on the wharf awaiting his return, so we checked the wharf . . . to no avail. He might be engaged in handyman work anywhere in town. I drove around the most logical spots, but struck out there, too.

Since it was near the noon hour, however, I figured the odds might be pretty good that Harmon could be found dining at the Wharf Rat Bar.

He and other not-fully-employed men-about-town made the Rat their personal club and "owned" the big round front table. There, they discussed *ad nauseum* the quotas on fish, the shortages of fish, the foreign trespassers upon fish and the cost of fuel for the boats to go looking for fish. Joe, the bartender, had dubbed them the "The Blues Brothers," and Harmon had added the subject of drugs to their repertoire.

He was convinced our small town was the drug capital of the world and that giant international deals were consummated hourly on every corner, by a multitude of unlikely people. His list of suspects had included a visiting movie producer, a born-again preacher, a retired botany professor, an undertakers' supply salesman and a Swedish hairdresser. Harmon protected us against them all, and drove my brother crazy with "reports." Harmon, according to Sonny, had reported thirty-six of the last three drug sales in Provincetown.

So I parked, and Fargo and I walked down the alley to the Rat, where I secured him to a large anchor outside, with his choice of sun or shade, and entered the building.

It was filled with tourists, apparently enjoying both the fare and the décor, the unmatched chairs, bare tables, uneven floors and the determined sea going atmosphere. Fishing nets hung along every wall, festooned with ancient boat hooks and oars, dried starfish and lobster pot markers, small kedge anchors and dried seaweed. In one corner stood an old ship's telegraph, harvested from a long-dead ferry. Its indicator was frozen on *Dead slow astern*, which really said it all for the Wharf Rat Bar.

Joe, the owner and bartender, waved and pointed toward an empty barstool. "Hi, Alex. There's no tables right now, this'll have to do. But I got a nice cold Bud, been sittin' on ice for you all morning."

"I'll take it with pleasure."

Joe uncapped the beer and poured it into a frosted glass. I did not think tourists received these niceties.

"Boy, this is nice and cold! It's getting hot outside." I turned on the stool and checked the front table. As expected, Harmon and friends were there. Harmon was halfway through a hamburger, and I elected to let him finish before bothering him. I tuned in to their conversation in time to hear Harmon pontificate on a new and different, yet not entirely dissimilar subject.

"Of course the alligator is real. How do I know, you ask? Well, now, you guys know I ain't no stranger to the criminal mind." He leaned back in his chair, hands hooked in his overalls bib, and took on a professorial mien. "Sonny Peres can tell you, I've worked on many a case with him. This ain't really so different. Same old trouble of a fallin' out among thieves. Why only this morning, Sonny said to me, 'Harmon, I can't *tell* you what all your help means to me.'" His listeners looked impressed. I suppressed a giggle.

"Early this morning," he continued, "right square in the middle of Pearl Street, I found an important message and took it di-rect to

20

Sonny, so he could get right on it. It were hand-printed on a piece of light cardboard and had two holes punched in the top, like a string had been put through it at sometime or other . . . so you could maybe hang it on a doorknob or the like. It said, 'Your stuff is at my place. If you want it, come and get it.' And it were signed, 'Al.'"

I was lost. So, it seemed, were the round table denizens. But not Harmon. He translated for us.

"You see, with all my experience, I tumbled to it right off. Some drug dealer up here owed a big bunch of money to a big Florida distributor and was trying to buy still more from him, without no cash up front. So the distributor, he planned a little surprise for the dealer. The message meant the drugs are here in town, if you want 'em, come on to our reg'lar meeting place. And 'Al' stood for alligator, but the dealer, he didn't know that. He had no idea his distributor had brought that four-legged thing right up from Florida with him."

Harmon took a swig of beer. "So when the dealer walked in on the supposed roundyview, there would be the gator, ready to kill him. These big distributors, you don't fool with them. But the alligator, he got out somehow and chased that lady instead. I tell you, Sonny was impressed!"

I could imagine that he was. Harmon had never been right yet about a drug dealer. The law of averages said that at some point, one of his outrageous guesses would be correct. Could this be it? I caught his eye and called out, "When you finish eating, could I see you a minute?" He nodded.

Sometime later I caught the sharp aroma of raw onions and beer and realized that Harmon had joined me. I told him of the problems with the deck, and he agreed it sounded like a job he could easily finish in two days or less. We agreed he would go to the cottage around nine tomorrow morning and look it over, then go get what lumber and paint he needed and come back and start work. "If there's any problem," I said, "Call me. Otherwise I'll see you tomorrow afternoon."

"Yeah, sure, Alex. Okay."

I knew he'd be there and do a good job. I bought him a beer and prepared to leave, when I realized I didn't have enough cash to pay my bill. It was no problem. Joe was always happy to run a tab, but it reminded me I'd best stop by the bank.

I collected Fargo and we mushed slowly through the summer traffic. Entering the bank, I looked around and spotted Cindy in the middle of the main floor. Neither Cindy nor I are inclined toward public shows of affection, even around close friends or relatives, so you can understand my surprise at finding my love locked in tight embrace with Mildred Morris. Mildred was a large-boned, athletic woman, ever cheerful, as if she had just leaped the net and cried, "Well played, well played!" She was a crackerjack accountant and handled the books of several small businesses in town, including mine. I think there had once been a Mr. Morris, but I'm not sure. Mildred was friendly, but she was private.

As Cindy patted Mildred's back in a baby-burping fashion, I realized with surprise Mildred was crying against Cindy's shoulder, and now felt somewhat less intrusive in joining the already-joined pair.

"Can I be of help?"

Cindy shot me a relieved look and replied, "Mildred has lost her cat, Hercules, and has reason to fear he . . . he may not return."

"Ah. Well, that's terrible. Why are we afraid Hercules is . . . permanently missing?" I had known Hercules a large part of my life. He was a giant, muscular tomcat, white with a gray saddle, and extremely pugnacious. He hated all dogs, most cats and a fair number of humans. And only the bravest didn't make way for his passage. He must be at least eighteen years old by now, but he had not mellowed with age. The only thing I could think of that might have managed to kill him was a semi or a nuke. Or maybe he was sick and had gone away to die, as animals sometimes will. I did hope he hadn't suffered. He had a certain nobility.

By now Mildred had straightened away from Cindy, blown her nose and hiccupped. "Oh, Alex, I'm sorry to cause such a scene. Cindy, dear, I've ruined your blouse and made a fool of myself in the middle of your bank. But you see, Hercules was all I had . . . everything to me."

This brought forth a new freshet of tears, and she collapsed again onto Cindy's now sodden shoulder. By this time, I too, was patting her back and muttering, "There, there."

Fargo wasn't all I had—not by a long chalk—but just the thought of losing him gave me a sharp pain in the stomach and a tightening of the chest I hoped was not a coronary. "Mildred, I'm so sorry. Is there anything we can do to help you find him, uh . . . whatever the uh, outcome?"

She finally got herself under some control. "Thank you, I don't think so. I've looked all over. Last night I let him out, and I thought I might have heard him cry out once, but I wasn't sure. He didn't come in all night, but that's not unusual." No, it wouldn't have been. There have been many kittens in this town that bore his distinctive gray saddle as an heraldic symbol of his nightly excursions.

"This morning," she continued, "I looked for him again, but there's no sign. He never misses his breakfast."

"Well, let's hope for the best," I said weakly. Mildred collected herself and went on her way. Cindy was talking to me, but I wasn't listening. In my mind, I was seeing a pitiful old tom dangling from the jaws of a drooling alligator.

"Are you hearing a word I said?" Cindy asked.

"Oh, uh, no. I'm sorry, I was thinking of poor Mildred. Whom will she talk to over breakfast tomorrow?"

Cindy's voice changed from annoyed to concerned. "Lord, Alex, is it that bad? Has she really got no one?"

"I kind of think so. She lives alone. I don't think she dates. I don't know of any family here in town."

"Well, we'll have to come up with something. That's too sad for words! Give me a day or so. What I asked you was, can you have me at the airport at seven thirty tomorrow morning? Choate Ellis is having Cassie fly us over for the seminar."

Choate Ellis was the bank CEO and Cindy's boss. Cassie was

23

my best buddy and president of Outer Cape Charter. She was also its pilot, secretary, reservation clerk and mechanic. If she ever called and said she needed me to fly 'round the world with her, I'd grab my toothbrush and run.

"Sure, I can do that." I must have looked wistful.

"Maybe you could ride over and back, so you and Cassie could play war games on the way home."

Now how did she know we sometimes did that? This woman consistently amazed me. "Thanks," I replied with total cool, "But I have some stuff to catch up with in the morning. Oh, you might want to check your blouse, your shoulder is covered with makeup." There, that would fix her.

She looked down. "Oh, my God, I'll have to go and try to wash it off. Dammit! I'll see you at the house for dinner, right?"

"Right." I angled off toward a teller to get some cash.

It was an evening of sixes and sevens.

Cindy swore she'd told me to pick up something to make for dinner. I swore she hadn't. I offered to go get something. She said she didn't feel like cooking. I suggested we order take-out. She said it was fattening. Finally, I made my famous ham and cheese omelets and a salad. The omelets were a little brown on the bottom, but I thought they tasted fine. In fact, I surreptitiously finished hers when I cleared the table. I wasn't very full. I guess she was.

I said I'd clean up, while Cindy packed. As she dragged a suitcase from the closet, Fargo began to pace and keen. He hates suitcases, knowing full well they mean someone he loves is going away, and he's probably not going with them. There was no shutting him up. I retired to the kitchen and picked up one of the scandal sheets Cindy consistently brings home and swears she never reads.

It was the usual intellectually challenging stuff. Several famous women were pregnant, apparently by all the wrong men. A Mississippi man had spontaneously combusted at a tent revival while speaking in tongues, and neither firemen nor doctors could explain the phenomenon. A woman in Germany had gotten locked in a restaurant freezer for two days, but survived. Doctors could not explain that, either. A dog in China had given birth to a litter consisting of four puppies and two piglets. I always wondered why these incidents always seemed to be in faraway countries, or perhaps Mississippi or West Virginia.

One feature caught my attention because of the photos. Dress and hairstyles indicated they had been taken a number of years ago. They showed a woman, standing in a courtroom as a jury foreman read out the verdict. She was stunning, obviously tall, and slender, with a regally long neck and well-defined features, dark hair slightly waved . . . and a totally blank expression. There were also insets, apparently school photos, of two children, a rather plain girl of perhaps eleven, and an absolutely beautiful little boy about seven.

The headline read: *Woodchopper Killer Dies After 30 Years in Mass. Mental Hospital.* The story, if you took away most of the adjectives, said that the woman discovered, or thought she discovered, her husband had been sexually abusing her son and possibly her daughter. The wife was in the backyard feeding her husband's various body parts into the woodchopper, when the two kids returned home from a neighbor's birthday party. They naturally followed the noise into the backyard, and rapidly went running back up the street, screaming hysterically.

Interestingly, the woman had not pled insanity, but instead had insisted on pleading self-defense, in that she was defending her two children, who were too young to defend themselves. It didn't work. They found her insane anyway, and gave her a life sentence at a state mental facility. Thirty years. My God, it must have seemed like an eternity!

By now Fargo had moved his own little anxiety attack to the kitchen, resting his head on my leg and emitting soft whimpers. I stroked his back. "Okay, okay." I raised my voice. "Honey, I'm going to take him outside for a minute before he has a nervous breakdown."

"Or gives me one," came sharply back.

By the time we returned Cindy was in the kitchen, having poured herself a glass of wine and made me a bourbon highball. Quickly, she pushed the scandal sheet aside. "I don't know why I buy those things, I never read them."

"I know." I sipped my drink. "What did you think of the guy down south who spontaneously combusted?"

"It grossed me out! Oops, you caught me." She gave me that smile that always makes me just a little short of breath.

I grinned back. "Feeling better?"

"I think you've caught me there, too. I can't seem to help it. I just get a little batty whenever one of us has to travel. It's so strange." She reached for a cigarette, something she does about once a month. She would smoke only that one. I don't know how she does it.

"Are you worried about an accident, or a bomb or something?" I asked.

"Oh, to a degree, sure, but that's not it. And it's not that I think either one of us is going to stray, although sometimes it sounds that way." She moved her wineglass around in a little circle.

"What's left?" I wasn't following too well here.

"I'm afraid when I come home, or you come home, one of us will be completely changed. One of us won't be the same at all . . . completely different. Our attitudes, feelings, needs . . . everything will have changed. One of us will be a stranger." Her eyes began to fill.

"Sweetheart! Please don't cry." I straightened in alarm. "You know I don't do well when you cry!" In fact I was frantic at the first tear. "We aren't going to change! Never! I'm Alex. What you see is what you got. It may not be great, but it's me . . . and always will be. And you could never be less than what you are. Never!" I reached across the table for her hand, but it was not enough. I went around the table to hold her, and she rose to meet me. I held her painfully tight. I could not lose her.

She took a shaky breath. "You don't think I'm nuts? Maybe I need a shrink."

26

"Maybe you just need a drink, and since it's out in the open and you've talked about it, it won't bother you so much. If it does, you can always see a shrink if you want. Or if you want to talk to me, love, I'm here. I'm always here. I love you, batty or not." I looked at her, and she nodded, and with one accord we drifted toward the bedroom.

And we talked, and we touched and then we slowly reached that ultima Thule that comes so rarely and so perfectly, when all things disappear into unbearable and absolute pleasure.

Chapter 4

Cindy looked very attractive and professional in her "Boston" clothes. I noted that both Choate Ellis and Cassie gave her an appreciative once-over as we walked toward the plane. It made me feel like I was escorting a movie star. We gave each other a light, and decorous cheek-to-cheek hug, and she climbed into the cabin with a gallant assist from Cassie.

"Safe trip," I said to no one in particular.

I watched as Cassie fired up the starboard engine and then the port and taxied to the runway's end. The small plane hurtled back toward me along the runway and cleared the ground just as it passed in front of me. Gaining altitude, Cassie waved and began a slow turn back over the bay to aim them toward Boston's Logan Airport.

Sighing, I walked to my car. "Fargo, why were we not born rich? Or at least rich enough to fly a plane like that all over the place?" He shrugged and sat down in the passenger's seat, ready to leave. I think he considered airplanes strange noisy cars that were best avoided.

I decided to stop by on the way home and see what Mom was up to on this nice morning.

I found her lopping branches off an old forsythia that bloomed magnificently every spring and then grew wild every summer.

She straightened up and eyed the shrub warily. "One of these days it's going to reach out and get me. Hello, my darlings." She kissed me as she petted Fargo. "And how are we this morning?"

"Well, we just saw Cindy and Choate Ellis off to Boston on Cassie's magic carpet."

She gave me a mother's look. "So you are on your own for a few days."

"Yeah." I started picking up forsythia clippings and shoving them in the plastic bag nearby. I thought about my conversation last night with Cindy. I was delighted she'd "confessed" and thought it boded well for anytime one of us had to be away in the future. I thought about my own chimera and wondered if I could muster up the courage ever to discuss it. The thought of *that* conversation was really beginning to bug me.

Mom stopped work, laid the clippers on the wall and then sat down beside them.

"You seem a bit quiet this morning, Alex. Everything all right?"

"Oh, absolutely, thanks. Yes, I'm fine. I was just thinking. Apparently, Cindy's had this little bugbear that has been chasing her around. Last night she told me about it. She felt greatly relieved afterward and was glad to realize what it was. Just silliness, really, but something that got bigger and bigger in her mind. It wasn't really a problem, you know, but I think we'll both be easier, now it's in the open. She had this nutty hang-up anytime either of us traveled."

Mom patted the wall beside her, inviting me to sit down.

"And you have a little bugbear chasing you around, but you can't talk about it?"

My mother knew her child.

"Well, yes." I told her of my fear that I would disappear as an individual if Cindy and I lived together. In the bright morning sun, it sounded a helluva lot sillier than Cindy's problem, which I had treated rather lightly.

Mom was silent a moment and then said, "I don't know that I'm the right person to talk to. I know that for years I felt I had gone from being my parents' daughter, to being my husband's wife and then my children's mother. My marriage was not a glowing success, as you know and frankly, I never really felt like 'Jeanne the Person' until after your father's death."

Nothing about my father had been a glowing success in my mind, either. He drank heavily but not happily. He was scathingly sarcastic. He was dissatisfied with his job as a supermarket manager, but not enough to do anything about it, and maybe he was depressed. God knows it had not been a joyous house in his lifetime.

When I was twelve and Sonny fourteen, Provincetown got the edge of a violent, fast-moving hurricane. If that was the edge, I would hate to have seen the middle. To this day I can remember the terror and helplessness I felt. Mom, Sonny and I spent the night glued to the radio, at least in some way attached to other people. Daddy Dearest spent it glued to the Scotch bottle. The next morning was drizzly and windy, but the worst, the trusty radio told us, was over.

A neighbor's tree had been a casualty, bringing wires down with it and partially blocking our driveway. After watching the wires for some time, our cold, hungover father pronounced the wires dead and went to pull them and the limb away from the drive so he could go to work. Standing in a puddle, he lifted the branch, did a nightmarish, seemingly endless little tap dance and fell dead on the asphalt, some thirty thousand volts having gone through his body.

I looked at my mother. "Did you ever miss him?" I hadn't.

"Oh, generically, yes. Of course I was stunned and appalled at his death. But feeling as if I had lost half myself? No. I vowed I would bring you and Sonny up to be your own personalities, and I managed to do that, although you each scared me half to death on occasion."

She smiled and continued. "I don't think your fear is entirely without reason. I seem to recall that one or two of your lady friends were a bit suffocating, and one so narcissistic, I was afraid she might destroy you. But, fortunately Cindy is none of the above. And you know, many people live out their lives together quite contentedly. I doubt you will ever lose yourself, Alex, but you could lose Cindy if you don't discuss this. Maybe you need to continue living apart for a while—or forever—but you need to be doing whatever you do consciously and by design, not by default."

I loved my mom.

Then I went to find my brother. I was worried.

I found him in his office, also worried.

"What do you think about that Withers woman?" he asked abruptly. "Is she crazy? Alcoholic? What?"

"I think she told the truth as she saw it, and originally I thought it was that she was upset, tired and drunk and just had a realistic dream she thought actually happened. Now, I'm wondering." I told him about Hercules.

"Oh, hell. Mildred has a house out near Harmon, doesn't she?" He got up and filled his coffee mug from the carafe behind his desk. I noticed his hand was slightly shaky. Obviously this was not his first cup. "Want some?"

"No. Yes, Mildred lives out that way. Why?"

"Earlier this morning I stopped by Aunt Mae's to drop off some big bags of potting soil I picked up yesterday for her. I knew she was at that convention thing, but some high school girl is keeping the shop open for her, so I knew the garage would be unlocked. I saw Harmon's truck at the cottage and walked over. He had apparently brought over some lumber and paint for some project, but when I found him, he was sitting on the deck, holding Wells in his arms and crying like a baby."

I jumped up in alarm. "What's wrong with Wells? Did you get her to a vet?"

Wells was Cindy's adorable young black cat, sweet and affectionate, complete with tuxedo front and a white chin that looked like a dab of whipped cream. Cindy would be heartbroken if anything were seriously wrong with her.

Sonny held up both hands. "Nothing is wrong with Wells. I think she was just comforting Harmon for the loss of his rabbits."

A few years back, somewhere in his wanderings, Harmon had found a pair of baby bunnies, obviously orphaned. He'd brought them home and managed to raise them into healthy pets. They were actually kitty litter trained, and lived in the house in cold weather. Now, they were outdoors in a large, grassy pen, complete with a cozy doghouse in case of rain.

"What happened to them?" I changed my mind and helped myself to coffee. This pet thing was turning into a nightmare.

"Harmon got home late last night. Something had broken into the pen, and they were gone. He looked all over—no rabbits. Poor bastard, he kept mopping his face with this grimy handkerchief and sobbing, 'They're all I had, all I had.' He damn near had me sobbing with him." He sipped his coffee.

"My God, the poor man! Sonny, what the hell is going on here? This all makes no sense. We aren't alligator country." I swallowed some coffee and no longer had any doubts why Sonny's hands were shaking. A jail inmate forced to drink it would swear his civil rights had been violated . . . and win.

Sonny shrugged. "I don't know. First the trouble was more or less downtown, now maybe it's out near the ponds. All we need is this thing to grab a kid."

"But no one has *seen* the alligator! Is he really there? Could it be a super big coon? Maybe he's rabid or something?" I lit cigarette four, and Sonny motioned for the pack.

"That's a great comfort. Now which do we want most, a six-foot alligator or a giant rabid coon?"

"I try. Say, Sonny, what did you think of that cardboard 'message' of Harmon's, signed by 'Al?'"

Sonny laughed. "I think some guy named Al broke up with his girlfriend and wants her to get her stuff the hell out of his apartment. What did you think?"

"I thought maybe some kid named Al was keeping a bunch of stuff for a buddy, and Al's mother told him to clean up his room or she'd bring in a backhoe, so Al wrote a note to his pal."

"Another good possibility. Believe me, I did not call the DEA. However, I did spend a long time on the phone just now to a fellow down at Mystic Marine Aquarium. Very helpful. He said if the gator is here, someone *had* to have brought him. No way could he have wandered all the way up here. Secondly, like all cold-blooded animals, the gator doesn't need to eat a lot frequently. He can live on water birds and small animals for a long time, depending on how big he is and how good the hunting is. Thirdly, he's probably been as scared as the rest of us, and if he finds a friendly waterhole, he'll lie low. At least for a while. Maybe nab the occasional Canada goose or small dog or cat. But eventually . . ."

"You'll have to tell everyone to watch their pets and children." I stubbed out my cigarette. "Sonny, you must!"

Sonny shook his head. "Wrong. Alex, I can't issue some frightening, horror-filled warning all over town, based on the disappearance of a couple of pets and the dream or delusion of a drunken woman who may also be emotionally disturbed. Every fool in town who owns a gun is already sitting on the front porch waiting for a gator to stroll by." He mimed raising a rifle to his shoulder and firing.

He stood up and turned to the window. "Hercules was older than God. He probably is lying peacefully under a bush somewhere. A dog or coon got the rabbits. Period. I do not," he continued slowly, "plan to be the person who single-handedly bankrupts Cape Cod this summer. There wouldn't be a tourist left any closer to the Cape than Taunton. We have beefed up all our night shifts. All our squad cars are carrying thirty-thirty rifles and making extra runs by all the ponds we can see from the roads. Everyone has extra-big flashlights, and if any foot patrol person is carrying a forty-five in their holster, I'm pretending not to notice it. Everyone is looking, looking, looking. They'll shoot if they have to. It's all I can do, Alex. The Chief agrees." His shoulders sagged.

I felt sorry for him. "You're probably right," was all I could think to say in farewell.

Reaching Nacho's desk, I picked up Fargo's leash to lead him away from the gourmet deli in her file cabinet. Nacho was busy on the computer, but turned her head to say, "He had three potato chips, two small pretzels and a cup of water."

"Thanks." I led Fargo slowly away, head, ears and tail down, a dog obviously in dire need of sustenance. "Listen, Barrymore, you had breakfast at home and a nice little snack with Nacho. Cut the starvation act." He trudged on, an abused animal if ever I had seen one.

We made it to a park bench without my having to carry him. I sat down. He flopped. "Listen, Fargo, it's think time. It seems to me, we've been hearing a bunch of sobs and moans and people saying, 'They were all I had,' or 'He was everything to me.'

"Now to me, that means they needed these animals a lot, but even more, it sounds like the animals needed *them* to care for them. As it stands, these people are stuck with nothing that needs them. And that's an awful feeling. Agreed?" He whuffled what might have been reluctant agreement.

"So what needs a lot of care? A baby, right?" No reply. I continued. "Now Harmon would love a puppy." Fargo looked up and gave a half wag. Sometimes I still called him my *good puppy*. "But a puppy wouldn't be right for Harmon. He needs something he can leave overnight when he goes out on one of the fishing boats or beachcombing after a storm. And Mildred is a cat person." The word "cat" got to him. He sat up and looked around alertly, ready for play, a chase, even supervised socializing, whatever worked.

"No, Fargo, I'm thinking in terms of kittens." He was still looking. "Let's go. You won't like where we're going, but you can stay in the car."

As we turned into the vet's driveway, Fargo curled up in a tight ball, getting smaller and smaller as I parked. I opened my door. "I won't be long, you stay." He closed the one eye he had cracked open.

Entering the vet's I saw that Victor was chatting casually with his office manager and a kennel boy. Good, I wouldn't have to wait.

"Hey, Alex, what's up? Where's Fargo?"

"In the car, he's fine." I explained the purpose of my visit.

"You're a good sport, Alex. That's a great idea. Let's see who's got some kittens." He walked around into the waiting room, where a large bulletin board took up most of one wall. He looked over a number of the notices pinned there, then removed one.

"Here we go, Alice Pennington. She takes very good care of her animals. She felt Melody deserved to have one litter and will have her spayed as soon as the kittens are placed. I believe Melody produced seven beauties. Let me call Alice and see who's left."

Four were left—three females and a male. I departed the vet's with two of those cardboard carriers, several samples of kitten food, and two booklets on the care of kittens, with a note penned on the front: *Be sure the kittens visit a veterinarian by Sept. 1, for booster shots and to arrange neutering.*

Alice Pennington was glad to see me. The kittens were now almost nine weeks old and full of energy. I picked out a sweet little tiger female and the gray and white male for Harmon. I figured a gray and white male might have been too reminiscent of Hercules for Mildred. For her I chose a sweet-faced calico, thinking a gentle female might also be better than Hercules in the affection department.

Alice gave a little *moue*, followed by some very unappealing baby talk. "Poor little tabby-kit is going to be left all alone and by her lonesome, isn't her? Oh-hh. Poor babykins. Poor little orphan kitty-pooh. And, you know, Alex, it's really easier having two. They entertain each other."

I knew I was being sweet-talked, but what the hell? I popped poor little tabby-kit into the carrier. I proffered Alice a twenty-dollar bill, which she made one weak gesture of declining, but then reached for, returning to normal-speak.

"Thanks, it'll help with Melody's spaying bill."

Chapter 5

Driving toward Mildred's house, I thought of names for kittens, while Fargo kept turning toward the backseat and whuffling. Since Mildred had named her old cat Hercules, I figured maybe she was into Greek mythology. Well, okay. We could do that. The little calico looked to be sunny-tempered, so we could call her Eos, the dawn goddess. And the tabby hadn't seemed the least bit pitiful to me. In fact, she had seemed quite sassy, so she became Eris, goddess of discord.

Parked in Mildred's driveway, I printed a stick-up note on the pad I kept in the compartment: "We are homeless and helpless. Won't you please take care of us? We know we will be happy with you. Love, Calico Eos and Tabby Eris." Making sure the little plastic bowl of food in the carrier was full, I filled the other small container with water from the jug I keep in the car for Fargo, and set the carrier on the porch in the shade. One down.

Making the short trip to Harmon's place, I repeated my actions. I didn't really think Harmon would be interested in Greeks of long ago, so I signed his note: "Tom and Geraldine." Mission accomplished.

It was late afternoon and I figured we had labored long enough for one day. We headed home for a game of tag with the hose, the thrill of picking one of my very own tomatoes, a big bowl of fresh cold water and a can of icy Budweiser. Cigarette number six, I feared, but I was in too good a mood to be very accusatory about it.

We continued the pleasant evening by ordering our favorite pizza—sausage with extra cheese. I made myself a salad and filled Fargo's bowl with dry food, which he ignored, knowing full well pizza was en route.

Retiring to the living room, I clicked on the telly. One of the cable stations was featuring a Bio-Drama of the Woodchopper Woman whose photo I had seen in Cindy's scandal sheet the other day. The thing that amazed me about such Bio-Dramas was not how bad they were, but how they existed at all. How on earth did the stations manage to collect so many pictures, so many relatives and neighbors and cops to be interviewed, in so short a time? Surely, they couldn't keep files and film clips on everyone who ever went to jail or a mental facility! It was truly incredible. Of course we were going to watch it while we ate. Cindy would never know.

It boiled down pretty much to what had been in the paper. According to neighbors, Virginia Leonard was the average American housewife, thought to be happily married, a good housekeeper and good mother, if somewhat overprotective of her two children. Her husband Jeff worked for an auditing firm and traveled frequently, but seemed to enjoy his wife and kids whenever he was home.

"And then one afternoon, it all changed for the Leonards," the commentator intoned ominously.

A neighbor joined him on camera. "It had been a pleasant summer day," she said. "A little girl over on Fourteenth Street was having a birthday party. My two kids were going and so were Elaine and Bobby Leonard." The screen flashed photos of the plain young girl and the beautiful little boy.

"I would have let my kids walk over to the party," the neighbor continued, "But Virginia called and suggested she would take all four, if I would pick them up. That was typical. Virginia hated her kids to be anywhere without adult supervision. So that's what we did. She took 'em and I picked them up after the party. I dropped them at the end of their driveway."

Her voice began to quaver.

"I'll never forgive myself. I dropped them off at their driveway, and those kids just walked up that driveway and right around the house to see their mother cutting up their father in the woodchopper. But I didn't know. How could I have known? I had just backed the car out and turned toward home, and then I heard them screaming all the way down the block. I backed up at about ninety miles an hour. I don't know how I did it. They were in the road holding each other and screaming. I jumped out and got my arms around them, asking them what on earth was wrong? They couldn't even tell me, they just fell against me, sobbing."

The screen now featured a picture of Virginia and Jeff Leonard in happier days—a slender young woman, slightly taller than her husband, who was a stocky young man with light brown wavy hair and an easy grin. She held a baby. He clasped the hand of a little girl.

Another neighbor next joined the interview. "I lived right across the street. A little earlier in the day I had been busy, and my then two-year-old Petey somehow unlatched the screen and got out of the house. He was always quite a little terror." She smiled, remembering, as if it had been some sign of greatness to come.

"When I realized it, I ran out just in time to see Jeff Leonard pull in his driveway, jump out of his car and run out into the street to pick up Petey. Jeff was laughing as he scooped Petey up. 'Now, Cowboy, where do you think you're going? You're going right home to mama, that's where! No more adventures for you today, pal.'"

The woman took a drink of water. "He set Petey down in our yard, patted his bottom and said, 'Now get along home, Cowboy, before you get hurt.' I ran down and got Petey and thanked Jeff. I had Petey in my arms and he leaned over and gave Jeff a kiss on the cheek. Jeff tousled his head and left. I called out an apology and he turned and laughed again. 'All kids get loose sometimes, no matter how hard you watch. I guess they have guardian angels.'"

She sniffed. "That was the last time I saw him alive. *He* was the one that needed an angel. Then later, Virginia tried to say Jeff was abusing Petey! Right there on the street with me watching. Poor woman was crazed, of course."

Fargo and I were doing pretty well. I was watching the screen and eating pizza and salad, with the occasional sip of beer. Fargo was eating the crusts and counting the pieces left in the box. The drama returned after brief commercials—about six minutes worth.

Our next guest was a retired woman police officer who had worked on the case. "Worst damn case I ever got assigned to," she began. "I had nightmares for years to come. When my partner and I got there, a man from a nearby house was already standing at the end of the driveway, stopping neighbors from going into the Leonards' backyard. When the kids had started yelling, he had come over and helped the neighbor woman herd them into her car again, and then he had run to the back of the Leonards' house to see what was wrong. What he saw was Mrs. Leonard with a butcher knife and a hatchet, dismembering her husband on the picnic table and feeding the smaller parts into a woodchopper."

The ex-cop made an automatic gesture toward her shirt pocket for cigarettes, remembered where she was and settled for water. "When Virginia Leonard saw the neighbor, she screamed something like, 'Go away! I must save the children from this monster!' The man saw the knife and hatchet and didn't argue. He ran back out front, hollering for someone to call 911, and waving people off . . . and barfing all over the place." That earned her a sour look from the commentator.

The ex-officer continued, with a faraway look, as if she were seeing it all again. "We were the first police car there. We talked her into turning off the chopper and telling us what was going on

. . . as if we couldn't see. She told us very calmly that her husband had often sexually abused their son and daughter. That he had admitted it and agreed to seek help. Then, just minutes before, she had seen him openly abuse the little two-year-old across the street and laugh about it with the mother, who must be abusive also."

"That had apparently put Mrs. Leonard over the top," the cop continued. "When her husband came into the kitchen his wife stabbed him six times with a butcher knife and dragged him into the backyard."

A social services worker appeared next. "It took us till the next day to calm the children sufficiently even to talk to them. And to this day, I'm not sure what part of that whole sad story is true. The daughter Elaine said that the mother was always 'nervous' and wanted to know where they were and what they were doing every minute. Elaine added that up until the last few months, things had been a lot more fun when Daddy was home. He helped with homework, took the kids to baseball games, swimming, hiking, etc. Sometimes all four would go to a movie or, occasionally a theme park." The woman stopped, put on her glasses and consulted some notes.

"Lately, things had been a mess, Elaine said, and blamed her brother Bobby. He didn't want to go anywhere without Daddy, or didn't want Mom and Sis to go along at all. He complained that Elaine and Mom didn't want Daddy to love him anymore. Then he told her that Daddy loved him best, man-to-man, now that Elaine was getting big and grown-up like Mom. Well, you can imagine what a can of worms *that* opened up, especially when Elaine flatly and consistently denied her father had *ever* touched either her or, she was sure, Bobby, improperly."

More commercials. No more pizza, and finally, the end of the Leonard saga.

The psychiatrist Jeff Leonard had agreed to see was never found and was thought to be a figment of Virginia's imagination. Elaine quietly stuck to her story. Bobby stuck hysterically but vaguely to his and was thought to be lying. Medical examinations showed no signs of abuse to either child. One shrink added that Bobby had perhaps somehow seen his parents having sex and thought his father was hurting his mother, especially if she had been making moaning sounds at the time. He was simply a very sensitive child. Yeah, I'd bet. The kid looked beautiful but shifty to me. I figured him for just wanting everyone's attention.

Virginia's insistence that Jeff's pat on Petey's bottom was sexually abusive didn't help her case. Neither did her plea that she had killed Jeff in self-defense, acting for her children who could not protect themselves. She was sent to a facility for the criminally insane, for life, such as it must have been. Solemn little Elaine and adorable blond, wavy locks Bobby were adopted—separately—in another state, and changed their names accordingly. Their whereabouts, the commentator smirked, were carefully guarded, letting us all know he could have found them if he wished.

Later, I let Fargo out for last call, and when he came in I patted his bottom. "I guess we'll have to start watching that," I told him.

He yawned and slurped some water onto the floor.

Friday morning I had snuck Fargo out for an early beach run and was back, sitting in the kitchen with a mug of my special Costa Rican coffee, when the phone rang. It was my mom.

After our hellos, she announced, "I'm at work. Mildred Morris was just here to drop off the monthly accounts. She looks ten years younger than she did yesterday."

"That's nice to hear, wish I could say the same." Pause. Pause. "Er, is there some reason I need this information?"

"Yesterday afternoon she found two adorable kittens left on her doorstep. A note said their names were Eos and Eris."

"What strange names!" I grinned at my mug.

"Not if you once knew a little girl who was crazy about Greek mythology," she said. "I just wanted to let you know, I know you did it. You're a softie and I love you. Bye." She hung up.

Cross Mildred off the worry list. One down, one to go. The phone rang again. This time it was Cindy.

"Hi, darling! Tried you earlier, but the line was busy."

"Yes, it was Mom."

41

"Everything okay?"

"Oh, sure. She called to tell me someone left two cute kittens on Mildred Morris's doorstep, and Mildred is recovering rapidly from Hercules' sad disappearance." I sipped the coffee, getting cool but still great.

"And I suppose you had nothing to do with that." I could tell she was smiling.

"Absolutely not."

"Alex, are you lying?"

"Absolutely."

"I thought so. You can be quite nice on occasion. It's why I put up with all the other times."

"All what other times?"

"I have to get downstairs. I just wanted to let you know, we'll be back around six or so. Choate says he will drop me off, so you don't have to worry about fetching me from the airport."

"I always find you fetching."

"I'm glad. I gotta run. I love you, cat woman. Bye."

"Me too. Bye."

My two phone conversations gave me inspiration to do a few things around the house. How had it gotten into a mess in just one day? Fargo had tracked up the kitchen. I had duplicated him in the bathroom. The empty pizza box and a dirty ashtray plus an empty beer can decorated the coffee table. Jeez! The couch pillows were squashed. Oh, Lord, give me strength. He did, I guess, until around noon, when I said the hell with it.

I wondered how Harmon was coming along with the deck and if he would be finished by tonight when Aunt Mae returned. I hoped she would have no reason to go down to the cottage, and assumed Cindy and I would be here overnight.

I took for granted that Harmon would be lunching at the Wharf Rat Bar. Maybe I should go down and ask about his progress. That was the only reason I was going. I certainly would have preferred to stay home and have a nice cucumber sandwich and some of Cindy's skim milk for lunch, but I really needed to know about the deck and should pay him if it were finished.

Leaving His Nibs ensconced in the shade with a bowl of water, I went inside and found a seat at the bar. Sure enough, Harmon had joined his *confreres* for luncheon and was, as usual, dominating the conversation.

"Well, o'course I ain't no expert on cats. But they was so little and helpless . . . what you gonna do? I brought 'em in and quick-like read that little paper that came with 'em, telling you what to do with them, and we was off to a fine start."

I began to relax and ordered lunch before I tuned back in. "Now that little cutie, Geraldine, she just curled up in my arm and looked around like a little . . . a little princess . . . and then fell right asleep. But that Tom." He sighed deeply. "I tell you, he's forever runnin' up my pants leg and jumping from my lap to the table and slidin' all over the floor." He shook his head heavily. "He don't give a man a minute's rest."

I turned to my sandwich and iced tea with a free conscience. Harmon was in love.

Shortly after six, Cindy barged through the kitchen door, dropping her suitcase, kicking off her high heels, and fending off Fargo's exuberant greeting. I got up to kiss her hello, and she gave me a peck and pushed me away. "Don't touch me! I'm sweaty and awful. Boston was an oven. The plane and Choate's car were worse after being parked in the sun for hours. I hate these damn shoes. I've always hated these damn shoes. I think I'll burn them. Don't even speak to me. Just pour me something cold while I shower before I die."

It was just Cindy letting down after two days of being terribly gorgeous and professional. I could wait. "What do you want to drink? A tall Scotch?"

"No." She was struggling to get out of her dress, but I knew better than to help. "I'd just belt it down and be a nasty drunk, along with everything else. Iced tea is fine." She sidled out of the

43

kitchen, dress still over her head. I guessed she knew where she was going.

I poured two iced teas from the pitcher we kept in the fridge and added ice and lemon. Then I took her suitcase in and put it on the bed. The shower was running, and Cindy was swearing like a sailor at something.

Fargo looked at me with concern. "Don't worry, it's not terminal. Come on."

We returned to the kitchen and took the iced tea glasses outdoors. Ten minutes later Cindy padded barefoot across the grass, dark curls still damp, dressed in shorts and one of my too-big T-shirts—looking about sixteen. She sank into my lap. "Hello, darling, did you miss me? I don't know why you would."

I kissed her and proved that I had. She sipped her tea and stood, pulling my hand to bring me up with her. "I don't know why you came all the way out here, just to turn around and go back inside . . . at least I think the neighbors would prefer we go back inside, don't you?"

"We must always be thoughtful of the neighbors," I agreed and walked quickly toward the door.

Chapter 6

Fargo was a bright dog who understood many things. Being barred from the beach in summertime was not one of them. Frankly, I agreed with him. As long as we went early, left early and were diligent about poopybags, I saw no reason to deprive us of our early morning visits. Fortunately, as Sonny's sister, I knew that any patrols passing the beach at this hour of sunup would carefully look the other way. I didn't ride Sonny's coattails in other ways and felt no guilt about letting Fargo get his exercise and fun, tourists notwithstanding.

Before we left, I sat down on the edge of the bed, gently patting Cindy's cheek, risking a fast pop with a pillow. "We're off for a lap around Race Point, honey. Want to join us?"

She snuggled deeper under the light summer quilt. "Uh-uh, but I'll be up and running when you get back. I have a lot to do."

That was the answer I had hoped for. I wanted her up early and over to the cottage. Harmon had told me yesterday, he'd finished the repairs and the painting. I wanted to see it—wanted her and Aunt Mae to see it.

We returned from the beach to be met at the backdoor by a whirlwind. "Hose him off if he's sandy. What did you two do to this house? Here, these go in the car to go to the cleaners. Here's a grocery list you can do at the same time. Actually, two of them, one list is for the cottage. I hope it's right. I can never remember what's where. What's that bag?"

"That bag, my dear, holds our breakfast—delicious, nutritious Portuguese fried bread."

"Nutritious? It should be branded with a skull and crossbones. Well, it *is* delicious. Come on, coffee's made."

"Thank you, kind lady. For a moment here, I was afraid we were out to beat the four-minute mile."

We sat down to coffee and the still-warm bread. I broke mine in two and began to savor it, while Cindy nipped a tiny piece of her own. "Sorry to be in such a rush, darling. I just want to get everything done so I can relax this afternoon. You remember we're going to Lainey and Cassie's for drinks and dinner, to inaugurate their new dining room furniture."

"Oh, yes, sure," I lied. Then I remembered. "And Peter and the Wolf will be there, too."

"Right."

"I hope to God it works out better than the last time this six-some was together for an evening."

Last fall, the six of us, augmented by Sonny and Trish, had gotten together here for dinner and it had been disastrous. Lainey and Cassie had started an argument that damn near got to the plate-tossing stage. Wolf and Sonny had got drunk. Sonny and Trish had a tiff over who was to drive home. Wolf and Peter had had a blazing argument over an Amelia Earhart movie, of all things. And Cindy had gotten mad at me because I'd had just enough to drink to think it was all quite funny.

"I hope so, too," Cindy replied with a sour look. "At least Sonny won't be leading the charge to the bar."

"Maybe Peter and Wolf will bring some nice, sweet old movie like *Fatal Attraction* or *Who's Afraid of Virginia Woolf*. They're always good for a real hoedown."

"Oh, no. Don't even think it." She cocked an ear toward the laundry room. "That laundry should be almost finished. I'll get it in the dryer and then go over to the cottage. I want to check on Wells. I know the girl who watches the shop for Aunt Mae has fed her, but that seems sort of . . . cold. She must be wondering where I am."

"Sonny was over there on some errand." I finished my bread and stole a small piece of Cindy's. "Said Wells was fine. But I'll wait and follow you over before I do errands, just to make sure everything is okay."

"That's very thoughtful of you, darling, and if you touch that bread again, I'll break your wrist. More coffee?"

Aunt Mae must having been watching out the window. The minute our cars pulled in, she came briskly across the lawn, wearing an accusatory little half smile and shaking her finger. "Now, Cynthia, just what have you gone and done?"

Cindy's eyebrows went up. "Hi, Aunt Mae. I don't know what you mean."

"Of course you do. And it really is my responsibility. Now just tell me what it cost and I'll write you a check right now." She patted the pocket of the green canvas apron she had already donned for her day in the herb shop.

By now we had turned the corner of the house, and the deck was before us. Harmon had done a good job. It looked sturdy and straight, and was painted a deep Wedgwood blue that looked great against the gray of the cottage.

"Aunt Mae, I didn't do this, or have it done. I *meant* to. We enjoy it so much, and you are so generous about the rent, I was *going* to have it done, but I just hadn't gotten around to it."

"Then who did it?" Aunt Mae asked.

47

Then they both looked at me. "A-a-a-lex!"

I bowed. "Guilty. I love ya both, ladies, and I didn't want you or anyone else getting hurt on it. My small gift. My great pleasure." I bowed again.

At first there were lots of statements to the effect that it wasn't in the least my responsibility, and lots of arms waving checkbooks. But then I got lots of hugs and kisses, and several choruses of, "You really shouldn't have." Wells ran down from Aunt Mae's house and leaped for Cindy's arms. Fargo ran around and barked. It was a Hallmark moment.

I soon escaped and went on my appointed rounds.

For years, Lainey and Cassie's so-called dining room had been "furnished" with a dilapidated old kitchen table with four unmatched chairs and two sagging bookcases. But now all was changed. It was a lovely room, with soft green carpeting and a small apple wood breakfront as its focal points. A shining dining room table and six chairs with pink, lavender and beige needlepoint upholstery, plus a buffet of rich pecan wood finished off the room. A bouquet of fresh tall pink coneflowers on the buffet added a nice touch of drama.

Cindy, Wolf, Peter and I had offered numerous compliments on the room, and had sat down to a dinner that kept us making admiring comments. On a warm summer night, Lainey had chosen a cold dinner menu that was both delicious to eat and lovely to look at. It was a meal to die for. And it probably tasted all the better for its lovely surroundings.

Conversation had been desultory. I noticed we stayed on safe subjects: the disappearing alligator—interest was dying fast on that subject, the joys and disappointments of gardening, a break up that had surprised no one and, of course, the weather.

Cassie and Lainey had a really great, funny surprise for dessert. We were all led into the kitchen and told to make the ice cream sundae or banana split of our dreams from the great array of ingredients spread before us. Suddenly, we were like a bunch of kids, nudging and laughing, saying, "Oh, that looks good, give me some of that," "Stop shoving!" and, "Don't be a pig, save me some of that."

I watched Cindy help herself to a small scoop of lemon ice doused with what must have been at least a teaspoon of chocolate sauce. Lainey, I saw, had dished up a bit of chocolate ice cream and a dab of raspberry topping. I won't try to describe what all the rest of us had, I just noted that our plates were filled dangerously close to the rims.

Coffee was a welcome closer, and we took it out onto the porch, so that those of us who wanted a cigarette could horrify Lainey in some degree of peace. Peter deftly got the conversation off Laincy's lecture.

"I guess you've heard the news? Paul Carlucci is coming to town and bringing his whole troupe!"

"Who's Paul Caruso?"

"He's bringing the cavalry? They still have a cavalry?"

"Or singing monkeys?"

"The opera singer? I thought he died back in the nineteen-twenties."

"Is he that guy who hunted crocodiles on TV? I thought he died, too."

Peter dropped his head and spread his hands in mock despair. "Ladies, ladies, you are so *provincial!*"

"Of course we are." Cassie waved a hand to include the area around us. "We live in Provincetown."

I laughed. "Very good, Cassie."

Peter sulked. Wolf continued. "It's Paul Carlucci, not Enrico Caruso. And it's his *t-r-o-u-p-e*, a group of actors, a troupe of players, and they're coming to town! This town! It's quite a deal. They'll be performing at the amphitheater, and if it goes well, it will become one of those yearly festivals that draws hundreds of people. He could put Provincetown on the map."

"We're already on the map," Lainey snipped. "And if we get many more people out here, we're going to sink."

"Lainey, Lainey, this is Broadway writ large!" Peter cried. "Right here in our own backyards!"

"If I wanted Broadway in my backyard I'd live in New York."

I sensed a little tiff brewing and hoped to avoid it. "Who's this Carlucci guy and what does he do?"

Wolf looked at me gratefully. "He's a writer/director in New York. He's done several off Broadway plays that everyone thought had great, great potential, but somehow he just hadn't clicked big-time. Well, he was being interviewed on some talk show a couple of years ago, and the emcee—an idiot, naturally—asked Carlucci if he thought Shakespeare was now outdated. Carlucci answered, 'A great play knows no calendar.'

"Well, he realized he'd gotten off a really good, quotable line, so he took it and ran with it. He swore, then and there, he could take any great play—Shakespearean or other—and make it work today."

"Not so." I lifted my cup for a refill as Cassie walked around with the coffee carafe. "Shakespeare works because of the way he shows human strengths and weaknesses that never really change, no matter when you live. You know, an otherwise great person fails and falls because of too much jealousy or ambition or greed. The one fault finally gets an otherwise great person. Shakespeare doesn't much deal with social issues *per se.*"

Cindy was nodding agreement. "She's right. Look at George Bernard Shaw. His plays were wonderfully written, clever and timely, but you just about never see one produced now, because the issues aren't exactly ours today. Unless you're really into the Shavian politics of the time, you're lost with old GBS."

Cassie emerged with brandies, which she passed around, and Peter broke the tension with a flowery little toast to the new dining room.

Wolf wasn't going to give up easily, however. "All right," he muttered. "But Carlucci has proven his point. He's done three plays and he's made them work. First he took Ibsen's *A Doll's House* and—"

"Oh, hell," Cindy laughed. "You've hit on the one possible exception. *A Doll's House*, to womankind's great misfortune, is still timely, as are one or two of his other plays. In fact, did you know that 'women's liberation' in Chinese is actually the word *nora-ism?*"

"You're kidding!" Cassie held a mug toward Peter for more coffee. "I didn't know the Chinese *had* a word for women's lib."

"Well, they had to borrow it, but I am dead serious."

"Aha!" Wolf crowed. "But in Carlucci's version it wasn't *Nora* who was made to feel less and less a necessary part of the marriage, less a real person. It was the poor *husband!* Carlucci changed the setting to the present and had Nora slowly take over every decision the poor man made. She even took over his business and left him stuck at home with the kids and housework. Finally, in desperation, he left the two kids and scarpered without even a note."

"I love your phrase, Wolf." Cassie had a glint in her eye. "If the husband was *stuck* at home with the kids and housework, what about all the women who are home with them everyday? Should they also *scarper?*" Somehow I felt we were working up to another evening of endangered crockery.

"Was the play a success?" I asked.

"Definitely." Peter took up the baton. "Ran nearly a year, great reviews. And *then* our genius Carlucci came out with the biggie! Remember Somerset Maugham's *Rain*, where the lady of rather ill repute slowly but surely seduces the young missionary on a south sea island during the monsoons?"

A couple of us nodded vaguely. A short story, I thought, and maybe a movie.

"Well, our *wunderkind* renamed it *Snow* and modernized the setting to a B&B in Vermont during a blizzard, with a young priest and a black drag queen, whom the priest thought was really a woman until Act Three! She looked just like Queen Latifah. It was *fabulous!* We saw it in Boston. It has become an absolute cult piece with gay men."

"I can imagine," Cindy said dryly. "But didn't Carlucci have a flop just last winter?"

"Well," Wolf admitted, "He produced *The Second Mrs. Tanqueray* by Sir Arthur Wing Pinero . . . called it *The Tanqueray*

Tragedy. In the original, around 1910, I think, this rich guy divorces his wife of many years and marries a young thing. He insists his social clique accept her, and he is powerful enough to get compliance, at least on the surface. But behind his back they make her life hell. She finally commits suicide." He got up and went to pour another brandy.

"Who cares?" Cassie asked. "People don't place that kind of importance on divorce or social acceptance today. They just make new friends. Today, Tanqueray is just good gin."

"You have a point. So, Carlucci updated the play and made the sweet young girl a sweet young lad." Peter sighed reminiscently. "It was deemed a great *succes d'arte*, a most moving piece."

"An artistic success?" I teased. "Isn't that French for box office failure?"

"Worse than that," Cindy recalled. "I remember reading one review that said, while the poor *laddie* offed himself in Act Three, the audience, unfortunately, had already done the same thing in Act Two." That got her a roar from the lesbian contingent and scowls from Peter and the Wolf. "Who's Carlucci's next victim, *Rebecca of Sunnybrook Farms*?" My lady was on a roll.

"*Hamlet*." Wolf almost spat. "And it will be earthshaking, I can tell you. It's set in a small town down in Georgia, where the old King Hamlet lived. He owned a bunch of discount stores throughout the south. His cousin and wife want to sell out to a big national chain. They kill the old man, but young Hamlet isn't sure exactly who killed him, isn't sure they should sell, feels—like his father—it would be unfair to the employees. Hamlet and Horatio are gay lovers, of course. Take it from there. Can't you just feel the tension! Oh, and it's a musical. Can't you just *see* it?"

"*Hamlet* is a musical, set in the rural south, about discount stores. Who is Ophelia, Miss Georgia Peach of 2007? I can't wait. 'To be or not to be,' set to rockabilly." Cindy stood and looked at me. "Take me home to Tara, darlin', I can't stand no more classic tragedy tonight, y'all."

We made our farewells and went home to an ecstatic Fargo. I

let him out for last patrol and turned to ask Cindy if she wanted a drink or some coffee. Usually, when we got home from any party or such, we dissected the evening over one of the two, and had fun all over again. This time Cindy shook her head. "I think I already had too many brandies or something. I feel numb."

"That may have been the subject matter, not the brandies," I suggested.

"Poor Ibsen. Poor Maugham. Poor Shakespeare. *Poor* Pinero. Nobody's done Pinero since 1930. Hell, no one has *thought* of Pinero since 1930. And *Rain*—I guess Wolf said they called it *Snow*—with a drag queen. I shall take to my bed with a case of the vapors. Good night, my love, and flights of angels sing thee to thy rest." She put her arms out, mimicking an airplane and giggled as she made a little misstep turning into the hall.

She stopped and gave the doorjamb an owlish look. "Damn door always was in the wrong place."

She continued toward the bedroom, singing a little song I devoutly hoped she would forget by morning:

The last camel died at noon,
Humming an old Cole Porter tune.
And while the trail was steep and sandy,
We all enjoyed the Napoleon brandy.

Alas, my ladylove was looped.

Chapter 7

I hate it when the phone rings in the middle of the night. I can never find it before the second ring, and by then I've had time to imagine that everyone I care for is either dead, injured or in a Turkish prison.

Tonight was no exception. It was ten to three, and when I finally got the phone to my ear, I couldn't quite understand what the person on the other end of the line was saying.

"Hello? What? Who's this?"

"Streak, darlin', don't be mean! It's *Bootsie!* And I'm in *town!*"

"I am not 'Streak' and I don't know any Bootsie. You have the wrong number and probably the wrong town, and why the hell are you calling anybody at three in the morning to say you're here? Good-bye."

Fargo picked that moment to jump onto the bed and land on my stomach. So I added a loud "Ooof!" to my farewells.

"What did you say, honey-babe?"

"I said oof. My dog just . . . Christ, why am I having this conversation?"

I heard Cindy give a smothered giggle as Fargo snuggled cozily between us.

"Streak, now be nice. I came just to see you, and this is the number you gave me, so it must be you!"

"I am trying to be nice. My name is Mergatroyd Mountbatten. And I do not know, nor wish to know you. Streak's number is 487-9773. Good-bye." I hung up.

"Whose number was that?" Cindy asked.

"Captain Anders's private line." Anders was outstanding proof that not even Ptown could have cops that were universally smart and dedicated. He was dumb and obnoxious. He had gotten the job through the political clout of a former chief. The clout was now long gone, but how did you get rid of Anders? He never did anything dishonest. He rarely did anything at all. Fortunately, retirement was only a few years away.

"Hopefully," I added, "Mrs. Anders will answer."

"You really are dangerous when somebody wakes you up." Cindy laughed. "Go back to sleep, Streak, darlin'."

"Oh, God."

We all sort of settled down and were quiet. Fargo was the first to begin to snore lightly. A short time later, Cindy's breathing became rhythmic and deep.

And I began to think those calm and happy thoughts that come to us all in the middle hours of the night. What the hell was wrong with Cindy's car? The mechanic had fixed it twice, but it still made that funny noise. The garage door opener moaned piteously with every use. I supposed I'd better get a new one before the damn thing stuck halfway. What had caused my back tooth to give a twang when the ice cream hit it earlier last night? God, I hated dentists! And mine had a billing system that made our defense budget look like Scrooge personified.

Then Fargo began to whimper and twitch his legs in his sleep. Automatically, I reached out and stroked his head. "It's all right, sweetheart. It's all right. I won't let it get you. Go back to sleep. You're safe in bed."

Cindy heaved a disgruntled sigh. "Why do you always wake him up? My brother says when they whine and paddle their feet like that, they're having a wonderful dream about chasing rabbits, or maybe squirrels or a cat."

"I have heard that," I replied loftily, "But no dog has ever been able to reassure me that it doesn't mean a five-hundred pound rabbit wasn't chasing *them*. Therefore, I go to their rescue."

"Oh. How thoughtful."

They both went to sleep again. I lay staring at the window. When I realized I could see things outside, I gave up and got up. After dressing quietly, I made a pot of tea and thought about getting my camera and going out. But it wasn't much fun alone. Before I could decide, two rather frazzled beauties joined me and all was normal.

After tea for two and a biscuit for one, we went to the beach.

As the dog ran ahead of us and we walked down to sea level, I was once again reminded of why I loved this place. A few miles offshore, a gray fog bank squatted on the horizon like a grumpy toad, and above it, cirrus clouds reflected the radiant orange-pink glow from a sun not quite risen above them. The ocean was almost calm, with no breakers out to sea, and only wavelets reaching the shore, rippling almost apologetically along the low-tide line. Even the breeze seemed shy, just touching your cheek and then fading, as if not wishing to intrude upon your thoughts.

Far down the beach, another dog appeared—maybe one of the Coasties had it with him overnight and felt secure in letting it run this early in the morning. It was a Dalmatian, I thought, lean and graceful. The two dogs spotted each other and began to run right toward each other, like knights in a tilting match. They covered the ground at amazing speed.

"Are they going to kill each other?" Cindy's voice held alarm. She grabbed my arm and pointed.

"I hope surely one of them will give way. God, they must have a closing speed of fifty miles an hour!" I was getting a little concerned about a collision myself, and couldn't decide whether it would be better to bellow at Fargo to come back, or not distract him.

Before I could decide, both dogs had slithered to a stop, scattering great clods of wet sand around them. Then began the sniffing ritual, followed by their backing off, facing each other and bowing with front legs low and extended, rear end and tail up in the air . . . the universal animal symbol of, "Want to play?" Yes, indeed! Fargo ran in a wide circle, the Dalmatian in hot pursuit. Then Fargo crashed into the water, leaping through the shallows and beginning that strong swim, which always makes me worry slightly that his next stop might be the Azores.

The Dalmatian followed him into shallow water and stopped, unsure whether she wanted to continue or not. She nibbled daintily at the water and shook her head in distaste. She took a few more tentative steps and stopped when a small wave splashed across her chest. Retiring to the edge, she barked and Fargo turned. I could almost see his shrug as he swam back to shore to rejoin his more timid companion.

They trotted over to us to say hello. The female Dalmatian was a friendly beauty, and I pulled out a couple of small biscuits for each of them. At that point a young woman appeared down where the animal had begun her run. She was waving and blowing a shrill whistle. The Dalmatian looked up, gently accepted the treat and turned for home. Fargo followed her a few steps, and I called him back. The three of us walked over to a half-sunken tree stump and sat down. Fargo stared down the beach.

"Do you suppose he needs a playmate?" I said.

Cindy gave me a look over the top of her dark glasses. "Don't even think about it. Let's go home and go to bed. You must be delirious."

I was in that sort of out-of-body state where you are so tired you are past tired and too wired to be sleepy. "Aha!" I leered. "The lady is propositioning me!"

"No, the lady has every intention of going to bed to sleep, per-chance to dream."

"Oh, Shakespeare. Right, the players are coming with their polyester-suited Hamlet. I can hear him singing that soliloquy now." I picked up a stick and began a rap beat on the tree trunk. Cindy wasn't the only one who could compose a song.

To be or not to be is the question, yessiree,
To off ol' Claudius or leave him be?
An' do I stab Polonius behind that drape?
Or watch sweet Ophelia wrap herself in crepe?
Of course there's always darling mother
To poison her or smother . . .

Cindy gave me a withering look and stood. "Come on, Fargo." She began to walk up the beach. "Let yo' mama sit there and suffer slings and arrows of outrageous fortune. You and I will stop and buy the papers, not to mention a few pastries, and then we'll have a lovely nap. Let's go, boy. Anyway, I don't like the looks of the alligator under that log."

I knew they wouldn't go far. They'd stop and look back and wait.

She broke into a jog, Fargo trotting happily by her side.

"Hey! Hold up! Wait for me!"

Chapter 8

Earlier in the summer a tourist had dozed off while driving his car through Provincetown's snail-paced traffic. One could hardly blame him, but my friend Marcia Robby—also understandably—was not pleased to find his ancient and large Oldsmobile sitting in the front room of her antique shop. It had been my pleasure, as well as my job, to expedite repairs and to find her a place to live while repairs were made. I picked Green Mansions. I figured that Peter and the Wolf, combined with their Victorian décor, would make a good blend. And I had been right, she loved it there.

Marcia made out well with the repairs, with a lovely big bow window replacing the three small ones that had been knocked out, and an inviting new walkway with neat landscaping leading up to the door. The interior was much brighter and seemed more spacious. She had presented Peter and the Wolf with a giant, kitschy Victorian lamp as a thank-you for their hospitality, and they were delighted. And she had given me a lovely small round table, which now sat under our dining room windows, providing an intimate little dining table when Cindy and I felt privately formal.

I was using it at the moment to fill out some forms for a couple of insurance cases I had just closed. They were both straightforward and basically dull, which suited me fine.

One was at an older B&B, where a young woman claimed to have tripped on a frayed rug and taken a header down the stairs, managing to break both her leg and her wrist. She was, unfortunately for the insured and insurer, quite right. I took photos, sent them in with a report and warned the owners to make repairs in a hurry before someone else took to the air.

The other one was more fun, for me, anyway. A man in his forties had been walking up the driveway of a house advertising homemade fudge for sale. He claimed to have fallen over a tricycle that was blocking the driveway, and that he hadn't seen. He claimed a painfully sprained back. I told the owners over the phone to make sure no one moved the tricycle until I could get down there to take photos. The way I saw it, the bright red trike was parked mostly on the lawn with one lone back wheel on the driveway, not even knocked over and leaving room to drive a small truck easily around it. And it was broad daylight.

I caught up with the victim coming out of X-ray at the hospital, clad only in one of those little hospital gowns, which he was trying simultaneously to pull down in the front and hold together in the rear. Well, don't we all? I cannot imagine anyone being a hero in these circumstances. I flashed my private investigator's license, my thumb carefully concealing the word *private* and gave him the bad news.

The insurance company would pay for whatever medical care he had received up to this minute . . . period. If he elected not to sign a release but to pursue the matter, the company would probably go after him for all medical and legal costs, plus my fee. When I showed him the Polaroids of the tricycle's location, he signed.

I went back to give the good news to the owners, and they gave me a small box of fudge in return. That night, when Cindy asked me where the candy came from, I told her I'd taken it from a baby.

This morning I sat idly adding items to a grocery list Cindy had given me at breakfast, and realized that suddenly it was almost the beginning of August, past the halfway mark in our Season, and still Cindy and I had not had *that* conversation. My talk with Mom about it had come back to me sharply only last night.

During dinner, Cindy had mentioned that the bathroom and the kitchen were strongly in need of painting, but somehow she had sounded tentative, as if she weren't sure she should bring it up. Like maybe she figured it was my house and she had no right to be telling me about the décor?

I felt awful. Had I made her feel she wasn't a full-time partner? What the hell was the matter with me that I'd rather go chasing alligators and the fraudulently injured than have a plain and simple talk with the woman I loved? Sometimes I really worried that I had a blank spot in my emotions somewhere.

My first instinct, upon hearing her comments, had been to reply that I thought the rooms did not especially need painting. Thankfully, I had not made that statement! I looked around the kitchen and agreed it was a bit shabby, and that I'd noticed a little peeling in one corner of the bathroom. Yes, we should run over to Jake's Hardware on Saturday and get some paint chips. Then we'd get Harmon in to do the work whenever he was free.

She had seemed very pleased and said she loved looking at paint chips. But I knew I had simply applied a Band-Aid to the wound. I *had* to get my act together. I poured more coffee and sat back down to rehearse my little speech. I was going to give it tonight, for sure!

A tap on the back screen door interrupted my rehearsal. It was Carla Brownlee, our next-door neighbor, a pleasant woman in her early fifties.

"Carla! Come in. How about a coffee?"

"That sounds good and, here, your favorite cookies—oatmeal Scotties." She placed a covered paper plate on the table.

"Are they ever my favorite! Thanks, I needed that." I put the mug in front of her, remembered she took milk and actually

61

poured some into a little pitcher, placing it neatly near her, along with the sugar bowl, napkin and spoon. Mom and Cindy would be proud. "So, Carla, what's new in the 'hood?"

"Well." She hesitated slightly. "Good news for Bob and me. You and Cindy may not agree."

"My God, you haven't gone and sold your place, have you?" My stomach gave a lurch. The Brownlees had been good, friendly— but not too friendly—neighbors for years. Who knew what their replacements might be like? Like reaching for a life preserver, I grabbed a cookie.

"No, no, not even a thought of that," she quickly assured me. "But we *have* rented it—the whole house—from next Thursday through Labor Day."

"How did you ever manage that?" The Brownlees rented six rooms to tourists and provided a lush Continental breakfast to start their days. The house was luxuriously furnished and boasted elegant table settings and accoutrements. Bob Brownlee had a museum-quality collection of seventeenth and eighteenth century snuffboxes which he kept displayed in a locked glass cabinet. All in all, the place was lovely.

Carla set down her mug. "Well, you know the realtor, Ellen Hall?" I nodded. She and her partner were friends of ours. "Ellen called me last week. It seems some big Broadway producer is going to do a Shakespearean play out at the amphitheater over Labor Day weekend. They've been rehearsing in New York, but will start rehearsing up here soon, of course, and they need rooms for the actors and the rest of their people. Ellen mentioned lighting technicians, and sound people, wardrobe folks . . . all sorts of people I never really thought of whenever I saw a play. They're renting out several houses in town."

She sipped her coffee and continued. "It can't be easy. I know we had a tough time canceling our regulars and finding other places they could stay."

I lit cigarette number two for the day, hard on the heels of number one. I'd have to watch it to stay within my quota of five . . . well, I would try.

62

"I hope to God we get the actors and not the band." I lifted my head skyward.

"Good grief, is there really a band? Well, yes, I suppose there would be, since it's a musical." Carla laughed. "Fear not, my dear, you are getting the leading actors, the *stars*! Shakespearean actors! Surely, Shakespearean actors will be well behaved. And the director himself will be in our own ground floor bed-sitter." She said "director" as if she were saying "emperor," and then sobered. "Alex, I really do hope they don't bother you and Cindy."

"I'm sure it will be perfectly fine. But seriously, Carla, things like Bob's snuffboxes . . ."

" . . . are in the bank. The rest of the silver and china and crystal are safely locked in a closet in the basement. Our tenants will be left with everything expendable. I think it's a win-win, Alex."

I wondered if she considered the grand piano, the carpets and the appliances expendable? Perhaps I was remembering the tale a friend from Connecticut told us about the amount of damage Liz Taylor and some husband or other once wreaked on a lovely summer rental by the beach on Blue Hill in Westport. He said the owner's wife went into a nervous collapse on viewing it when they returned home. And there were only two of them!

Carla finished her coffee and continued. "We're making about as much as we would if we rented daily, at full capacity, with none of the stress. Ellie and Betts, our regular maids, will continue taking care of things, only *we* don't have to pay them! And Thursday bright and early, Bob and I are off to spend the rest of the summer at my sister's place out on the Michigan peninsula. Now, Alex, if you have any problems at all about the tenants, call Ellen. She's handling everything about the rental. Tell Cindy bye for us." She stood, smiling, arms outstretched.

I got up and gave her a hug. I wished them well and hoped they'd gotten a sizeable damage deposit. Little did I guess that no damage deposit existed that would cover the events the players would bring to town.

❧

Cindy and I did not have *that* conversation that night. We were too busy wondering what our new neighbors would be like. Neither Cindy nor I were sure that "Shakespearean actor" automatically translated into "desirable neighbor." And even if it did, we weren't too sure that people one thought of as *Shakespearean actors* would be doing a modern *Hamlet* musical set in rural Georgia.

Thursday morning, Cindy left for work with great regret. I had strict instructions to call her the minute the players arrived, with full descriptions of what they looked and sounded like and what they were wearing. Did she think they would be in Elizabethan attire? She had hinted strongly that I should spend the day weeding the flower bed along our driveway, so that I would just happen to be out front and could casually make them welcome when they drove up. Would they say things like, "Fie, my good fellow, parkest not in front of yon fireplug?"

I finally got her out of the house—late—and had just decided on another coffee, when the phone rang. It was my mother. She knew both Cindy and I had busy schedules, so if we were inviting the travel-weary actors over for drinks and nibbles this evening, she would be happy to make up some canapés and bring them by. I told her I thought it might be just a little premature to strike up friendships so early in their stay, and we parted rather stiffly.

Moments later Aunt Mae took her shot at it. She believed that little pots of herbs always made such thoughtful welcome gifts. If I would like her to select some especially unusual ones and later bring them by, she would be more than willing to do so. Just let her know how many were needed. I told her I didn't know which, if any, of the actors might be into cooking, but if I heard of any interest in herbs, I'd let her know. Her good-bye seemed just a little cool, also.

I gave a drooping Fargo his breakfast. He ignored it and sat by the back door, head down, a picture of despair. He had somehow deduced he would not be running errands with me. "Angel Dog," I explained, "It's too hot to leave you in the car when I'm going into stores. Parking lots are like ovens. You would melt."

Ready to go out the door, I offered him a farewell biscuit. He sniffed it and looked away, so I put it beside his dish. As I went out the door, he staggered weakly toward his bed, overcome with terminal depression. I knew damn well he would scarf down the biscuit the minute I was out of the driveway. I knew he also had food, fresh water, a rawhide, a cool kitchen, and I'd be back in two or three hours, so I really felt no guilt. Much.

Still alive upon my return, Fargo circled the yard in apparent restored health, checking for two- or four-legged intruders, rolling in the grass, taking a playful nip of a tomato plant, just to tease me.

I made several trips carrying the groceries, the cleaning and the wine into the house and nobly stowed them away. I put the grass trimmer line in the garage, and noted I'd forgotten to buy mulch. Then, back inside the house, I sat down beside the answering machine, to calm its nervous twitters.

Cassie just thought I might want to advise the actors she was always ready, should they need a fast trip anywhere. Cindy wondered if anything was going on yet. Billy Whitmire reminded me he had tuned Carla Brownlee's piano back in June, but if any of the actors felt it needed some small adjustments, he'd be happy to run over. Free of charge, naturally. Mildred Morris wasn't sure the cast would have brought any office personnel along, so if they needed help in keeping track of local expenses, filing invoices or anything like that, she could come by almost any time and would be happy to help out. Cindy wondered crossly where on earth I was.

I ignored the other calls and called Cindy to report all quiet at the front lines.

I popped a Bud and went out to join Fargo. He had forgotten his earlier pout and trotted over, ready for an ear-fondle.

I complied, and now it was I who sighed. "Fargo, my love, our thespian troupe ain't even in town yet, and already they're driving me crazy. What the hell will it be like once they get here?"

He rolled onto his back, my signal to provide a tummy scritch. Projection is never a problem with dogs.

Chapter 9

My plans for Friday morning had been to mount a bunch of photos and put them in their frames, ready to go to the various shops and galleries that carried them and needed replacements for those they had sold. Actually, I spent most of the morning on the phone.

Vance called. He and Dan just wondered if we were all right. We had been with them—and in perfectly good health—last weekend at the Poly/Cotton Club, but I thanked him for his concern, and no, no actors had yet arrived.

Lainey called, just wanting to make sure the blister on Cindy's heel had healed properly. It had, nearly two weeks ago. No, no actors in sight.

Even Mary Sloan called. She and Ann hadn't run into us in ages and were just wondering how we were. And had we met anyone famous yet?

Peter and the Wolf called, just to say "Hi." "Hi" included a subtle question about "Anything new going on?" No, nothing new. Except our newfound popularity.

I looked at Fargo, who took that moment to walk to the door and give me a quizzical glance. "You are right, Dog of Dogs. It's lunchtime, and I have accomplished nada. I think I'll repair to my 'other office' and let the answering machine do what those clever people at G.E. built it for." I eased around him and was out the door before he realized he was left behind. "I'm sorry, Fargo," I called. "We go through this every summer. It's just too *hot!*"

Ever efficient, I took the car and stopped by Gammon's Nursery to pick up the forgotten mulch. Then, with incredible luck, I got a parking space right at the head of the alley leading down to the Rat.

The day was having trouble making up its mind what it wanted to do. I'd awakened to clouds, which gave way to sun. Now the clouds were moving in again.

Even at the Wharf Rat there was no escape from the world of drama. Joe's opening words were, "Are they here yet?"

"Not as of half an hour ago, and I'm already sick of hearing about them. Just give me a Bud, Joe. My phone has rung off the hook for two days. How does word get around so fast?"

He beat his hands on the edge of the bar and intoned, "*Boom*, boom, boom, boom, *boom*, boom, boom, boom. Okay, one Bud. Want a pastrami? It's nice and lean."

"Why not?"

"Hi, Alex." The aroma of garlic and beer was a sure ID.

"Hello, Harmon, how are you?"

"I understand you got a bunch of actors movin' in next door at Bob Brownlee's place."

"Yes, but they aren't here yet." Maybe I could just tape this sentence and play it when asked.

"Well, Bob, he ast me to look after the yard while they's away. I'm glad to do it, of course, they're nice and they always pay good. But it's a perfect excuse to be there a lot and keep an eye on things."

Unthinking, I replied, "Oh, I think all the valuables are safely locked away, Harmon. You don't have to worry about theft . . . not that I have any reason to think they'd steal anything. They're probably perfectly honest."

"Maybe, maybe not." He raised his chin and straightened his stance. "I'll be on the lookout, never you fear. You tell Sonny there ain't no drugs gonna go in nor out of that place but what I know it. You tell him I'm on the job."

"I will do that, Harmon." And I knew Sonny would be thrilled. I had no idea if our unseen actors enjoyed an occasional recreational drug, or shot up heroin four times a day, or were clean as arctic snow. But I did know one thing: Bob Brownlee was going to have the best kept lawn in Massachusetts.

The weather had finally reached a decision. By the time I got to the car, the dust on the windshield was beginning to spatter into mud. By the time I got home, the rain had settled into a slow drizzle that looked as if it might stay a while. Pulled up in front of the Brownlees' were two white vans. Or, more accurately, one van was parked in front of the Brownlee's, the other was behind it, blocking my driveway. Eight or nine people milled around the vehicles, unloading enormous amounts of luggage.

I stopped in front of my house and opened the car door, to hear Fargo barking lustily and ceaselessly out the dining room window. What really intrigued me was that he seemed to be sitting on the little antique table Marcia had given us, and I wondered what had happened to the lamp that ordinarily sat on it.

I got out of the car, to be greeted by a good-looking big, tall guy with his hand extended.

"Hello. We've blocked your driveway. I'm sorry. I'll get one of the drivers to move the van as soon as I can find him. We're not quite organized yet. I'm Noel Fortnum, by the way."

We shook hands. I knew who he was. I'd seen him in a revival of *Mame*, where he'd played Mame's ill-fated millionaire husband. He'd done some TV stuff, too, I recalled.

"Welcome to a rainy Provincetown. I'm Alex Peres, and don't worry about my car. It won't melt." I smiled. "Nor will I."

"Well, let me at least see what I can do about getting some luggage out of here." He turned toward the van and then back. "Oh, hi, Terese. Some of this stuff is yours, isn't it? Point it out and I'll get it out of the van for you. And Terese Segal, meet our next-door neighbor, Alex Peres."

"Everything has an ID tag, all you have to do is look. My room is Number One upstairs. You can put it there. Careful with the laptop." Ms. Segal, wearing a raincoat and hat with her wispy, carrot-colored hair now frizzled around the edges like some long-unstarched lace trim, gave me a head to toe look and dismissed me as one of the dull natives. We did not bother to shake hands.

"That your dog?"

"Yes."

"I hope he's not going to be a nuisance. Why is he barking so much?"

"His original owner was a porn film maker. It traumatized the puppy so much he still is frightened of actors." Actually, Fargo's breeder was a lovely retired postman with a farm in Vermont, who probably thought Doris Day films were daringly risqué. And I had owned Fargo since he was eight weeks old. He wasn't afraid of anybody. He assumed everyone he met loved him. Mostly, he was right. With the charming Ms. Segal, I wasn't so sure.

"You wouldn't believe what I've spent on shrinks for him. What part do you have in the play? Lady Macbeth?"

I heard Noel smother a laugh. Ms. Segal tightened her already small mouth and answered, "No, I'm not one of the troupe. I'm an embedded journalist for the *A-List*." She favored me with a slight wiggle of her somewhat pointy nose, a professional prerequisite, perhaps.

I knew the *A-List* was one of those weekly magazines filled with information, disinformation and misinformation about various celebrities and wannabe celebrities and used-to-be celebrities. My only question was: with whom was Ms. Terese Segal currently embedded?

She took me aback with her next question. "Tell me, are there a lot of drugs in Provincetown?"

"I really am not up on that," I answered. "They've never been my thing." And then I had one of my ingenious, but not always wise, thoughts. "However, I know a fellow who does undercover work for the Ptown cops . . . closest thing we have to a narc, I guess. He hangs out at the Wharf Rat Bar, says he gets lots of tips there from the fishermen. Just ask the bartender to point out Mr. Harmon Killingsly, and he'll be glad to help you, I'm sure."

She scribbled Harmon's name into a notebook, nodded and turned away without further comment. I had served my purpose, I no longer existed. Well, thank you, too, Ms. Segal.

Noel was at my side again, having unloaded the contents of the van onto the sidewalk. "She'll be waiting awhile before *I* carry her bags up. I haven't bellhopped since my college days in the Poconos. Since you're here, why not meet the rest of us? We aren't all that bad."

"I'm sure." I laughed. "Just let me go and see why my dog seems to be sitting on the dining table. I'll be right back."

Inside, I did indeed find Fargo sitting on the table, nose stuck through the blinds like that of a curious old woman. The lamp was lying on the floor, and paw marks smudged the tablecloth. I shooed him off and quickly turned the tablecloth over, picked up the lamp, more or less smoothed out several small dings in the shade and put it back on the table. There! All good as new. I leashed Fargo and we went out. I wanted to be able to give Cindy as full a report as possible.

My next introduction was to Teri Malewski, who was to play Ophelia. She was a pretty blonde in her early twenties, standing beside her luggage, which consisted of a battered duffel bag and an obviously new and expensive suitcase. Her bags rather summed her up, I thought—newly into stardom, yet with personal experience perhaps far beyond her years. She was polite but distracted, obviously looking for someone.

Her search ended as a navy blue Porsche pulled up behind my

car, and a tall, slender man got gracefully out. "Oh, Paul, thank God you're here! For some reason they've put me way up on the third floor with Nick Peters, you know, that creepy stage manager. We've got the only two rooms up there, and I have to share a *bathroom* with him!"

She leaned her head against his chest. "Oh, Paulie, I'll be way up there all alone with him, and he's *weird!* Can't you do something?"

"Yes, yes, darling, you'll be quite . . . Don't worry. Nick is sometimes just a little hard to . . . Stay cool, Paulie is here and you know I . . ."

During all this, Paul Carlucci managed to absorb Noel's introduction and offered me a firm warm handshake, topped off with a salesman's smile. "Ms. Peres! Delighted . . . heard such lovely things about you from Ellen Hall. We must have you and your friend for drinks . . . getting settled today, but soon, soon . . . looking forward to it! Yessir, very soon . . ." And he was gone, still smiling and nodding, with a comet's tail of people behind him asking questions and wailing problems. He must have infinite patience. The hullabaloo around him didn't seem to bother him in the least.

My next introduction was to Elaine Edgewood. Both her name and face were familiar to me, but I couldn't place her. She was fairly tall, with a long and graceful neck, and rather average looking at first glance—straight brown hair in a ponytail, but with lovely brown eyes and an expressive mouth that gave her an elusive beauty. I put her at plus or minus forty-five.

Noel gave her an affectionate hug. "Elaine is Hamlet's mother, Gertrude—my *inamorata* in the play, by the way. Unfortunately, in our little play she's usually called *Queenie*. Silly name."

Elaine raised her eyebrows and grinned. "There are those who might say it's a silly play. Not I, of course. I think we may present a *Hamlet* that will make more headlines than the original ever did."

She and Noel laughed at some private joke, and I smiled politely. "Ms Edgewood, I'm sure I've seen you somewhere recently. You look very familiar, but I'm having trouble—"

"Please call me Elaine. I'm getting ancient enough, fast enough, as it is. Well, my most recent Broadway role was Sylvia, the older sister in *Fondly Remembered*. Or, a few months back on TV, I played Molly, the half-Indian woman in the *Follow the Sun* miniseries."

"Oh, that's it, I'm sure. Yes, I enjoyed your role. She was quite a character."

"Thank you . . . oh, excuse me a moment." She turned toward a rather short, almost pudgy man standing behind her, apparently listening to our conversation. "Nick." She smiled. "I tried to shift your footlocker, but it's a mite hefty. If you could just take it out, I could get my stuff out, and I think that would empty this van that's blocking Alex's driveway. The driver could take the van wherever they're going to keep them, or you or Noel could just move it out of the way. At least let the woman get to her own garage and out of the rain."

"You do love things neat and orderly, don't you, Elaine? Anything to have everything in a tidy little box, so it looks like all's well with the world." He put out his hand to me. "I'm Nick Peters, the stage manager, the only plebian in this august group. I hope we'll all make good neighbors." His smile was sweet, contradicting his sarcastic speech, but I noticed his light blue eyes seemed watchful and did not warm up with the smile. Elaine looked pained and turned away.

"I'm sure you will make lovely neighbors." I smiled back. "The problem may be the other way around. Just about everyone I know is all excited about having a theater group in town. By tomorrow, they may be lined up along my wall, hoping to meet you."

"Oh, they won't even notice *me*," Nick almost simpered. "My name is in small print in the Playbill. But they're sure to be begging autographs from our leading man, won't they, oh, royal Prince Hamlet?"

"Not unless the weather improves." The subject of Nick's snipe sauntered across the lawn to us. The rain had dwindled to a fine mist, and he wore no hat, revealing blond curls flecked with raindrops. He was tall and broad-shouldered, with narrow hips clad in tight jeans. His tan flattered his deep blue eyes, and as he neared us we received the full brightness of his smile. He was quite gorgeous and well aware of it. "Hi. I'm David Willem."

"Alex Peres," I answered. "And trusty companion, Fargo."

"Hello, trusty companion. I'll bet you take very good care of your owner. Watch out, Elaine, there'll be no sneaking over the wall at midnight with Fargo on guard," he teased.

"Don't be bitchy, darling. And if I go sneaking over walls I always carry a doggy biscuit."

Well, that answered one question. I had thought Elaine might be gay. About the men, I wasn't sure yet.

Carlucci appeared on the porch. "Sorry to interrupt, but I need you all inside for a moment. Let's get things settled in here, and maybe go over a few ground rules. Come on, my happy band of brothers—and sisters. Dear Alex, you will forgive us . . . just dull, dull business . . . drinkies soon . . . perhaps tomorrow . . ." Did he ever finish a sentence?

Fargo seemed happy to get home. So was I. I felt some tension in the air, like an approaching electrical storm—not about me, but surrounding my new neighbors. They had all been very nice to me, except for the *embedded* journalist, and I felt I had handled that well. I was sure she considered me a dull and stupid local and wouldn't bother with me anymore, which was exactly what I preferred. And once she found Harmon, she should have no trouble thinking up headlines.

As for the troupe in general, I wasn't sure they were in the least a happy band.

Chapter 10

By now, everyone had a favorite name for that summer: mad, weird, crazy, scary, nutty. The swarms of tourists, the belching tour buses, the crowded ways, the ear-splitting music issuing from nearly every building along Commercial Street, were just part of Ptown's daily life in midsummer.

But now we had the troupe of players come to town. We had recovered from the fright of the unseen alligator, and I had the feeling that any one of our lately arrived thespians might be more likely to chase a naked lady up a tree than any aquatic beast.

Determined not to rearrange life around a bunch of strange people who would be living next door for six weeks, Fargo and I made our usual early morning beach run, and picked up the weekend goodies on the way home. On our return we had a croissant, which we shared, and kibble, which we did not. By my second cup of coffee, Cindy joined us.

She kissed the top of my head, and then the top of Fargo's, which pleased us both greatly, and poured herself a cup of coffee.

Joining us at the table, she cut an almond croissant and transferred half of it to her plate, where she broke off a tiny piece and chewed it slowly.

"Good." She nodded, and broke off another mini bite. "By the way, I noticed the strangest thing. The cloth for the little dining room table was put on wrong side up. When I took it off there was dirt and maybe paw marks on it, and the lampshade has a couple of dents that weren't there when the lamp arrived. Isn't that strange?" She looked at me quizzically.

"Really?"

"Yes, really. Alex, what on earth were . . . ?"

"Well." I stood up briskly. "I've got to get going on framing those photos. Fargo, here, you go outside for awhile."

That was the way the day went. We met, parted, and met again. Late morning we gathered outdoors, where two of us had iced tea and one of us had a bowl of cool water and a biscuit.

Cindy called Fargo to her side and told him to sit. "Now, confess, Fargo, so I don't have to beat you. Did you jump up on the table for some reason and knock off the lamp? And did Alex rearrange everything and really think I wouldn't notice a dirty, wrong-side cloth and bent lamp?"

He knew he was being asked if he had done something bad, but since he had long forgotten that he had, he simply grinned and wagged his tail.

"I thought so," Cindy said, and gave him a pretend spank on the hindquarters. But she couldn't help grinning back. "What were you doing, fella, checking up on our new neighbors along with everybody else?" Turning to me, she asked, "Do we have anything special on for today?"

"Nope. Nor tonight."

She looked askance. "You mean we are actually home on a Saturday night? Do you suppose this is just some social oversight, or should I check the expiration date on the deodorant?"

"I think it's the midsummer doldrums. I suppose we could stir up some action," I added without great enthusiasm.

She shook her head quickly. "No, not unless you really, *really* want to. It's been a long week. Maybe I'll just run over to Evans's Market and pick up a roast chicken and some pasta salad. We'll slice some of your prize tomatoes with mozzarella, and we'll just have a private backyard picnic for you and me and Fargo and Wells. How's that sound?"

"Per-fect-o!"

And again we parted to mulch the garden, prepare clothes for the next work week, patrol the wall against invaders.

Around five thirty Mom and Aunt Mae just dropped by, Mom with a big Cobb salad with seared scallops and shrimp, Aunt Mae with one of her richly magnificent applesauce cakes.

Then, in rapid succession, we accumulated Peter and the Wolf, with an enormous chunk of Jarlsberg cheese, some fancy crackers and two bottles of wine. They were followed by Cassie and Lainey with another of Evans's chickens and a bunch of corn muffins. And finally, we acquired Trish and Sonny, bearing a small ham and four six-packs of beer.

It would seem Cindy and I had a dinner party underway, which no one had bothered to tell us we were going to host. We knew, of course, the devious reasoning behind the arrival of these people. But I wondered what they thought they would accomplish besides feeding us all a veritable banquet. Had they concealed telescopes somewhere in their clothing? Were they carrying cameras that looked like cigarette lighters or phones or pencils? Were they planning to speak in pear-shaped tones, hoping to be hired as extras?

Did they really think there might be some rehearsal taking place in the backyard next door, complete with armor and dueling foils and cries of, "Take that, you dastardly villain!" Or did they figure our semi-famous neighbors would simply hop the low wall and join the festivities when they got a whiff of the food?

In point of fact, that was exactly what happened, in a small way. I noticed Elaine and Noel come out onto their back porch and sit down with the evening papers. They looked sort of lonely and I called over to them.

"Elaine, Noel! We're having a kind of impromptu picnic here. If you're not busy, we'd love to have you join us."

They seemed glad of the invitation. I introduced them around and got them drinks, and everybody seemed to be quite at ease. At some point, I heard Elaine and Aunt Mae discussing herbs. Noel and Cindy and Sonny were talking about college funds for kids. I heard Trish offering Elaine a ride in her boat, and then Peter was inviting Noel to one of their soirees, although Noel seemed to be delicately declining. Mother helped rescue him with a question about mastering different dialects.

Finally, we had all eaten our fill. Dusk was falling as we sipped coffee or beer or whatever. And silence fell comfortably over us as well. After awhile, I spoke.

"Well, Elaine, Noel, tell us. Why are you here?"

"Oh, my good lady," Elaine quickly answered. "We are but a poor troupe of players, come to entertain you with our dramatic antics. We bring you now a tale rife with greed and passion, falsity and betrayal, and, alas, of murders most foul. Our play is called *Hamlet*."

"And if you listen closely"—Noel set down his beer—"you may recognize some small resemblance to an earlier play with the same title. *Our* play is set in the present, in a small city in northern Georgia, named Dalton. Some years before the play opens, a businessman named Fred Hamlet made his home there and opened a discount store. It did well, and he opened another, and another, and another, until he had some thirty stores around the south and was a very wealthy man. Fred called his stores *KustomerKing Stores*, and he soon earned the nickname King Hamlet."

Elaine took up the tale again. "A giant chain named *Big Mart*, sometimes called *Pig Mart*, wanted to buy him out, but King Hamlet was uncertain. He had a feeling this corporate giant would not be economically good for the various small town independent merchants in his areas, and he was afraid the large corporation would not treat his KustomerKing employees well when the behemoth took over his stores. Fred was a good man."

She bummed a cigarette from Sonny, who actually had a pack, and continued. "Some of King's executives and certain family members who owned stock in *KustomerKing* disagreed. They wanted to take the money and run. Among them were his wife, *Queenie*, and his cousin, *Duke Hamlet*, who was very, *very* fond of Queenie. Wanting *not* to sell was the CFO, Joe Polonius, who for years had been skimming millions off the profits and into his personal offshore accounts, and was afraid Big Mart's audit would find him out. Undecided was King Hamlet's son, Prince Hamlet, although he seemed to be tilting toward his father's side. As you can see, we have a volatile situation here and much intrigue and possible treachery."

Sonny and I freshened drinks all around, as Elaine went on. "Suddenly, on a weekend fishing trip to the family cabin on the lake, King Hamlet drops dead of a heart attack. The only other person with him is the Duke. The coroner is uneasy about the cause of death and wants to have the body examined by the Georgia Bureau of Investigation. The local police chief pooh-poohs the idea. After all, didn't the Duke have a big barbecue for the police and firemen every year? Wasn't he a member of the NRA and the Slippery Elm Baptist Church? The Duke was a good ol' boy who wouldn't never hurt nobody, and that was that. There was no investigation, but there was a wedding." She reached for her coffee.

Noel stood up and began to walk around us. "Indeed, wedding bells chimed for Queenie and the Duke, so hard upon the heels of King's burial, that many people said the leftover funeral meats were simply sliced into cold cuts for the wedding feast."

He paused and leaned on the back of Mom's chair. She looked up and gave him a smile. "Er . . . uh, well . . ." He lost his train of thought. I imagined Mom's smile could do that to you if you were a man. Recovering, he continued. "Now comes Prince Hamlet home from college for the funeral and into a hornet's nest. He discovers the coroner's misgivings. He finds that Polonius's son Laertes, called Larry, has maliciously 'outed' Hamlet's affair with

Horatio, while Polonius is busy cooking the books. Lovely family. Prince Hamlet is now disgusted with, and untrusting of, his mother, his uncle and Polonius and Larry. He is sure of only one thing: he has inherited sufficient stock to swing the decision either way."

I put down my beer and raised my hand, as if in class. Noel smiled and nodded for me to speak. "I always thought Hamlet and Horatio were gay anyway. I mean in the original play. Remember at some point Ophelia can't figure why Hamlet won't give in and marry her? She says something like, 'You had promised me to wed, but would you have tumbled me if I came into your bed?'"

Noel paused in his perambulation and now rested his hands on the back of my chair. "Aha, ladies and gentlemen, a Shakespearean scholar among us!" My mother and aunt gave a couple of hand-claps. I felt myself turn red and buried my nose in my coffee mug as Noel went on. "Many of us have held that thought, but somehow it never took off with most scholars. My personal opinion is that the NRA squelched it. Probably figured it would be fatal to the male bonding they all find so masculine, yet so *terribly* satisfying."

Noel got a good swell of laughter out of that one, combined with several calls of, "Hear, hear!" He bowed and took up the tale again. "Now Prince Hamlet starts his fatal downhill run. First, Ophelia kills herself, leaving a note that she can't face her family and her social world with everyone knowing the Hamlet she so loved threw her over for another man."

Sonny handed him a beer. He nodded his thanks and took a sip. "Then one night, as Hamlet comes home, he hears his mother scream, 'Someone is on the balcony! They're going to kill me. Help!' Knowing his father kept a pistol in an end table, our brave prince runs in, grabs it and fires at the figure struggling to free himself from the folds of the draperies. And who falls out, dying, but poor old felonious Polonius? His last words are, 'But, Queenie, you knew I was coming. You told me to meet you here so we wouldn't be disturbed.'"

"But," Elaine added regally, "I insist that Polonius was simply dying and confused, that I had told him nothing of the sort. And of course, the ever-faithful local cops write the incident off as a sad accident. That's fine for the public, but Hamlet now is almost certain Mummy helped Duke with the king's death and set up Polonius."

She sank gracefully into a chair. "A few days later at a family 'business' meeting, Laertes bursts in, back from a trip to their Caribbean bank and shoots Hamlet to avenge his father Polonius's death. Mortally wounded, Prince Hamlet fires back and kills Laertes, who manages first to blurt out that the Duke gave him ten grand to out Hamlet and Horatio. Hamlet blows the Duke away, turns to me and says I have no right to live after all I've done, and kills me. Finally, Hamlet collapses and dies in Horatio's arms."

"And there you have it, my lords and ladies." Noel pulled Elaine to her feet for his bow and her curtsy. "A typical Shakespearean tragic ending—blood and corpses all over the stage."

There was a spontaneous round of applause. My mother, however, shook her head. "Do you think, as they say, that it will fly?"

Noel looked embarrassed. Elaine gave a rueful smile as she spoke. "My dear Jeanne, *A Husband's House* has been reviled by every women's group on the planet. *Snow* has a dedicated, but small, cult of gay men who laugh at all the wrong lines. *The Tanqueray Tragedy* is not mentioned in polite theater society. If Paul Carlucci has another *succes d'arte*, the only thing that flies will be Paul's backers getting out of the country before the loans and the bills come due."

"Let me put it this way," Elaine completed. "To say we are all nervous is the understatement of the year. We're already snapping at each other like turtles, daring anyone to make a mistake or upstage us by an inch. That's not necessarily bad. It can make for very keen performances, as long as everyone knows his lines and his moves and is very, very—*up*. But if one of us makes a blunder, the timing will all go to hell, which will throw us off our lines, and we'll go down considerably faster than the Titanic. And I must add, having a nosy, second-rate, dirt-sniffing *journalist* privy to our every move does not help us hold it together."

Noel muttered, "Oh, Christ!"

I assumed it was the evening's closing prayer.

Chapter 11

I suppose if you lived next door to Buckingham Palace, you would eventually cease to pay attention when the Queen motored forth, or Prince Phillip came out to sneer or one of the Corgis picked out a tree and peed.

In any event, we grew used to our new neighbors and ceased to be intrigued by impromptu backyard rehearsals. The actual ones were held at the amphitheater, of course. Perforce, we heard Ophelia practicing her scales and songs. She had a good voice, and evidently had some good training, as opposed to so many of our current American performers. She hit her notes roundly and firmly, could exercise power without screaming and actually enunciated lyrics clearly.

Hamlet had a well-trained voice—both speaking and singing— but somehow he seemed emotionless to me, almost as if he had something else on his mind. Maybe I had just seen overly dramatic interpretations of that role. He seemed cold, though, on stage and off. Horatio, who came to the house next door frequently to work on his scenes with Hamlet, seemed like a lovely, friendly puppy. I thought he and Ophelia were going to make "young" Hamlet look pretty pale.

I assumed Duke Noel and Queenie Elaine would certainly turn in commendable performances. I had seen both of them in other roles. But even these two professionals were having trouble with a love duet, sung just before their wedding and confessing their years of love for each other. Elaine kept chiming in on Noel's lyrics before she should, and he kept mixing up two lines, which made her responses idiotic. I guessed they would work it out.

We saw little of the other players or crew. In fact we saw little of our neighbor, the stage manager. Nick was gathering what props hadn't been shipped from New York and storing them in the garage, which he noisily and gratingly and repeatedly declared off-limits to anyone who drifted within twenty feet of it.

He and Harmon had several rumbles about Harmon having access to the yard equipment stored in the garage, with Nick insisting Harmon leave it all outdoors, put it in the basement or, for all he cared, in the effing living room. Finally, Harmon simply put on his stolid, I'm-a-stupid-local face and did as he pleased. If nothing else, he had Nick by about three inches and thirty pounds.

One morning Ophelia called across the wall to me with a horticultural question. Positively *thrilled* that anyone would ask *me* something about plants, I cleared the wall in my best Errol Flynn style and went to her aid. She had a tiny pot of dill she had been given by "this sweet old lady" (who was probably my aunt and not all *that* old, if you don't mind!). She was learning to cook, Ophelia explained, and thought if the plant grew big enough soon enough, she could clip some of it to make scrod with dill sauce when her boyfriend came up to visit.

Well, that pretty well answered one question about Ophelia. She was straight. But what the hell, I liked her anyhow. Some of my best friends were straight. Sure, I'd be glad to help with the planting. Noting that the van was gone, which meant Nick was also probably gone, we ventured into the garage and found a small trowel. We got the little plant gently into the ground and watered it, with Ophelia kneeling to give it a final maternal pat, when our resident journalist strolled up behind us. And the morning had been so pleasant!

"What a charming bucolic scene! What are you doing, my dear, praying you finally will stop fucking up your dialogue?"

Ophelia stood, smiling sweetly. "Oh, I may pray for this and that. But at least I'm on my knees only when I'm praying, not while I try to remember what's being said during what I euphemistically call an 'interview.'"

It took Terese, not to mention me, several seconds to catch on to what Ophelia meant. When she did, she gasped and her face turned an alarming red and she screamed, "You cheap little bitch! How dare you insinuate I'd have to do that to get an interview with any man!"

Obviously, I had no idea *what* Terese might do for a juicy quote, but certainly her anger was genuine, as evidenced by her intended swipe at Ophelia's cheek. The younger woman grabbed her arm and held it. "Don't fuck with me, lady. I was raised in a section of New York where you'd just be pigeon goo on the windowsill." She flung Terese's arm roughly away and walked toward the house, calling back, "Alex, thanks for your help. Sorry we were inter-rupted."

I saw Terese's eyes drop to the nearby trowel. I stepped on it heavily. "Don't even go there. You started it. All she did was defend herself."

"What are you, the peace police?"

"If need be, now let it go." I picked up the trowel and walked toward the garage as Terese turned and moved toward the front sidewalk.

Entering the dimness of the building, I nearly walked right into the firm, stocky body of Nick Peters. Whoever was away in the van, it wasn't the stage manager. He'd been around somewhere all along.

"Oh!" I said. "I'm sorry, I didn't see you." I held up the trowel. "Just putting this away. I won't bother anything."

He nodded. "No problem," he said with surprising mildness. "She's a real bitch, isn't she? Good thing you stepped on that garden thing."

"You think she might really have hurt Ophelia?" I laid the tool back where I'd found it.

"Terese would willingly do anything she thinks would further her impressive career as what she considers a Pulitzer-quality *journalist*," a voice behind me said bitterly.

Hamlet had come out of the house, unseen, and quietly joined us. "I have a word for her, but women hate to hear it, so I won't say it. But she will pry, lie, play one person against another, never minding whom she hurts, nor how badly, if it gets her one more column inch of space in that filthy rag! You'd think she *was* out to win the Pulitzer Prize for the junk she writes."

If David gave half the emotion of that little speech to his stage speeches, his Hamlet might indeed go down in history.

"She always looks at you like she knows something about you," Nick added. "Something you don't know she knows. I think she gets her jollies off on that."

"I think you may be right," I said. "That type would rather have you on edge about an unprovable rumor than to face you down with facts. It's more fun to watch you squirm."

"She probably does know something about you." David laughed shortly. "After all, we've all got a thing or two in our lives we'd like to keep quiet, and she's just the one to ferret it out. So just watch your back, Nick!" He punched the smaller man playfully on the shoulder.

Nick reacted as if he'd been plugged into a light socket. In a nanosecond he had the front of David's shirt bunched in his hand and was poking him hard in the chest with the forefinger of his other hand, as he backed him out of the garage and onto the concrete driveway. "What are you talking about? What did that goddamn woman say? Well, it isn't true, whatever she claimed!"

David grabbed Nick's arm and tried to stop the poking. "Nothing! Nothing! I just meant what I said. Stop that, Nick. It hurts!" He threw a clumsy punch at Nick's head, and they went down together, rolling on the driveway, David screaming, "Don't get my face in the gravel!"

And Nick screaming back, "Then tell me what she said!"

"She said *nothing*. I just meant she'd love to have something on you, like she figures she does on me, and Elaine, and everybody else! Christ, I could kill her for this!" They continued to roll, grapple, punch. Obviously neither man had spent much time in the ring.

I was still debating whether to get in the middle of this scuffle, when Paul Carlucci catapulted out the back door and onto the drive. He pulled them apart. "Nick! David! Quit this! Right now! Nick, do *not* hurt his face. Both of you, *quit!* All right, all right. That's better. What on earth started this?" He looked curiously at me.

"Don't look at me, I was just returning a garden tool." I lifted both hands in innocence.

"Terese." Both men spat out the name simultaneously.

"Oh. Well, I'll handle it later." He sighed with heavy resignation. And suddenly I was quite certain where Ms. Segal was embedded. "David, come get in the car. I want you to see a doctor about that scrape."

"It's nothing, Paul. Some Neosporin will do it," Hamlet said rather wearily.

"David, I said get in the car. We can't neglect this. It could get infected, and I have no intention of your going on stage looking like the phantom of the opera. Nick, I'm sure you have things to do. Alex, perhaps you'll forgive us if we leave now?"

And the theme music came up on *Father Knows Best*.

And I realized he actually had finished a sentence.

I went back to the house, suitably abashed, to be greeted by a worried Fargo. He wasn't used to hearing yells and seeing fights, and apparently he didn't like them. Neither did I. I was strangely shaken by the two arguments I'd just witnessed. I felt as if the four people were all yelling and fighting over one thing, with something else not said.

Picking up the kitchen phone, I called Cindy and suggested we spend a night or two at the cottage. She obviously heard something in my voice, and simply replied, "Of course. Why don't you go on over now and I'll pick up some take-out for dinner. If you'll take over my yellow dress with the white jacket for work tomorrow, that'll do it. See you there around six."

I took Fargo and the dress and went over to the cottage and opened windows and doors and then went out to play with the *kinder*. I would roll/bounce a small ball down the little dock. Fargo would trail along behind it and jump into the pond to retrieve it. Wells would try to catch it en route, and was sometimes successful, in which case she would grab it and make a soccer run onto the lawn, guiding it with her paws. Then Fargo and I would have to chase her and get it back. I guess they enjoyed the game. I did.

Shortly after six, I made a small pitcher of bourbon old fashioneds, and, yes, I know it's better to make them individually. I put pitcher, glasses and ice onto a table on the deck, moved two chairs close together, lit a cigarette and sat down to wait. But not for long.

Cindy came around the side of the cottage and up the steps, bearing a plastic bag.

Fargo and I each got a glancing pat as she went inside, saying, "I wasn't very inspired. We've got fried chicken, coleslaw and potato salad. Plebian enough?"

"We didn't have to cook it. I don't care how plebian it is. I made old fashioneds, want one?"

"Ah, yes, now that ain't plebian. Be right out."

And she was. Now attired in shorts and T-shirt, she gave me one of those special Cindy kisses that could never be perfunctory and sat down with her drink. I told her of the day's events and she nodded. "No wonder you wanted to get away. I don't know how people live as actors. You know, they're trained to be able—in a play—to turn on any emotion required for X-number of minutes and then just turn it off again. How do you simply stop being angry or scared or in love or . . . evil, right on cue? And in real life, how do you know if you're responding to a situation with *your* emotions or the actor's? This drink is delicious." She took another sip.

I recalled, "There's an old song my grandfather used to sing: *I was a fool when I believed you, when said you'd never leave me, when you've never told the truth in all your life.* Not that actors are necessarily liars, at all. But it would raise the question, wouldn't it?"

"Yep. Of course, sometimes we all do it to a degree. We act interested in a business meeting when we're bored stiff. Or we get it together to be gracious and charming at some party we could sleep through. But we're pushing, doing it deliberately because it's part of our job, or to be courteous to our friends. We are fully aware of what we're doing. With actors, I wonder if there isn't a gray area where they either don't know exactly what it is they're feeling or don't admit it. Hand me one of your cigarettes. I feel dangerous."

"I don't know how you do that. Once you smoke one, don't you want to go out and buy a pack?" I lit one for her, passed it over, and lit another for myself.

"My strength is as the strength of ten because my heart is pure." She removed the cigarette regally from her mouth, posed and blew a delicate puff of smoke.

"Yeah, sure. You in your Bette Davis mode?" We sat quietly for a while, watching some gulls circling off to the left and a pair of Canada geese moving lazily on the pond. Fargo had his eyes on the geese but couldn't quite be bothered. Wells pounced across the grass after some unseen critter. The sun started down behind the dunes, like a round, red lens saying "Smile."

"We'd miss this if we didn't have it, wouldn't we?" Cindy asked.

"Yes, indeed. I know it sounds silly to have a 'getaway' place just a mile from your regular house, but at times like this, it's priceless." I waved my hand to encompass everything in sight.

"Sometimes we both need it, sometimes I need it for myself alone. Do you ever need it alone?" She held up her empty glass.

I got up and gave us both refills. "No, not alone, not yet, anyway. Sometimes I like being here just with the animals before you get here."

"But you might need it, and it should be here if you do. We *can* afford it, you know."

"Yes, in a way, of course I know we can. At least for now. But what about thirty years from now, old age creeping up. Seems like you should start saving for it in kindergarten." I looked over at her.

"Nursery school is better."

I swished the ice in my drink. "And it seems a bit extravagant, sort of conspicuous consumption, you know? A couple of people have made some veiled comments. It would be different, maybe, if it were up in New Hampshire or Maine, I guess. It's just that it's so close."

She shrugged. "Let 'em talk. We need it, we can pay for it, we got it. We're well invested. You've got your own IRA now, plus you're putting away the money we save having you on my medical insurance. I've got a good 401K at the bank. Leave old age up to me. When you start doddering, we'll be able to buy you a cane." Her words were light, but her voice was very firm.

"You sound very certain," I said.

"I am. We need a getaway Alex, for us, for me, and in a sense for you, even if you never spend one night alone here. You need to think you have some safe little escape hatch, or someday you'll get up a head of steam and make a big breakout we'll both regret." She ground out her cigarette emphatically.

Hey, wait a minute, I thought, those are my lines. "Darling," I began haltingly. I wasn't ready for this. I needed time to make sure it would all sound the way I wanted it to. "I love you and—"

"I know you do," she interrupted. "And I love you. That's why I'm saying all this. It isn't exactly easy. Remember my bugbear about one of us coming home changed by a trip? It wasn't easy for me to admit that, but it did seem much less frightening in the light of day. I think we've all got bugbears that may seem silly to other people, but can scare us into doing really stupid things. Like my getting bitchy or needy every time one of us is going away."

"I suppose so. I guess it's just a matter of working through them," I hedged.

"Well, you've got a similar one you won't even talk about at all. You're afraid of being tied too tight, right? You're afraid of losing yourself. You're afraid you can't hack it, right?"

I clutched her hand as if it were all that was keeping me from falling off a cliff, and maybe it was. "Well, maybe in some ways . . . yes . . . oh, hell, you're right." And suddenly it all came bubbling out. Once begun, it would not be stopped. She listened, without laughing or criticizing or getting angry or teary, without disagreeing or adding her own little interpretations.

So there were all my fears and doubts, spread before her like the unappealing wares left on a tag sale bargain table. She still remained silent, merely bending forward to pick up her glass and drain it. I wondered if she were trying to think of a nice way to say good-bye.

Finally, she spoke. "I was trying to think of a good way to put this, and I can't, really. But think of this: visualize a giant piece of paper with a graph on it. Starting at the left margin there are two lines, one blue, one red. They go across the paper, sometimes together, sometimes one moving a little up or a little down, crossing, re-crossing, going along together or slightly apart till they reach the right-hand margin." She took another cigarette from the pack on the table, but I made no comment.

"That's us, Alex. Sometimes we're closer than others, but we're basically together until the paper runs out. Together, but definitely one red line and one blue line. We do not turn into a purple smear!"

I poured the small remains of the old-fashioneds into our glasses. "I like that. Together until the paper runs out." I smiled.

"Don't be flip!" Her face was serious. "It's *you* I love, Alex, not some featureless blob of an extension of myself! You don't have to live scared. You know, loving someone who doesn't swim in your own gene pool or have four legs and a tail is *not* a terminal illness!"

"I believe you." I spread my hands in a helpless gesture. "It's simply that I have spent the last ten years, in and out of relationships, doing the same thing over and over and wondering why I got the same catastrophic result each time. Now—well, you and I have a relationship unlike anything I've ever known. I want it. I love it. I treasure it. And what if I'm not big enough, or adult enough, or stable enough or something enough to handle it?" I sank my head into my hands. I couldn't believe I'd said that to anybody, much less Cindy.

She lifted my chin and leaned over to give me one of those Cindy kisses that said she was both lover and friend. "I think you're something enough. *Being* together does not necessarily mean officially *living* together. Loving each other does not mean forsaking our own self to meld with the other. We shall be together until the paper runs out, under a multitude of roofs, in a plethora of beds. We'll even dine at separate tables if we feel like it, especially if you and Fargo keep wrecking the one in the dining room."

I grinned at her, and then felt a sudden shyness. "Ah, you think it would hurt dinner if we postponed it for a little while?"

She stood and held out her hand, giving me a smile that was sexy and impish and yet, somehow, kind.

"Dearest Alex, nothing could hurt that dinner."

Chapter 12

We went back to the house a few days later. I'd been picking up my phone messages two or three times a day, but really didn't like to be out of touch even that long this time of year. This was my time to do at least preliminary investigations on fairly numerous insurance injury claims. It was my bread-and-butter income, and I couldn't be unavailable.

After the season's bizarre start, the cases had all continued to be blessedly predictable. A woman took a quite legitimate fall on a wet spot in a supermarket. That incident would be handled out of Boston. A man had tripped and fallen over a barstool. Probably faked, but the unthinking bartender had served the guy a drink when he was already drunk. That one was settled on the spot with two of the crisp new bills I kept available for such times. A man claimed "food poisoning" after lunch at a local seafood stand. The clinic said it was more than likely too much hot sun combined with the giant banana split that had followed the mayonnaise-heavy lobster roll and fried onion rings. I always tried not to think of exactly *how* the clinic arrived at such diagnoses.

I even took a cheating spouse case because I felt sorry for the older man who was "absolutely certain" his pretty young wife was cheating on him. I had hopes of proving she was not. He was, however, absolutely correct. Only two nights of surveillance revealed that the young woman had reunited with a doubtless more virile and, according to her, more romantic partner. I wasn't sure which of the two spouses I felt more sympathy for.

After a late night, thanks to the illicit lovers, and an early morning, thanks to Fargo, I set out rather groggily on my errands. The cleaners, the post office, the drug store. As I walked toward the drug store, I was startled to see my mother and Noel walking from the supermarket toward her car, Noel pushing a loaded cart. He grinned and waved. Mom blew a kiss, but made no effort to come over. I assumed she had run into him inside, picking up some snacks for himself and the others and, knowing he had no car, she was giving him a ride home. She was always considerate.

Returning from my parking lot encounter, I got my second surprise when I saw that Cindy had come home for lunch.

She was hunched over the small dining room table—now with a pristine new tablecloth and lampshade—eating a salad and reading some magazine. She barely looked up long enough to explain, "This is the new issue of the *A-List*. I want to finish it so I can leave it for you. Your salad is in the fridge. It needs dressing. There's a pitcher of tea, too, if you want some." She returned to her reading.

"Oh, okay, thank you." I'd been thinking of a salami on pumpernickel and some chips and a pickle, and maybe a cold beer. Oh well, a salad and iced tea were nice on a hot day. Refreshing and healthy, just what I wanted, really. Maybe if I kept saying it, I'd believe it.

I took my now-dressed salad and a handful of club crackers and glass of cold tea into the dining room and sat down.

I hate watching someone else read something I can't see. Cindy sat across from me, so of course the copy of the *A-List* was upside down to me. As she read, Cindy favored me with little exclamations and opinions. *Uhmnn. Oh-oh. I'll be damned. Oh, really. Te-hee. Oh, no way. Wow. Hah.* Since there was no way for me to guess what these remarks referred to in the article, I was getting more irritated by the moment.

"Cindy, please either read the damned article out loud, or be quiet. Your conversation is not quite understandable."

"Well, pardon me! I thought I was doing you a favor. These things are probably all sold out by now. The guy at the newsstand said he could have sold twice as many as he had in stock."

"Sorry, do continue to enjoy your mumbles." I punched a fork into my salad.

"My *mumbles?*" She looked up and burst out laughing. "You are just envious that I got it first and ticked off that you didn't get a thousand calorie sandwich and beer for lunch. Now be good, you'll get this in a minute."

I sipped my tea sullenly. How did she know? How did she *always* know?

True to her word, she finished the article quickly and passed the magazine across to me. "It's interesting and just about what you'd expect, I guess. A lot of people in this town are not going to be thrilled. Neither are the cast members. I've got to get back to work. Bye for now."

I tried to look disinterested and not to grab the magazine. At least not until she got into the kitchen. I vaguely heard her put dishes in the dishwasher and say good-bye to Fargo. I was already turning to an article entitled, "The Life of a Play." There was a subtitle reading, "Survival in a Small Town." Already I didn't like it.

Terese did not plagiarize her description of the Provincetown area from the Chamber of Commerce brochure. She referred to our rolling dunes as giant sun reflectors that hurt the eyes. Our roaring surf and sparkling beaches were the Coney Island of New England. She referred to the Brownlees' lovely inn as "stripped down living quarters." She harped on our plethora of souvenir shops, with no mention of our interesting and good quality gift shops and art galleries and museums. She didn't think much of our restaurants or various boating and fishing activities either. I got up and added some more ice to my tea. I needed something cooling.

Terese did approve of the amphitheater. "A starkly perfect setting for the multi-talented Paul Carlucci's latest dramatic triumph. He has written a masterful modern adaptation of *Hamlet*, so in touch with so many of today's emotions and challenging issues, it defies description . . . a classic which will prove timeless." Wow! Was she talking about the script Noel and Elaine had described to us the other night?

The cast, Terese hoped, would live up to the writer/director. Professionals all, she assured us, but having just a few problems along the way. She phrased her gossipy items in a tone of high-minded concern for the production. Actually, she shot them down like ducks at a carnival booth.

To her, David Willem seemed to be having difficulty maintaining his focus and projecting his depth of feeling for his role, perhaps due to the lack of his "aristocratic" founding father Dutch family and his "artistic" wife to keep him company and provide support in free moments. I wondered exactly what that meant.

Could Teri work past her upbringing in New York's more difficult environs to portray Ophelia as the truly delicate and sensitive young southern belle of the play? It would take, Terese feared sympathetically, a quantum leap.

Noel seemed to be just the teeniest bit stiff in his love scenes with Elaine. Could it be she brought back painful memories of his first wife? I didn't get that one, nor did I fully understand her crack that Nick Peters thought he'd make a better Hamlet than stage manager. Was Nick a wannabe actor? I didn't know.

Terese then moved on to the locals. When I noticed Sonny's and Harmon's names in type, I went and got a cigarette before reading it. It was a good move. A stiff bourbon might have been an even better one. I began to read.

Is he gay? Who knows? He turned down this reporter's dinner invita-

tion because he was "too busy." Did he possibly think I was asking for a date? But he wasn't too busy to have a drink that afternoon with our endearing young Horatio, whose sexual orientation is so well-known so intimately to so many. Maybe this was Detective Lieutenant Edward (Sonny, what else?) Peres's "busy-ness"?

Oh, Sonny was going to love this! His buddies would be teasing him for the next ten years! I read on to see what else Terese had to offer.

I asked Sonny about crime in Ptown. His reply was, "We try to keep our town safe for everyone." I pinpointed Provincetown's drug problem, and he answered, "What drug problem?" Really!

Actually, Provincetown has a horrendous drug problem. Nearly every day, the so-called fishing fleet leaves the docks to rendezvous with mother ships over the horizon. They then bring the drugs ashore where they are transshipped across New England and New York. And sales are made locally in broad daylight on most any street corner."

I laughed aloud. Terese had swallowed Harmon's determined belief in mother ships hovering offshore to load up various fishing vessels with drugs. Our hardworking fishermen were likely to lynch her, if Sonny didn't beat 'em to it. He'd really love the crack about drug sales on every street corner! I had a feeling Ms. Segal might be un-embedded and headed home very shortly. And possibly on the end of Sonny's highly polished boot. I went back to the article.

And who is the lone warrior in an attempt to slow this flood of narcotics? He is a so-called, pseudo undercover agent of the Ptown police, a true diamond in the rough who drifts around town doing odd jobs and picking up information wherever he can, with little or no assistance. He is, for instance, now posing as a groundskeeper for the inn where Paul Carlucci, the stars of the troupe and I are staying. Harmon Killingsly is his name, and even his casual conversation leaves no doubt where his interests lie. I suppose he assumes a theatrical group might provide a ready market for these busy drug dealers, though I've seen little evidence of it.

Harmon may be the simple rustic, but he's all that Ptown has.

More next week from Provincetown. Where Terese Segal sees all.

I laid the magazine down in disbelief. Terese had swallowed my off-the-cuff spiel and Harmon's ramblings hook, line and sinker and put a spin on them that wouldn't have occurred to me by the next millennium.

In one medium-length article, she had managed to infuriate various shopkeepers, restaurateurs, innkeepers, the fishermen, the entire police department and doubtless the board of selectmen. And that didn't count the people connected with the play! Only Carlucci had come out well, and unless his entire endeavor here was beyond my small town comprehension, he was teetering on the edge of a resounding disaster with or without Terese's help.

This called for a beer. I looked at the fridge and decided the Wharf Rat was a better choice. "Let's saddle up, Fargo. I feel the need for companionship. I do believe we may be under attack by foreigners." Ever faithful, ever ready to go, he waited and grinned and wiggled by the back door until I got his leash, and we were off.

The Rat was still busy with late-lunching tourists, but there were a good number of locals at the bar, and the front table had every seat filled with a group of fishermen, a few local workmen and a tight-lipped Harmon. Conversation at the table was low-pitched and solemn. I waved as I passed, but I don't think they even noticed me.

Looking around for a table for myself, I didn't see one, but I did spot a table for two, occupied by my mother and Noel. I walked over to say hello and accidentally nudged a couple of shopping bags tucked under the table.

"Presents for my kids," Noel explained. "Jeanne was nice enough to help me pick them out. Now all I have to do is mail them."

"I think I've got an empty carton at home that's just about the right size to hold them," Mom said.

Noel made a circle with thumb and forefinger and smiled. "Alex, shall we try to find an extra chair? We can make some room here."

"No, no, finish your lunch in peace. People would be tripping over me in the aisle. Enjoy your meal. Talk to you later, Mom." I leaned and gave her a peck on the cheek. She smiled and gave my head a pat, and returned to her clam cakes. Well, at least Noel was gentleman enough to buy her lunch after she drove him and his groceries home and then helped him shop. At least I assumed he was buying.

I found a seat at the bar next to a man whose name escaped me. I thought he owned a small shop downtown. As I sat down and Joe set a Bud in front of me, the man pushed his half-filled lunch plate and coffee mug toward Joe.

"Nothing wrong with Billie's food, Joe, but that damn magazine article's give me heartburn. Sayin' the town's fulla dope and junk souvenirs and bad food. How many people you think read that thing?"

Joe shrugged. I swallowed a sip of beer and answered for him. "Not enough to cause us grief unless it goes on for another issue or two."

"I wouldn't be so sure," the man disagreed. "It makes us all sound like a bunch of drug lords and rip-off artists, and stuff like that, it spreads."

"I'll be surprised if there's a second one like it," I said in an effort to placate. "I imagine there will be a bunch of phone calls to the *A-List* from the Town Manager and the Coast Guard and the Massachusetts Board of Tourism. Maybe even a Senator or two. I think Terese's next article will be pure whipped topping."

"She oughtn't be allowed to write a next article at all," the man grumbled, sliding off the barstool and turning toward the door. "She should be stopped. Maybe some of us should get together and just see to that."

Joe flashed a sour grin and leaned toward me to speak softly. "Don's upset. Some tourists in his shop this morning were laughing about the *A-List* and calling his so-called merchandise 'junk.' Of course, it *is* junk!"

I laughed. "Hurts worse when it's true, huh?"

"Alex, I'm awful worried." I turned to see Harmon now seated beside me.

"What's wrong, Harmon?"

"That damned woman, that's what's wrong. Here I thought she was just a nice lady, up here to write stories about them acting people, and look what she's gone and done!" I thought he might cry. And I felt very guilty. I certainly hadn't helped matters with my clever remarks to Terese.

Signaling Joe for a beer for Harmon, I patted his hand. "I don't think there's any great harm done. Most people have sense enough to take magazine articles like that with a big grain of salt."

"I'm afraid Sonny's gonna be real mad at me, Alex, but I never—I *never*—told that damn red-headed snake I was a cop. She was all sweet and worried about drugs in town, and I told her how I kind of kept an eye on things. Just trying to make her feel safer. You understand?"

Sadly, I understood only too well how a well-meaning, innocent Harmon and a conniving, spinmeister Terese had produced a believable wicked fairy tale that would make perfect sense to anyone who didn't know Ptown.

"Well." His face tightened with an anger I had never seen him show before. "She's done made fools of all of us, even Sonny. It don't matter about me so much, but Sonny, he's an important man in this town. People look up to him like he's a rolled model, and that bitch ain't got no right to make him look bad. We can't let that go on!"

I pushed the bottle in front of him. "Sonny won't be mad. He understands that kind of person, and he knows you wouldn't lie about being on the force. Don't worry. It's not a big thing. Here, Harmon, have your beer and tell me how Tom and Geraldine are coming along."

At least I hoped it wasn't a big thing. Too many people feeling like Don and Harmon would not be good—for themselves or the town. Maybe not for Terese either. I hoped the Governor of Massachusetts would draft a firm letter to her editor.

Chapter 13

I had to admit that Terese Segal and the *A-List* had certainly made an impression on the town. By the next day, I think everyone over the age of six had read the damn piece, and everyone had a grumble. From Aunt Mae to the mailman, I heard the chorus: *She must be stopped.*

It began to sound like one of those weird movies where the entire village unites and burns the evilly possessed woman at the stake, while the police force studiously looks the other way. I wouldn't have been surprised to see a lynch mob proceeding up my street with grim, silent determination. The only thing that really bothered me about that scenario was my niggling desire to join it.

And the merry band next door was anything but. Only Carlucci seemed to be on good terms with Terese. The others all seemed to speak in whispers among themselves, except for Nick, who spent most of his time closed in the garage, probably with a cross and a bulb of garlic.

She had them all scared, and after a day or so, they began to take it out on each other. Hamlet, while sunning in the backyard, was joined by Polonius, with some complaint about Hamlet's "trampling, absolutely *stomping* on my lines, and I will not have it!"

Hamlet stood, I presumed to cash in on his height advantage over Polonius, and insisted he was merely "answering briskly, as any young college man would reply to some old trout droning on about what to do or not to do once you get to college."

Polonius simpered. "*Young college man?* You'd better put some dye on the sideburns, then. The gray is showing."

"It's nothing, but I'll take care of it. Many people start to gray in their twenties."

"Twenties! You're thirty-five if you're a day."

Hamlet then literally stamped his foot and screamed, "Am not!"

I had taken my laptop out to the picnic table, assuming that Fargo and I would enjoy a little fresh air while I completed some reports that were rapidly approaching the overdue mark. It seemed I had made a mistake. I might as well have brought out the little TV and watched soaps. Although I didn't need to watch one on TV. I felt I was living in one.

I looked over at the now empty yard and tried again to finish the reports. I was about halfway through the second one when I jumped at the sound of the back screen door crashing open across the way as Nick Peters stormed through it, and crashing again as Ophelia came out hard on his heels.

"It's bad enough I have to share a bathroom with the likes of you under any circumstances, but you make it impossible! The maids clean it every morning, and by noon it's a mess again. Get up there and clean up your stuff and wash that tub! I want to take a bath later."

"So take it." He walked on toward the garage.

Ophelia grabbed his shirt and spun him around. "I am going over to Jake's to work on my solo. I will be back in an hour. If that bathroom isn't clean, I'm going to take all your smelly, icky clothing and soggy towels and put them on the sidewalk with a big sign saying, 'Plague! Nick Peters's filthy clothes. Beware of lice!'" She released her hold and walked away.

"In your dreams!" he called after her. "You wouldn't dare." But I noticed that as soon as Ophelia was out of sight, Nick walked back to the house.

I gave up and returned to mine, but not before I had been treated to a small tiff between Noel and Elaine. Elaine complained that when she ran to the Duke in one of their many love scenes, he caught her the wrong way and hurt her back. He replied in an ultra-patient tone that if she would merely lean into him rather than collapsing into his arms, he wouldn't have to support her so tightly—to the point of wrenching his own shoulders.

At that point Hamlet sat up in a deck chair he had placed beneath a small shade tree. "You know, Elaine, if you would pace yourself to end up with your weight on your right foot, then when you turn to the left to embrace Noel, your balance would be better and—"

Elaine's head snapped around almost audibly. "What did you study in that so-called acting school, ballroom dancing?"

Placatingly, Noel intervened, "Actually, Elaine, he may have something. We could try it."

"Fine, you two try it. You'll probably love it!" She stormed into the house, and the poor screen door crashed again.

I got a beer from the fridge and sat down at the kitchen table to light a cigarette. I was sick of the whole bunch of them at this point. Every dandelion was bigger than an oak tree to them. Cindy had spent last night at the cottage because of a screaming match between Carlucci and Laertes that seemed to go on for an hour. I was not getting my work done as scheduled. I was into a cigarette I didn't need and about to open a beer I didn't really even want. And it was barely noon.

Then I got mad at myself. Why did I let them control my life?

I would go back outside, do my work, and if anybody else started a ruckus I would simply tell them to take it elsewhere. And so I did, snubbing out the cigarette and replacing the unopened beer.

I was whizzing right along in the dull insurance-ese my employers preferred. Real day-to-day English was too easy to understand. At one point I saw Terese, apparently strolling among the flowerbeds in the noon heat. I shook my head. To each his own. Nick came out of the house, the back screen door now squeaking loudly each time it was opened and closed. He got into one of the vans and drove away. Sometime later, I noticed Ophelia coming up the drive, finished with her solo work, I guessed. And I would have bet the tub had been scrubbed.

But these things didn't bother me. I was, in fact, pleased with the progress I was making. I finished another report and sent it winging, in some manner I would never understand, to Boston. I started on my last one, which I would shortly aim toward Plymouth and hit *Send*.

And then—it was bound to happen—Ophelia screamed.

"O-ooh, no!"

She was pointing at something in the driveway. I figured perhaps Nick managed to run over a field mouse, or perhaps a dead bird had somehow got there. I told Fargo to stay as I approached the wall. I didn't want him walking around for half an hour with something small and dead in his mouth, finally burying it, and then digging it up five minutes later to start the process all over again.

By the time I reached Ophelia—Teri, she had picked up the victim and was clutching it to her chest. I hoped she wasn't one of those people with a strange affinity for roadkill. We used to have a woman in town who took it upon herself to pick up roadkill, sometimes quite decomposed, put it in her car trunk and bring it home to bury in her backyard. You could smell her car before you saw it.

I braced myself as Teri opened her hands to me. And all I saw was a small, uprooted plant, obviously run over by the van and now far beyond resuscitation. It looked like a clump of grass, and for a moment, I couldn't understand her tears. Then I realized it was her little dill plant.

"What a miserable thing to do!" She gulped. "An innocent little plant! They only did it to hurt me. Why take it out on my sweet plant? Nick or Terese! It's got to be one of them. I'll find out, and they'll be sorry. Oh, will they be sorry!"

I thought back over the past hours. I didn't think it was Nick. When he came out of the house a little while back, my thought was that he went directly to the van, walking on the side of the driveway away from the dill plant's spot. But I wasn't a hundred percent sure, and I didn't really want to put the finger on Terese if she hadn't done it—although I'd bet she did it—because I didn't want to start World War III over a dill plant, rotten trick that it was. So I said nothing.

Nick picked that moment to drive in. As he got out of the van, he wore an unfortunate smirk as he asked, "Satisfied, now?"

"You bastard!" She uncorked a punch that knocked him onto his back and into the flowerbed.

He sat up, rubbing his chin. "Are you crazy? I clean up the damn bathroom, like you so nicely asked. Then I ask you are you satisfied and you knock me into next week. What the hell is the matter with you?"

"Didn't you do this?" She held out the now disintegrating plant.

"What's that?" He struggled to his feet, still coddling his reddening chin.

"My dill plant. Didn't you pull it up and then run over it?"

He hesitated. "I—I might have run over it, Teri. I didn't see it. But I wouldn't have pulled it up." His face crumpled like a little boy's about to cry. "I wouldn't deliberately kill anything like that." I believed him.

"Then it was Terese," Teri said. "Did either of you see her out here?"

I decided Terese could look after herself. I wasn't going to lie. "Yes, sometime around the noon hour."

"Uh-huh." Nick nodded. "Just after noon, walking around the flowers."

Teri gave us each a sort of bow and walked into the house, still holding the plant.

Nick shook his head. "Teri's tough as nails in some ways, and she can be a pain in the ass. But she did love that little plant. She watered it every day and even talked to it, like it was a cat or something. I feel sorry for her. She's still only a kid, really. This is her first feature role and she's nervous about it. All on her own up here. Damn that woman! Did you see that article she wrote?"

"Yes. I didn't understand it all. Like what she said about Noel . . . and about you."

"Oh, the thing about Noel was a double whammy—also about Elaine. Noel's ex-wife is gay. Her lover and she are raising her and Noel's two kids. No problem. Noel sees the kids as often as he can, and they have a stable home, I guess. Once in awhile Noel brings them into New York for a weekend or takes them to his cabin up in Maine or somewhere. Everybody seems friendly enough. And of course, the poke at Elaine is because she's gay, too, and she and her lover raised the lover's daughter. That's all. Of course, Terese likes to make it sound like everybody is at everybody else's throat."

"I see," I said, motioning for Fargo to come on over. "And what about your wanting to play Hamlet?"

He rubbed his chin and winced. "I don't know why Terese even bothered writing that." Nick spoke smoothly, but his eyes looked suddenly hard to me. "It's cold porridge. When I was in my teens I thought about becoming an actor, but . . ." He laughed a little too heartily. "I was the world's worst. Made a much better stage manager. Well, I gotta get to work here." He nodded and headed toward his friendly cave. Fargo and I recrossed the wall, and I felt I was gaining a new understanding of how Dorothy and Toto felt on returning to Kansas. Our yard seemed marvelously safe and sane and familiar.

I stood looking fondly at my sturdy tomato plants, heavy with ripe red globes and smaller still-green fruit, like Christmas tree balls adrift in the wrong season. I remembered how frail the plants had been last spring, and that I, too, had found it natural to give them verbal encouragement. If they had been vandalized at that point, I would have felt almost as if a helpless child or animal in my care had been harmed.

And I agreed with Nick. Hiding somewhere inside the tough broad was the vulnerable child that was Teri. Toughness is learned. Vulnerability is one of those mixed blessings some are born with. I knew a little about that.

So of course, I opened the car door for Fargo, and we headed for Aunt Mae's to find another dill plant.

Three cars were lined up outside Aunt Mae's little shop, and translated to eight customers inside. I browsed around until she was finally free, getting an appreciative hug for my wait.

"Hello, my dear, how nice to see you! It's my day for the Peres family, I guess. Your mother and Noel were just here to get some rosemary. She's going to make her rosemary and white wine chicken for the Hamlet people to snack on, though I imagine," she laughed, "that most of it will have Noel's name on it. And now you—"

"You mean now Mom's *cooking* for that bunch? Boy, Noel has some nerve! She's been chauffeuring him around and helping him shop, and now she's cooking! I expect any minute to hear he's just moved right in."

Aunt Mae gave a little stutter of a laugh. "Well, no, dear, I don't think you have to worry about that right now. So . . . to what do I owe the honor?"

I told her of Ophelia's little murdered dill plant and she clucked with disapproval. "People can be just plain mean! It's too bad that Segal woman doesn't simply pack up and leave! Certainly nobody wants her here." As she was talking, Aunt Mae was walking toward the back of the shop. She picked up a nice six-inch pot, scooped some soil into the bottom, dumped a dill plant from a smaller pot into the larger one, filled it with more soil and packed it down.

"There, this will live nicely on a bright windowsill, so she won't have to worry about planting it outside. Just water occasionally and give it a little food once in a while. Here's a little sample packet of food."

I reached for my wallet, and she waved her outspread hands from side to side. "No, don't be silly, Alex. It was kind of you to think of her loss. I'm happy to provide the little plant. It must be hard on a young girl, alone in a strange place. She told me this is her first important role, so please be sure to tell her the little plant will bring her luck. I know she'll do beautifully in her performance next week."

"Yes, thank God it's only eight days away. It seems like light years. I may give a block party when it's over and they're out of here . . . except the whole town would probably show up. Well, thank you, favorite aunt. I won't keep you." I nodded toward a car as it disgorged three customers-to-be and took my leave.

I thought a casual stop at Mom's would be a good idea. Mom was so openhearted. I wanted to make sure our summer visitors were not truly taking advantage of her good nature.

As I walked into the kitchen, the aroma told me the chicken was about done. Then I heard chords struck on the piano. Mom's pleasant voice sang a line I assumed was from one of her beloved Broadway show tunes. Then Noel's picked up on the second line and I realized just what show it was from.

So many years, I had to hide my love for you.
So many years I hoped you knew my heart was true.
Careful whenever others were near us
Always in fear lest they see us or hear us,

But now at last we are together forever
Wherever we go.
Together . . .
Forever . . .
Wherever . . .
We go.

I walked into the living room applauding. "Sounds great! Gee, Mom, are you replacing Elaine?"

"Don't be silly." She was, for some reason, blushing mightily, one of the few traits she had passed on to me that I wished she hadn't. "I was just helping Noel work through some timing problems in the duet."

Noel was rapidly gathering his sheet music from the piano rack. "Yes, yes. All much better now, Jeanne. I thank you a million . . . must run . . ."

"Noel, your chicken . . . oh my God, is it burning?" Mother ran for the kitchen, Noel and I following. "No, it's all right, but it was close!"

"It smells wonderful," I said pointedly.

"Thank you, dear. We're lucky it's not smoking. Well, 'seared' is popular nowadays." She laughed. Then Noel laughed. Then they both laughed for a while. What was so funny? By now she had most of it transferred to a platter, so I simply grabbed a drumstick from the second large skillet. And they laughed some more. Finally, she got plastic wrap around the platter and Noel got out the door, carefully balancing the hot platter on his stack of music, thanking her again as he left.

My drumstick now was cool enough to eat, and I took a bite. "Oh, so good!"

"Thanks, dear," she murmured absently. "I wonder if I should have driven him home. I hope he doesn't drop the platter."

"It's only a couple of blocks. Surely he can make it that far. You're now chief cook for the actors?"

"Not hardly. But I guess they're not really eating too well. It's time-consuming and expensive to eat out all the time, and sometimes they eat at oddball hours, and mostly nobody cooks. I guess it's nearly all TV dinners and snacks. I just thought a couple of chickens might be welcome."

"You're too nice. Cooking, shopping, rehearsing songs. I hope Carlucci has you on the payroll." I gave her a fond, if slightly greasy kiss on the cheek.

"Hah. Is everything all right with you? Any special reason you're here?"

"Nope. Aunt Mae told me you were making chicken, and I came to rob. Plain and simple. My mission is accomplished," I fibbed, dropping the bone in the garbage.

Looking desperate, Fargo pawed my leg. "Oh, Fargo, I was so hungry I forgot to save you a bite."

Mom smiled. "Here, Fargo, I cooked the gizzards for you, but I think they are outdoor food, if you don't mind." He didn't mind at all and crouched happily in the grass, chewing mightily.

As I pulled out of the driveway, with Fargo still licking his chops, I gave Mom a wave. But she was looking absently up the street as if still concerned that Noel might be strewing pieces of chicken along the way.

She really *was* too nice. Next they'd have her making dinner every night.

Chapter 14

Cindy and I were sitting in the backyard, swapping our accounts of the day. Two of her clients had brought in their month-old baby girl to introduce her to Cindy and set up a college account, "Remember?" she asked. "I told you people started younger and younger. I expect to be called into a delivery room any time now."

"Well," I said, "as long as they don't want you there at the moment of conception."

She laughed and tousled my hair. Obviously the event had put her into a good mood, so I skipped over the tale of the dill plant. I knew it would only make her sad. However, I did tell her of Mom's helping Noel with his lyrics and making chicken for the group at his B&B.

"He's as slick as a used car salesman," I grumbled. "First she's doing his grocery and souvenir shopping, then she's driving him around. Next she's helping with his songs and making chicken for that whole bunch. I'm surprised she hasn't told him off."

Cindy looked at me curiously. "Why would she tell him off? Nobody is *forcing* her to fry a chicken."

"Well, she's not stupid. Surely she knows he's using her."

"I think not, darling girl. I've seen them having lunch downtown a lot, and the other day I ran into them on the pier, going out to the whale watching boat and giggling like kids, and Lainey saw them one night at the movies. Dating, my angel, it's called dating."

"Dating? My mother, dating? Don't be absurd, Cindy. She doesn't *date*. And an actor at that? Never! Anyway, he's younger than she is." I nodded abruptly. Certainly that settled it.

Cindy flashed a smile that tried not to become a laugh. "Well, Alex, somebody is often a little younger than somebody else in a twosome. And last I knew, dating isn't limited to people under thirty who have not yet been married or procreated. Trust me, they're dating. And having a wonderful time of it! *Vive* romance! Don't you dare be a surly grouch to her about this!"

I squirmed in my chair. "God, Cindy, do you suppose—oh, hell no, couldn't be. Well, I suppose a few lunches and a boat ride just kind of make up for the favors she's done him. Anyway, they'll all be gone in a week and I guess no harm done. I wouldn't call it dating, Cindy, I really wouldn't."

She gave me a look that was simultaneously knowing, pitying, irritated and amused. "Whatever you say, dear, whatever you say."

At that moment the back screen door of the actors' quarters wailed its minatory opening squeak. Cindy glanced up. "Oh, it's Elaine. Shall we ask her over for a drink?"

"No!" I said vehemently, deliberately not turning to look. "All they've done all day over there is fight and scream. I've had it with actors. And you're trying to tell me my mother is dating one! I can't wait for next week. I'll escort them all to the Bourne Bridge. Peace, all I want is peace."

"Alex, she's sitting on the back steps, all by herself and—oh, dear—she's crying."

"Oh, sweet Jesus in the foothills, go see what's wrong now. She probably sprained her toe."

It seemed only seconds before Cindy and Fargo returned shepherding a sniffling Elaine across the yard. "Darling," Cindy called brightly, "We've decided on vodka tonics, and Fargo asked nicely for a biscuit. Would you oblige us?"

I stood and managed a smile. "Certainly," I replied with great heartiness. "My pleasure. I'll be right back."

In the kitchen, I put together their drinks plus a hefty bourbon for myself, and reached for the dog biscuits. "Asked nicely, did you? Are you sure?" Fargo did a little two-step and grinned. It was enough for me. "You're the only sane one around this place. Here."

He took it gently, and I followed him out the door with the tray of drinks. "Well, here we are," I said cheerfully, handing out the glasses. "Is something wrong, Elaine? Can we help you with anything?" I really did like her. Cindy was nice. I would try to be nice.

She sipped her drink and sighed. "I truly guess I have to talk to someone. I've held this all in for so long, it's simply consuming me. I hate to burden you two, but I guess I'm going to, aren't I? Please promise me you won't ever tell anyone what I'm about to say!" She looked at each of us seriously.

"Just Cindy, Fargo and me. It goes no further, I promise you." I took a preparatory swallow of bourbon and braced myself for some silly tale of woe about somebody getting better billing than she did.

She placed her hand on my wrist. "You know who I am, don't you?"

My God, had she got amnesia? Was she having some sort of breakdown? Was she going bonkers on us?

"Er . . . ah, yes, I guess so." Maybe if I reminded her subtly, "Elaine Edgewood, Queen Gertrude, Queenie!" I laughed slightly. "Take your pick."

"No, I mean who I really am."

And all of a sudden, I did know.

At once, I was back in the early summer, with Fargo in front of the TV, while Cindy was away in Boston. One of those *bio-dramas* came on the telly, "The Woodchopper Widow." The drama opened with the trial some thirty years ago. I saw the expression-less wife, who had been tried for stabbing her husband and feeding parts of him into a woodchopper. She had done so, she said, to protect her children from his sexual abuse of their children. And I remembered the tall, rather plain young daughter, swearing that their father had never abused her or her brother. Now, nearly three decades later, she sat before me, having acquired her mother's long and graceful neck and rich, dark hair. Her plain looks had grown into a tall, quiet beauty. She had her mother's intensity without the somewhat wild eyes.

"You're Elaine. Elaine Leonard. Your mother . . . well, I mean . . . your father . . ." I could think of no way to end the sentence. "You've grown up."

"And then some." She smiled faintly. "I thought you recognized me when we first met. You looked at me rather sharply and said something about my seeming familiar. I thought you knew me and were just too polite to blurt it out."

"No." I sipped my drink. "I did think you looked familiar, but just assumed it was because I had seen you on a TV series. I didn't recognize you as Elaine Leonard until just now. Although I did see that so-called bio-drama one of the cable stations did when your mother died."

Cindy was looking from me to Elaine and back with total lack of understanding. I was sure Cindy had read about the event in one of her scandal mags, but had simply forgotten. Elaine took pity on her.

"When I was twelve and my brother was seven, Bobby told my mother that my father did 'bad things that sometimes hurt' to him and to me. He made matters worse by adding that I liked the bad things he did. My dad traveled a lot on business, and Mother had several days for this too terrible news to stew in her mind and let her imagine all sorts of horror scenes."

She took a deep breath and went on. "Then, on a Friday, just as Dad pulled into the driveway from being away all week, a toddler across the way got loose from his mother and ran into the street. Dad dashed out and picked him up, and returned him to his mother with a playful swat on his bottom, for which the kid gave him a big smooch. Mom saw this from the kitchen window and decided it was a sign of further abuse, approved of by the toddler's on-looking, smiling mother."

"My God!" Cindy said. "Your poor mother must have simply been over the edge from worrying about it and imagining things that might have happened. If only she'd spoken to someone before your father came home!"

"Yes, that might have helped, but I think she was too mortified. In some way, certainly, she had cracked. She had never been terribly stable. Apparently, when my father entered the kitchen, she caught him completely off guard and stabbed him several times and then dragged him to the backyard. About that time Bobby and I returned from a birthday party, we saw Dad's car in the drive, heard the chopper running and figured he was doing some yard work. We ran around the house and—"

"Stop, Elaine." I put my hand on her arm. "Don't put yourself through any more of this. How can we be of help to you?"

"By listening a bit longer, actually. I'll skip the gory details and the trial. Moving right along . . . we had no close relatives, and a psychiatrist recommended Bobby and I be adopted separately. I was against that at the time, but later was very grateful. As they say, I really lucked out. Could I have one of your cigarettes?"

"Sure." I pushed the pack and lighter across the table toward her. It seemed to be my role in life to supply cigarettes to people who had "quit" smoking. What would happen if I quit? Where would any of us find the stray, rare, necessary cigarette? It could change the world, cause nervous breakdowns, increase unemployment, turn farms into wastelands. Best I did not quit just yet.

Elaine lit one and continued. "My new family was great. I wanted to keep my first name, and they agreed that Elaine Edgewood was a fine name. They had a natural son a couple of years older than I, but had been advised at his birth to have no more children. Tim was a great brother. Just slightly bossy, protective and a great deal of fun. Mom and Dad had wanted a daughter, but kept putting it off till they heard of me, and the story

114

moved them, and we were immediately attracted to each other when we met. They own a maple syrup farm in Vermont, and it was *such* a wonderful place to grow up! I loved—love—the place and them and my big brother to pieces. They were all supportive of my wanting to be an actress, although Tim used to tease me about it. Not anymore. Now he's very proud. And somehow my parents found the money to give me a year at the American Academy of Dramatic Arts after I graduated college."

"Do they know you're a lesbian?" Cindy asked.

"You bet, and they have treated my lover, Joan, as if she were their daughter, too. They are truly splendid people. They understood when I was grown and asked where my birth mother was. I went to see her. I guess I made peace with her. It helped some. I didn't see her again. She seemed rather content the way things were. She seemed calm, and they weren't very strict with her. But I sent her little notes about my career and a small present now and then. It all helped." She was sounding much calmer, and I was considerably relieved.

"How did Bobby make out?" I asked.

"Bobby had big problems. He swore to the end that Dad was abusive. I assure you he was not. And Bobby had no physical marks of abuse, nor did the shrink think his story held up. Unfortunately his hysterical babbling didn't help Mother any, either. Anyway, the shrink saw him for a while, tried to help him and hoped he'd grow out of it. I guess maybe he did. We don't discuss it."

Cindy picked up our glasses and headed for the kitchen. "Don't say anything important till I get back." We didn't, and on her return Elaine once again picked up her weird tale.

"Bobby was eventually adopted by a lovely, somewhat older couple who had no other children. They owned a big old family drugstore in a small Pennsylvania town. It was a great place. I visited once when I was in college. They sold everything in the world in it, and even had one of those old-fashioned marble ice cream counters with those wire stools that look so rickety. And when Bobby was the soda jerk, it was probably the one time in his life he was really popular and outgoing and had some fun. It's too bad he didn't stay there. I think he knew everyone in town. Actually, they changed his first name as well as his last, but I can't seem to call him anything but *Bobby*, although I try not to in public."

"Sounds like he made out pretty well, too." I sipped my drink slowly. I still didn't know what we were leading up to.

"Yes, for some time. I'm afraid my visit didn't help, unfortunately. When I told him I was going to be an actress, he said *he* was going to be an actor. Just like that. Like you'd decide to have mustard on your hamburger because I put some on mine, and it looked good. But his parents went along with it, planned on college and a year's acting school."

"What happened? Did he do well?" I had begun to wonder just how long this saga was going to be.

"A big discount store moved into the area, and downtown businesses went downhill. Some even had to close, although the drug store managed to survive. It's ironic, that our play here has the same theme, and it's probably not helping Bobby's emotional state. Anyway, there was no money for acting school, and university turned into a little community college in the next town over. And Bobby, grateful boy that he was, sued his parents for breach of contract!"

"He *sued* them?" Cindy's eyebrows were on the rise again.

"Yep. Sued them for breach of contract. He said they had a verbal contract to send him to the University of Pennsylvania and then to a year in acting school. His grades were good enough to get into Penn, ergo, they had to send him. He had lived up to his part of the bargain."

"I assume nobody allowed him to pursue that madness." I pulled my cigarettes back and lit one, scolding myself silently on general principals. I had long ago lost count.

"Well, yes, he actually found a lawyer who was willing to represent him, but a judge threw it out before it ever came to court. Can you imagine the precedent it would have set? It boggles the mind! Kids would be suing their parents over a new bike! Unfortunately, word of it spread all over town. Bobby's parents were very popular and well thought of in the area. While most people looked on it as just a stupid teenage trick by a spoiled brat. Bobby immediately became a treacherous young villain to some. He actually received threats, to the point where he decided to leave town."

I sipped my drink and groused, "I'm surprised he wasn't tarred and feathered and ridden out on a rail."

"No, it never got violent." Elaine sighed. "But his parents were afraid it might, and gave him a couple of thousand dollars they couldn't spare. He came to New York to become an actor."

"I'm afraid they were much more generous than I would have been," Cindy added. "I think my only expenditure for him would have been a one-way bus ticket to Burnt Cactus, Arizona."

"How did he make out as an actor?" I sucked on an ice cube and hoped the end of the tale was in sight.

"He spent a few months at some third-rate acting school, and then thought he should be leading man in every play scheduled for a Broadway run. God! After four years as a drama student in college, one at AADA and three years doing off-off-Broadway walk-ons, *I* had finally gotten the part of a salacious maid with about twelve good lines in *A Goldfish Bowl* on Broadway. I was so grateful, I walked around saying 'Thank you, God,' over and over everyday."

Cindy nodded in understanding. "Did you see much of him at this time?"

"Too damned much. He was living with a couple of guys who wanted to get rid of him, and he wanted to move in with us. But Joan was teaching, I was trying to get my own career going, and we had her little girl Katie, so fortunately, we had no room, or time, to help him. I tried to help him get parts, but he messed up the few he got. His attitude was that he knew it all, and no director had anything of value to tell him. He seemed to have no future in the theater at all. Of course, he has apparently found his niche and is doing quite well."

She filched another cigarette and looked at me as she returned the pack. "May I presume you've already guessed that Bobby is here with us?"

Chapter 15

I stared at her, my mind racing like a runaway engine. Bobby Leonard. There was no Bobby Leonard in Carlucci's group. I was sure of it! But no, he wasn't Bobby Leonard anymore. I visualized the stocky little boy with his golden curls and big blue eyes and full lips, and unexpectedly I saw a tall, handsome, broad-shouldered man with blond wavy hair and light blue eyes and a sexily sulky mouth. I saw Hamlet . . . David Willem.

And my speeding thoughts ran on to the *A-List's* comments about him, as if his claim of an old, aristocratic Dutch family were a lie and that his wife might well be fictitious as well. Then I recalled his superior air, his comments about his years at Princeton and his great Shakespearean training at the Royal Academy of Dramatic Arts in England, his arrogance toward the other actors and toward the stage manager, his condescending courtesy toward the locals. Oh, yes, I knew right where our Bobby was!

I wondered how he could keep all his stories straight and why someone who knew him as a boy hadn't faced him down with them years ago. Finally I realized Elaine had begun to speak again.

"So you see, all this stuff Terese Segal has been publishing, well, about all of us, really, has me especially worried about her comments on Bobby. He's not the most steady boat in the river. I don't know what he would do if the whole distasteful story came out. She hinted to him the other day that she knew something about his schooling. If she knows that, she may well already know or find out everything and blast the whole sordid account across the front cover of the *A-List!*"

Her eyes welled over. Tears rolled unheeded down her cheeks. "I can't let that happen to him, he's still my brother. I think I could survive it if I must. I have Joan, and her daughter Katie's grown and married now, with a fine life of her own. She's expecting their first child shortly. We would make it through, I think. But Bobby . . . on the bottom line, Bobby has no one except me. I have to stop Terese, but I can't think how. Can you *please* help me stop her?"

I had never felt sorrier for anyone in my life than Elaine at that moment. As for Hamlet, one side of me thought he had it coming. But I supposed I shouldn't judge anyone who had been through what he had suffered as a child.

What I felt or thought or judged was really academic. The truth was, I hadn't the foggiest idea how to shut up Terese short of a thirty-eight-caliber revolver, which was sure to put Sonny in a bad mood.

"Well," I said, "I know there have been many complaints about her first article—I mean from the town selectmen, the Chamber of Commerce and, I believe, from certain state organizations, plus a Congressman and Senator or two. I can't believe the editors won't be awfully careful about what they publish in the future. There are some people you just wouldn't want to provoke."

"But, Alex," Cindy countered, "If Terese's information is *correct*, there really is no legal reason to stop her, is there? I mean, they can't stop you from publishing something if it is true, can they?"

"No, darling." I smiled. "You are quite right. There isn't." Oh, how I would have liked to put an ice cube up each of her nostrils at that moment! "But pressure from those in high office usually makes people think twice about antagonizing them. I think it may well work out. Or, Elaine, you might simply try to talk to Terese. Surely there is a heart or at least some sense of social responsibility in there someplace. Just tell her the truth. This could put Bobby over the edge mentally. I can't believe even Terese would want to be accountable for that."

"Yes." Elaine stood. "I guess that's about the best move." She didn't sound convinced, and I didn't blame her. "Well, maybe I'll have a brainstorm. We can hope. Thank you both for listening to my screed. I feel better, even though nothing is really solved."

"Elaine, believe me." I gave her a hug. "It will all work out. Somehow these things always do."

"If all else fails," Cindy promised, "I'll get one of the tekkies at work to hack into the editor's computer at the *A-List* and publish a sizzling tale about *her!*"

We all managed a weak laugh on that, and Elaine left us, walking carefully across the now dark yard.

Within two minutes we had cleared the outdoor table, gone into the house, and I had ordered an extra large sausage and pepper pizza, without a word of protest from Cindy. Within five minutes I had filled Fargo's bowl with kibble, and he was chomping sturdily through it. He'd be happily surprised at the pizza for his second course.

Cindy poured herself a glass of milk and sighed. "What a terrible mess for poor Elaine. Do you think she can talk Terese out of using whatever information she has? Or can fabricate?"

I shook my head. "As you so pointedly said, my love, not if it's true. Just think how Hamlet is always strutting around, just letting it drop oh-so offhandedly, that he went to the RADA and to Princeton. If it turns out he's a graduate of Split Elm Community College and Ramon's Stairway to the Stars, that alone would be worth twenty thousand extra to the *A-List* circulation. If Terese has found someone who knew Hamlet as a teenager, she may easily find out the whole miserable thing, and I don't know what would stop her from publishing it, except decency, and we know that ain't in 'er. Ah! There's the pizza truck."

I met the deliveryman at the back door, armed with the correct change plus tip. I wanted nothing to slow this late dinner down. We concentrated on the pizza for a time. Fargo was so attentive, making sure he got every crust. Most with a bit of meat, cheese and sauce left on. His nose was quivering.

Eventually, we slowed. Finally, we stopped. We were replete.

Cindy got around to the subject we hadn't quite explored with Elaine. "Do you think Hamlet will have some sort of emotional break if this tale goes public?"

"I think Elaine is very worried that he might. With good reason, I fear."

"Why?"

"Well, he's built up this whole façade about an Ivy League school and a founding father family, that kind of half-British accent, etc. That would be quite a tumble for him. He does seem edgy. He had a real wingding over nothing with Polonius the other day. And I heard him arguing with Carlucci, too. Carlucci wanted Hamlet to sound sweeter and gentler when he broke up with Ophelia. Hamlet seemed genuinely confused when he asked Paul, 'Why should I be sweet? I'm through with her, aren't I?' That almost scared me when I heard him."

"Whew! Makes you worry a bit, doesn't it?" Cindy polished off her milk and stood up. "Want coffee?"

"Yeah, great. It is frightening, especially when you figure he's only acting, anyway. And then there's the old genetic thing. Mama was bonkers. Daddy may or may not have been a pedophile. God, I'll be glad when this is all over and they all go back to New York. I'll never complain about plain old tourists again."

Before Cindy could answer that, the phone rang.

It was Sonny.

"Well, hello," I said. "I wondered where you'd been of late. Where are you? Hiding from Terese?"

"In a way. I've been in Boston until this morning. Home now. Remember my old army pal who's head of security for INN-TV over there?"

"Vaguely." I nodded my thanks to Cindy for the coffee and took a sip.

"Well, he and I talked to one of their producers and convinced him to do a little special on our great theatrical weekend coming up. He thought it a good idea. It's summer, news is slow. Great publicity for the town. For Carlucci, too, of course." I heard ice rattle in a glass.

"Since when are you a PR expert? What's this all about?"

"Oh, I have been known to have the rare creative idea. This was just one of my better ones." He was very smug about something. "It's a great little piece. It'll be on at six tomorrow. I just wanted to make sure you didn't miss it. And try to make sure all your people next door remember to watch . . . just in case Carlucci forgets the time. He's always sort of in a fog."

I took a gulp of coffee and burned my mouth. "They are anything but *my* people," I sputtered, "But if I see anybody, I'll remind them."

"Okay, Sis, I'll see you soon."

We hung up. I wondered why he called me *Sis*? Usually he reverted to that childhood name only when he was very excited or upset. I shrugged and turned back to Cindy to announce our TV plans for Monday night. Neither of us could figure out how Detective Lieutenant Edward J. Peres could be involved in a TV program promoting an *outré* version of a Shakespearean play. Finally, we gave up guessing and went outdoors to enjoy the cool evening.

We sat quietly for some moments, letting the peace of the evening settle around us. Fortunately, our cast of players was all at the amphitheater for a rehearsal. Fargo meandered around his estate. I stretched out and lit a cigarette, which I generously decided was number five. Cindy stretched and sighed.

"I know it's *Macbeth* that is supposed to be the bad luck play, but I don't have a very good feeling about this one."

"Why would you?" I laughed. "The whole cast is a nervous wreck. Paul is fighting for his professional life. And dear embedded Terese holds us all in thrall as to what she may say next. I would say that hardly bodes a smooth, balanced performance."

"Yes, that's all true." She shifted uneasily in her chair. "My unease is different, I think. More personal, maybe. Hard to explain." She straightened and laughed shortly. "And really not my worry, is it? Let's go in and call Lainey and Cassie and maybe Vance and Dan, so they can be sure to watch Sonny's first TV production. He may be starting a whole new career."

I stood up and grinned. "Yeah, and I may be the next American Idol."

We collected ashtrays and straightened chairs and started inside. "Are we on the way to bed?" I asked. "Maybe I could be the American Idol there."

"Maybe. As long as you don't sing, darling. Please don't sing."

"I don't see why I can't sing. I sing as well as any of them." I closed the door behind us.

"It's different, Alex. You try to carry a tune and can't. They flatten the letter *I*, drop the letter *G*, hold the mike an inch from their mouths and scream without moving their lips. Tune doesn't come into it." She put the cups and saucers in the sink with a so-there clatter.

"Dearie me, lady, you sound worse than that judge Simon Somebody who's so sarcastic. I guess my singing days are over," I pouted.

"No, sweetheart, I take it back. You can sing to me anytime."

"Even in bed?" I kissed the back of her neck.

"Even in bed, but it will cost you."

"I'll pay, I'll pay.

Chapter 16

Fargo did not get his morning run. I figured that for the two weeks before Labor Day, the beach would probably be crowded from dawn to midnight. So after an unhappy stroll around the yard he came back in the house and jumped in bed with Cindy. With wet, dewy paws and warm, slurpy tongue. She was not amused.

She got up, and while I was in the shower, she made coffee. I took a generous swallow and almost spit it out. It tasted like a combination of cough medicine and some laxative I had been given as a child.

"What the hell is this?" I stared at the cup with some alarm.

"It's a delicious new breakfast drink, all organic, much healthier than coffee, with a brisk, enlivening, wake-up flavor."

"What did you do, memorize the commercial?" I asked. I carefully moved the cup under my nose and sniffed. "Alfalfa, ammonia and syrup of figs."

"You needn't be sarcastic." She sipped her new breakfast drink with apparent pleasure. "You automatically hate anything new or healthy. At least give it a chance."

"All right." I lifted the cup once more. I sipped and grimaced. "God, Cindy, it's awful. It really is. You drink that, you're going to spend the morning in the john. One way or another."

"Don't be crude."

"Sorry. Look, I'll just run down to the Coffee Mill and grab the papers. Back in a couple of minutes." Fargo and I trotted to the nearby café, where I purchased a large container of plain old coffee and a paper. I perched on the wall at the end of our yard and sipped my coffee at leisure.

Entering the kitchen later, I smelled—but had the good sense to make no comment—coffee. It seemed our latest trip into the organic wilds had been cancelled. Cindy and I began to chat about the day's activities, which apparently included considerable house-work. I had almost forgotten she was taking a vacation day. As she outlined her plans, I almost wished she hadn't. It didn't sound like my idea of vacation.

I had to go to WellHeet. The art gallery there had called yester-day to say they had only one or two of my photos left. Could I bring down eighteen or so this morning? I surely could. I had anticipated, or at least hoped for, this need and had matted and framed a bunch of photos last week. When I mentioned this most necessary errand, she nodded.

"Well, since you have to fight the traffic anyway, how about doing some grocery shopping while I clean?"

I tried very hard to maintain a neutral expression. Actually, I would gladly have driven to Hyannis to get one little three-ounce jar of her favorite lavender honey if it would keep me far, far away while she cleaned.

"Why not?" I shrugged. "Might as well combine what we can. I'll probably run the car through the Speedo-Lube while I'm out. You got a grocery list?"

She had. Plus an armful of clothes for the cleaners and a request for me to pick up a dress she needed brought back from the cottage for a Thursday meeting. Oh, it would be a glorious, errand-filled morning! With any luck at all, it would be two o'clock before I got home.

"Come on, fella, let's go!" We exited briskly as the vacuum started in the back of the house.

I returned home in the early afternoon to learn that Cassie and Lainey would be coming over to watch the news with us and was glad I had purchased some sliced Smithfield ham and lemon pepper turkey breast so we could make sandwiches, cut up a salad and call it dinner.

With some grunts and groans, I moved our "small" TV from the kitchen to the little table in the dining room so we could watch both the screen and the next-door neighbors on their front porch. The Brownlees had wisely placed their LCD wide-screen in storage, and the only other downstairs TV was a small one in their kitchen. The actors wouldn't all fit in that room, and I hoped they would opt for bringing the TV out to the large, cool front porch.

I put out the ice bucket and mixers. I arranged some marvelous Stilton cheese and water crackers, carefully trimming some rough edges and feeding them to Fargo and me. A year ago, my hors d'oeuvres would have been a chunk of supermarket cheddar and saltines stacked on a dinner plate. Cindy had definitely been a civilizing influence.

She was duly impressed upon entering the kitchen. "Darling! How nice! I think later we can just all make our own sandwiches and have some sliced tomatoes and chips and that will do it."

We just had time for our own drink, quietly together before Lainey and Cassie arrived, bearing bakery-hot cherry tarts. Our menu was complete.

We made our drinks and turned the TV on, without the sound. "Keep your voices low," I said. "I'd just as soon the neighbors didn't know we are eavesdropping."

As we crowded around the small table and looked out the

window, Laertes, Polonius and Horatio came up the walk and went inside. Horatio reappeared shortly, bearing their kitchen TV, which he placed on a table facing away from us. That meant the viewers would be facing *toward* us. Good, we could hear their comments better.

The men brought out various chairs to add to those already there. The women brought drink trays and passed them around. Terese brought herself and sat in a chair closest to the TV.

"I don't know why we're going through all this fuss to watch this thing," Terese complained, although I hadn't noticed her going to any fuss. "Nobody from the TV station talked to *me*, and I would have been the logical one to provide information. Except, of course, for you, Paulie darling."

Paulie darling was his usual placating self. "Well, they talked to several of us, plus a number of local people. It could be some very nice publicity for all of us. We'll know in a minute."

I looked at my watch. So we would. I reached over and turned up the sound as some music started and a title floated up: *Provincetown, Not So Far Off-Broadway As You Might Think, An exclusive INN Monday Night Special with Ray Cartell.*

Cartell came on-camera and began to tell the history of Provincetown as a town friendly to artists of all schools for nearly two hundred years. When he reached the present, Paul Carlucci joined him, standing above the top row of seats at the amphitheater. The camera was down on the stage, giving a long-distance shot and silhouetting them like small figurines against the setting sun. Very dramatic.

Carlucci was good, sounding rational, sincere and enthusiastic. According to him, Ptown would soon be the Shakespearean capital of the world. Both traditional and modernized versions would flourish. He ended with his favorite phrase, "Just visualize it, Ray. First Hamlet, then Julius Caesar, Lear, Othello! We've proved it, and we'll prove it again and again. A great play knows no calendar!"

Cartell went on to interview Hamlet, Ophelia, Horatio and

Nick in various scenic spots. All of them praised Carlucci, praised the people of Provincetown and sounded very upbeat about the production. Even Nick managed to smile and make nice. Then they broke for commercials.

On our neighboring porch, the conversation seemed to alternate between teasing those who had been interviewed—about how they looked, or that they sounded like they were doing a paid infomercial—and agreeing that the publicity was all very positive. The commercials ended and Cartell returned.

He was walking through the town with none other than my brother. Sonny had on a navy linen blazer, a white collarless shirt and khaki chinos. He looked very masculine and quite handsome. They strolled out onto MacMillan wharf, where Sonny propped his foot up on a bollard, displaying those spit-shined low boots he so dearly treasured. He gazed out across the bay with an expression that would have done credit to Drake.

Cartell stood beside him, intoning, "I'm strolling around Provincetown with Detective Lieutenant Sonny Peres. Sonny, how does it feel to have a busy tourist town under your care?"

"I love this town, Ray. Born and raised here. I know every foot of it. I know every beach, every inch of waterfront." He gestured out into the bay toward various fishing and recreational boats. "I know the piney woods and the dunes and where to find the best beach plums. I love the smell of the Portuguese bread frying in the bake shop, or the fog starting to send its tentacles through the town. I love the ocean when it's green and surly and working up a temper. It's my absolute pleasure to help keep this town safe for the people who live and who visit here."

Cartell leaned on a guardrail and grinned. "You sound a little Shakespearean yourself, Sonny. But how do you feel about a bunch of actors descending on you?"

Sonny turned on the full wattage of the Peres smile. "I think creative people are different from most of us. I think they see things differently. Like maybe colors are brighter and clouds are darker, you know? I think they may have nerve endings nearer the surface. But how do I feel about this group?" He made a circle of thumb and forefinger.

"I feel just fine about them. I've gotten to know a few of them, and I feel I've made real friends. In fact, I have only one un-good feeling."

"What's that?" Cartell asked.

"Traffic, Ray, traffic. I'm afraid we may be parking cars a mile out to sea to accommodate everyone who wants to see this fantastic play."

Both men laughed. Then Cartell sobered. "I can see how you might have made friends, Sonny. You're a nice, friendly guy. But you and even Provincetown itself seem to have made one very vocal enemy of a certain magazine reporter. Any comment on that?"

Sonny put on his hurt little boy face, which he did very well. "I don't understand it, Ray. I don't expect a portrait of Ptown not to show some of the warts. Sure we have a couple of kinda sleazy bars and some shops that sell junky stuff and a couple of food joints I don't much care for, but we have good shops and restaurants, too! Fine ones, in fact. Not to mention our museums and art galleries. We're a tourist town, Ray. We cater to lots of different people with different budgets and different tastes."

Sonny put out his hands as if he were balancing something. "I wouldn't have minded if the reporter had presented a proportionate picture of the town, but she just chewed us up and spit us out."

On the porch across the way, I heard a male voice say, "Aw, Terese, see how mean you were. That nice boy looks like he might cry." A chorus of laughter went up.

Terese answered with a snort. "Smarmy little bastard!" More laughter.

Cartell continued, "Yet this reporter learned that she invited you to her hotel for drinks and dinner. And when you refused, she let it be known that your refusal was because you are gay."

"Yeah, I heard that, too."

Cartell leaned closer to Sonny. "Is that true? My information indicates you are not gay. Did the accusation insult you?"

129

"No, Ray, to both questions. I'm not gay, but I certainly wasn't insulted that she assumed I was gay. In fact, I imagine quite a few men have pretended to be gay upon receiving that particular invitation." Sonny gave that Peres smile again, and once again the camera faded for commercials.

It took a second for Sonny's reply to sink in. Then the four of us looked at each other and roared. A similar burst of sound went up across the way. In the midst of it Terese jumped up, overturning her chair with a loud *crack*.

"I'll have his balls for this!" she screamed.

"No, honey," Ophelia replied. "You already tried that."

More shrieks of laughter followed her into the house. And I thought I heard another screen door bite the dust on her exit.

Cartell was back, speaking with the Town Manager and various merchants and innkeepers, but none of us were listening.

Cindy and Lainey were freshening drinks. Cassie and I were still wiping our eyes.

Lainey patted the TV as if Sonny were somewhere inside. "Absolutely brilliant! If I weren't gay, I think I'd marry him."

"Not if you're smart," I answered. "He's a great friend, a wonderful brother, a lousy husband."

"Anyway." Cindy grinned as she handed me a glass. "He may be leaving us shortly for New York and stardom. We've got Judge Judy and Doctor Phil. How about Lieutenant Sonny?"

Chapter 17

Tuesday morning found Provincetown basking in the bright glow of Sonny's reflected glory. Mom and Aunt Mae were on the phone early. Other friends were close behind. Cindy left for work saying, "I feel I should be wearing a big 'I Love Sonny' button."

I smiled and laughed and agreed with everyone I spoke with. Finally, I let the phone answer itself and went into my office to mat some additional photos to take over to Tellman's Gallery, near the lighthouse up in Truro. As I worked, my grin faded, and I became less certain how Terese would react to Sonny's humorous, but sharply cutting, put-down.

Frankly, I was concerned about what she might do. I didn't think Terese would be swayed by a phone call from Ted Kennedy suggesting veiled repercussions, any more than one from Billy Graham asking for a little Christian mercy. I had no idea of Terese's background, but I was pretty sure she didn't get where she was by crying herself to sleep and then giving in to anyone. I had the feeling this next article in the *A-List* might be smoking.

I would be willing to bet that by noon today, Terese would know all about Sonny's two divorces, his two kids, his gay sister, his father's bizarre death and his mother's . . . well . . . *dating* Noel. Her nasty little shovel might even dig up the fact that sweet Aunt Mae once went out with a man who later became a killer. And I would bet it would all be in the next edition of the *A-List*.

Furthermore, if she and her research people could gather any factual evidence about Elaine and Bobby's background, that would make the cover headline. Not to mention, the six o'clock network news with a nice exclusive for Terese on a show like *Jerry Springer* or *Geraldo*. Elaine and Bobby would then both have good reason to go off the deep end, but dear Terese would have been telling only the truth, which, of course, would make it all perfectly okay.

I wondered what Elaine thought Hamlet might do if the whole sordid story came out. All the sympathy that would go out to him for his childhood experience would be negated by the lies he had fabricated as an adult. Did she think he would get violent? Collapse? Go off and nurse his depression? I rather opted for the last. Hamlet might yell and scream and stamp his foot, but I didn't foresee much more.

Finally, the photos were done. I showered and dressed, and Fargo and I took off. He looked disappointed when we didn't turn for Race Point, but I explained, "We are going to break the law, angel dog, and so we must be very careful. After we drop some photos off at Tellman's we are going to sneak into The Beeches the back way and have a little run." He grinned and let his tongue hang out just a little.

When we reached Tellman's I tied him to a statue of Eros in the front yard. As I went through the door, I called back. "Don't bite'em off."

He gave me a dirty look as if to say, "Why not? Somebody bit mine off!" I laughed and went in, to be deluged with more talk of actors and reporters and Sonny and how handsome he looked on TV. Maybe Cindy was right. A new career might await him.

At last we drove slowly down an unpaved back road into the far reaches of the hiking area of The Beeches. "Now," I said, "You have to be very quiet and not bark. When I blow your whistle you have to come at once. I mean at once, and then we scarper. Got it?" He looked at me with totally intelligent eyes. I would swear he knew exactly what I had said.

I quietly released the dog with a whispered, "No bark!" I sauntered innocently along the trail down which Fargo had already disappeared and settled onto a bench under a beech tree with leaves that would soon lose their dusty green patina and turn to copper, like a giant Christmas tree hung with newly minted pennies.

I would have been happy to enter by the main gate and pay the fee, but I knew this time of year, Fargo was *canis non gratis*.

I heard a couple of distant barks, but figured they were too far away to be heard back at the entrance. I had a passing worry that he had met up with the alligator along the edge of the large pond, but discarded that quickly. If the gator hadn't shown up by now, he was probably in downtown Bangor.

I had a cigarette, probably number two, then carefully put it out, field-stripped it and put the filter in my pocket. Then I stood and gave a mighty blow into the silent whistle. A couple of minutes later Fargo appeared, tongue lolling. I grabbed his collar before he could dash off again, and we jogged to the car. We drove away, not having seen another soul, our crime du jour successfully complete.

Heading back to town, I realized I was very jumpy, even after my little adventure with Fargo. I don't know why this Terese thing was bothering me so much. Sonny was a big boy. If he wanted to bait her, that was up to him. Anything she spread about our family wouldn't be all that bad, and nobody in town would give a hoot. They all knew it anyway. As for the rest of the world, I'm sure it could care less about the little peccadilloes of the Peres family.

As far as Elaine was concerned, I felt great sympathy for her, but there wasn't anything I could do. I sincerely did not think my trying to talk to Terese would accomplish a single thing except to make matters worse. My connection to Sonny alone would be enough to make her hate me. And, frankly, I planned to stay as far from her as possible.

I didn't feel like going home. I didn't want to hear all the love songs to Sonny being sung at the Wharf Rat. The cottage would be lonely without Cindy. What to do to get out of this mood?

Suddenly I remembered I promised my mother I'd move some iris from the front yard to the back for her. I'd do that now. Maybe doing something physical and sweaty would calm me down. I made the turn onto her street.

In the driveway, I let Fargo out, and he ran immediately for the picnic table in the backyard—where sat Mom and Noel, drinking iced coffee. Jeez! This guy was turning into the old bad penny!

"Hello, darling!"

"Hi, Mom, Noel." I gave Mom a kiss on the cheek and Noel a nod. "Well, madam, your gardener is here. Tell me what you want done with the iris, and I'll punch in on the time clock."

Mom gave a little grimace and pointed to the back fence, along which now ran a neat little line of iris plants. "Darling, you are so sweet to remember! But Noel was here . . . and I mentioned them . . . and, well, he did it. But I thank you a thousand times, anyway."

"Oh, okay, just so it's done." I gave Noel a look that probably wasn't terribly friendly.

"I'm sorry, Alex, I didn't mean to do your job for you. Let me confess, I have absolutely nothing to do until tonight, when we have a run-through for lighting cues, and I am jumpy as a cricket. When Jeanne mentioned the iris, I practically ran for the garden fork, just to have something physical to do. I hope you'll forgive me." He sipped his coffee and looked penitent.

I laughed. "Well, I can hardly be irritated, considering that explanation. It's why I'm here, too. I ran out of things to do and was about to jump out of my skin, when I remembered the iris. Gee, Mom, you want a well dug, or something? You've got two eager workers here."

"You wouldn't like to clean out the basement, would you?"

"No," we chorused.

"Look, I've got a better idea." Noel smiled. "Why don't I take you two ladies to the Rat for lunch? We will speak only of pleasant things, and a glass of wine will steady our nerves. Okay?"

"Sounds good to me," I said. "Are things that bad back at the ranch?"

"Please." Noel groaned. "Nick is in the garage with the door closed. I can't imagine how he's breathing. Ophelia is on the front porch guarding her dill plant and talking to it. Hamlet is in his room pacing, and moaning from time to time. Elaine keeps going to Terese's door and saying, 'May I please come in, Terese? I need to speak with you.' Terese doesn't answer. Elaine goes away and comes back ten minutes later with the same request. Terese has had the phone tied up all morning, between talking and using her noisy little fax. It's been lovely."

Mother put her arm through his. "No wonder digging up iris sounded like such fun. You poor thing! Of course we'll go and have some lunch."

I put Fargo in the house with his bowl of water and a biscuit, and left him looking totally outraged. How quickly he forgot his run through the beeches. With Fargo it was, "So what have you done for me lately?"

The three of us strolled the couple of hundred yards to the Wharf Rat and walked into a wall of noise. The Blues Brothers were gathered at the front table and had obviously been there for some time. As I entered, Harmon bellowed at me full blast, "Hi, there, Alex. See that boy over there? Now ain't he somethin'? I reckon he fixed that carrot-topped you know what, didn't he?"

"I reckon he did, Harmon, indeed." When I recovered from the beer fumes I looked over and saw my brother, sitting alone at a table for four. I turned to Mom and pointed. She nodded and we went to his table.

"Hello," I said. "May we join you, or are you waiting for your agent?"

"Mom and Noel are welcome. I assume you can find a place at the bar."

"Now quit it, you two, or Noel and I will find a place at the bar." She turned to Noel. "I went through eighteen years of this. I'm not going to ruin my lunch with more of it. Now, can you two behave?"

"Yes, Mommy Dearest," Sonny lisped.

"Yes," I replied, cowering. "Please just don't beat us with the coat hangers."

"Oh, God." Mom sat down and picked up a menu.

"Reminds me of my two," Noel said. "They're just not quite old enough to have any subtlety yet."

"You call this subtlety?" Mom stared Sonny and me down, and said sweetly to Noel, "Now about that wine . . ."

Lunch really was enjoyable, except for the parade of people coming by to congratulate Sonny on shooting down Terese Segal. If he, and we, had accepted all the offered drinks, we'd have been face down for a week.

Despite his statement that we should speak only of pleasant things, Noel at one point did tell us what worried him personally about Terese's next article.

"All kidding aside about bratty kids." He lifted his glass to Sonny and me. "I worry about what La Segal might publish that would affect mine. Several years back my wife decided—or discovered—she was gay. That's why we divorced. She had met a woman she fell in love with."

"My goodness!" Mom looked startled.

"Yes. The divorce was about as amicable as they can be, I guess. I suppose neither of us had any very serious feelings left for each other. Mainly we were together for the kids, I think, and we weren't together all that often, anyway. At least the divorce wasn't cutthroat. Karen is a good mother. I saw no reason to start some sort of custody battle. So Karen and her partner have the kids, and seem to be doing a good job with them. They own a women's sportswear store near White Plains and do quite well. They also make sure one of them is home every day when school gets out."

"Do you see the kids?" Sonny asked.

"Yes. We have no problem with that. The only problem is that I'm away so much. I would like to spend more time with them, but that's not Karen's fault. Anyway, I bring them into New York or to my place up in Vermont whenever I can. Everything is pretty smooth. The kids love both women and vice versa. At first, there was some talk at school, but now everyone just seems to accept it. Schoolmates, teachers, other parents—no problems, except with an occasional right wing religious type, and the kids have learned to handle that."

He sipped his wine and laughed. "They just lean over and whisper in the other kid's ear, 'Be careful what names you call us. There's more of us than there are of you. You just don't know it yet.' But you can see why I don't want Terese spreading news of that arrangement all over the *A-List*. People would read it and start the gossip up all over again. I have no desire to hurt my ex-wife and her lover, and certainly I want to protect the kids. I'd really like to gag Terese, and I don't know how to do it. With a bath towel, maybe."

Sonny stared dreamily at his beer bottle, not his first, I thought. "Sometimes I think it really would be nice to have a police state."

"No, it wouldn't," Mom countered. "Then I'd have to wear a big badge and carry a nightstick to keep you in line."

I walked back with Mom and Noel to pick up Fargo and the car. It had been a nice long break, but the three of us were quiet and thoughtful as we walked. Personally, I'd be awfully glad when the play was presented and Terese had packed up and gone. Surely then she'd find some other target for her poisonous little darts. I wished Carlucci and his jolly troupe the best of luck, but I wasn't the least certain I wanted them back every year for a series of Shakespearean soap operas.

Thanking Noel for lunch, I asked if he wanted a ride back.

"No." He smiled rather sadly. "I think I'll just start cleaning out the basement."

I could almost get to like him.

⚭

Arriving home, I was startled to see Harmon mowing our lawn. It didn't particularly need it, nor had I asked him to do it. I always did it myself. And I was pretty sure Cindy wouldn't have asked him. Even more surprising was the speed at which he was striding around the yard, almost throwing the lawnmower out in front of him and then yanking it back the other way. Harmon was not noted for rushing through any job, but with his current reckless approach, I had some fear that flowers, vegetables and small shrubs would all be at ground level before he finished.

"Hi, Harmon," I called. "What's up?"

He throttled back the mower and came over, pale and sweating hard. I wondered if he were having some bizarre kind of heart attack. "Harmon, are you all right? Sit down for a minute."

"Let me just finish this. I'll be right there."

"Okay, I'll go get you a beer."

He shook his head. "No, I better not have no alcohol. Ice water would be fine." He roared off at a half gallop, and now I was really worried.

I brought out his glass of ice water and my iced tea as he finished. He gave the mower a cursory brush-off and propelled it toward the garage, nearly taking off my car's front bumper and trailing grass clippings as he went. What the hell was the matter with him?

He flopped into the chair opposite me and stated without preamble, "She's gone too goddamn far, Alex. I shall take action."

"What are you talking about, Harmon? Have some water. Cool off a little."

He took a sip, his hand so shaky he dribbled some down his shirt and never even jumped when the icy water hit his chest. "You remember my older brother Rob, that was killed in Vietnam?"

"Sure," I replied. Actually I didn't. I'm not sure I had even been born then, but I had heard about him over the years. Another war where we seemed to have no clear idea what we were doing or why.

"Well, a few days back I was over to the cemetery, clipping the grass and puttin' out some flowers like I had promised my mother

138

I always would, and here came Miss Nosy wanderin' around, reading headstones. She asked who Robert was, and I told her. You got a cigarette, Alex?"

I handed him the pack and lighter. I wondered whether I smoked half as many as I seemed to give away. Didn't anybody carry their own anymore? Or did they just wait for Alex?

"Well," he said, "I told her about him . . . how he was hit himself, but kept firing at the enemy while they helped some of our wounded get in the helicopter, and then when it was his turn, he couldn't make it. I told her how they sent him home with all them army men for the funeral, and how he got a Purple Heart and a Bronze Star that I still got in that little velvet box. She actually said she was sorry for my loss and went on."

Amazing, I thought. Was Terese a closet patriot? Could she actually feel for a young boy's loss of his only brother and a middle aged man's lonely task in the cemetery? Maybe underneath that leather tough exterior beat a heart of—

"But then, this afternoon right after lunch," he interrupted my sweet dream. "I was mowin' their lawn next door and she come running out screeching like a barn owl. Said she couldn't work with me making such a racket. I told her this was the only time I had to do it. Then she gives me this smirk and says she found out Rob weren't no hero, that he was a coward . . . shot in the back runnin' away! All that hero stuff were just a cover-up, and she was going to write it up in her next magazine article! Making everybody think Rob were a coward, when lotsa the men in his platoon wrote and tol' our mama that he saved them! Alex, Rob wasn't no coward!" He burst into tears.

"Oh, God, Harmon, don't you see she's lying! She was just pissed you were making a bothersome noise and knew that was a sure way to hurt you! She wouldn't be able to get that information from the government, even if it were true . . . or any information at all, in such a short time. She was just making it up as she went along. And no way is she going to publish it. You could sue her for millions! Forget it, Harmon. We all know what a hero Rob was!"

I finally got him sort of calmed down, although I'm not sure he really believed me, and he left. I spent the rest of the afternoon cleaning the mower, raking up the clippings and stomping the divots back into the lawn. That felt good. Every stomp was a kick in Terese's butt.

Cindy's arrival home at day's end was laden with clues for the trained observer.

Her car door slammed with great vigor. As she walked across the driveway, I heard her kick at something and send it skittering. She came through the door fuming, "Fargo, if you keep leaving rawhides in front of the door, you're going to kill somebody." She came into the kitchen. I braced.

"Why is the outdoor grill lit? I hope to God we're not having company. Would it be possible to get a Scotch and soda?" She continued toward the bedroom. "It's stifling in here. I hate these damn shoes." She disappeared.

Highly skilled investigator that I am, it was almost immediately obvious to me that Cindy had put in a bad day. I doubted that it had anything to do with Fargo or me, and she would figure that out shortly. So I simply made us both a drink, and Fargo and I went outside to put the steak on the grill and await the transformation.

It didn't take long. Wearing shorts, a T-shirt and no shoes worked wonders.

"Hello, my darlings. I'm starring in a new production of the Seven Dwarfs, and guess which one I'm playing? Uhmm-m, that steak smells luscious." She kissed us both, murmuring mea culpa, as she gave each of us a hug. "Good grief, what a day." She sat down at the table and absently ran her hands through her hair.

"The bank was robbed and they think you did it?" I asked.

"No, they know exactly what I did. I did it right in front of half the bank." She sighed.

"You . . . ah . . . had an accidental intestinal eructation? The elastic broke in your underpants? Your opium pipe fell out of your purse? You jokingly pinched someone you thought was Lainey on the butt, only it turned out to be Mr. Ellis's sister?" I ran out of ideas.

"Worse than all of the above. It all started with this nice looking, very well dressed man who arrived unannounced at my office door. I tabbed him at about forty and medium-well-to-do. He informed me he'd had a 401K just sitting in some bank in a money market account, getting virtually no interest. He grinned and said it had been there quite awhile, just due to his own laziness. He wanted me to advise him how to diversify it into various mutual funds, bonds, stocks, so he would be getting good returns for his retirement."

She took a deep drink of Scotch. She *must* have pulled a big boner. "He was quite presentable and spoke well. I aimed him into a chair and asked him about how much money we were discussing, and he said a bit over four hundred."

"Alex, can you just imagine an extra four hundred thousand-plus on my accounts at the end of the week?" Her eyes went dreamy. "My bonus would support us for six months. I sent Marianne for coffee and pastry. Choate Ellis happened to be in the hall, and I called him in and introduced them. I introduced him to both our young brokers." She reached for a cigarette, then muttered "No" to herself and continued.

"I worked out a nice portfolio with him. He was a bit conservative for his age, but I figured I could get around that later. Then I handed him a form, told him to fill it out, and we would arrange transfer of funds from his bank." She looked up at me with an expression halfway between laughter and tears.

"He smiled and said, 'Oh, that won't be necessary.' He reached into his pocket and laid four crisp hundred-dollar bills on my desk, plus two twenties and a small pile of coins. I asked what that was and he answered, 'My 401K. I took it out of the other bank yesterday.' Alex, I really thought I was going to faint. That was it. Four hundred and forty dollars and seventy-eight cents. *That* was his fabulous investment . . . a bit over four hundred!"

"What did you do?"

"I looked at my paperweight and my letter opener for a long time. Then I tore up his little pie chart and we got back down to business. He works for a florist. That suit set him back two months pay, at least. I put him on a budget that had him in tears, opened a Roth plan, and he's supposed to sock one fifty a week into it. That's one hundred and fifty dollars. I hope he likes that suit, he's going to be wearing it a long time. Your steak is about to burn."

So it was. We took care of that, made a salad and nuked a couple of potatoes, and there we were. We ate outside, there being no signs of the merry troupe next door.

We just finished when the rain started, and I wondered how they did lighting cues outdoors in the rain.

After we cleaned up, more or less, we actually found a decent movie on TV and curled up on the couch to watch it. It was still raining gently when we went to bed, a soft and swiftly working lullaby for two tired warriors.

I was having a lovely dream. Cindy and I were in Venice, coasting leisurely past beautiful palaces on a wide canal. Our gondolier was a stunning woman who sang some sort of operatic air as she poled the boat along.

Suddenly, instead of singing, she began to scream. And scream. And scream again. By the third scream Fargo was on the bed barking, and I was pushing him aside, trying to get up.

Chapter 18

I wrestled my way into yesterday's jeans and tucked in the T-shirt I had slept in. One boat shoe was at the edge of the bed. I slipped it on and began feeling under the bed with the other foot. There! Glancing at the clock, I noted it was six twelve a.m. I thought I might want to remember that.

Cindy was making her way up from sleep. "What . . . ?"

"I don't know, somebody's screaming next door." The screams subsided to a somewhat hysterical sobbing as I spoke.

"What should . . . ?"

"You should get dressed and make some coffee. If Fargo wants out, take him in the front yard on lead. Don't let him loose in the backyard. Don't let him loose anywhere. Keep him right with you. And you stay here!"

"You're so bossy. Are you mad?"

"No, sweetheart, scared."

"Then come back to bed." She pulled Fargo down beside her and began to quiet him. "See? We're okay."

"I see and I'm glad." I couldn't resist a grin and a kiss for both. Then I ran through the early morning light.

I cleared the wall at a leap and took a good skid on the wet grass and damn near went down. I pulled up limping, with an ankle that hurt. Fine. Heroic Alex races to the rescue, unfortunately breaking her ankle in the process. How dear Terese would love to write that blurb!

I burst through the back door and into the Brownlees' kitchen, to find Ophelia clutching the side of the refrigerator and sobbing, and Elaine in her nightgown, kneeling on the floor by a pool of blood.

It occurred to me fleetingly that Terese wouldn't care if I broke my ankle or my neck or made a trip to the moon on gossamer wings. She was lying on the kitchen floor, in what looked like buckets of blood, barefoot, shortie nightgown pulled up around her waist and a large chef's knife sticking out of her chest.

"Elaine! Don't touch that knife! Don't touch anything! This is a crime scene. Anything we do will just fuck it up. Come here!"

"Don't be mean, Alex." The tears started to roll. "I just wanted to see if there was a pulse . . . if we could help her somehow . . . or get help, but I think she's gone. My God, she looks so frail."

And so she did. Face pale and pinched, eyes expressionless, like one of those old Queen Elizabeth I portraits. White, white arms and hands at her sides, palms up as if in some mute acceptance of her fate. Bony white feet, skinny white legs and hips, and a tiny tuft of orange pubic hair that seemed more a pathetic afterthought than a guidepost to any past sexuality.

Elaine began to stand, and I noticed a small rim of blood on a portion of her nightgown's hem. Immediately, the thought flashed into my head and lingered: how long had it been there?

Once again she bent over Terese. "I'll just straighten her gown. This looks so . . . so violated."

"*Elaine!* For heaven's sake just come over here and *leave things alone!* You can't just rearrange the body to suit your genteel feelings. The police need to see things as they are, not as you think fitting. How long have you been down here? And how did you get that blood on your gown?"

She stepped past me, chin in the air, great actress about to perform, I thought. "Only a minute. I heard Teri scream and ran down to see what was wrong. And I haven't *rearranged* anything. I guess I touched the blood when I felt for a pulse. I did not put that knife in her chest!"

Turning to Teri, I said, "Oh, so you were the one who found the body?"

That resulted in renewed sobs and a collapse into my arms. At that moment, Noel fortuitously stepped into the little alcove by the refrigerator, and I shoved her into his arms.

"Here, Noel, throw some cold water on her and take her over to my place for some coffee. Cindy is up." I hoped.

"Yeah, okay. Just let me go get some shoes and a shirt on. What's going on? What's all the racket?"

"Terese is dead, apparently killed. You don't want to see it."

"Good God, what did she do, manage to electrocute herself? Slip and hit her head?"

"No, she was stabbed." I had the feeling I'd be using that sentence a lot of times throughout today.

"You're kidding!" That call of disbelief came from Nick Peters, standing on the bottom step clad only in a pair of rumpled khakis, revealing a surprisingly hairy chest. "What was all the yelling? Who was she fighting with? Who did it?"

"The yelling was Teri having hysterics from finding her. Nobody is fighting. We don't know who did it." And we never would if I didn't get on the phone to the Ptown cops. But I did want to try to keep the area as clear as possible. It seemed as if people were coming out of the woodwork.

I had one of those absurd moments, which I tend to do in crises, remembering a fellow on TV who complained to a reporter, "Originally I was leading a small group in a peaceful anti-war protest. Then all of a sudden I was running for my life to keep ahead of the mob."

145

Figuring Noel was the sanest, I spoke to him as he was coming down the stairs, now wearing shoes and struggling into a shirt. "Please get everybody out of here as soon as you can. This place is a madhouse."

Elaine put her arm around Ophelia. "Come, my dear." She looked at me coldly. "We will infringe on your hospitality as little as possible." They turned, and I watched them move slowly across the wet grass, barefoot and in their nightclothes, looking like a pair of bedraggled evicted angels that had suffered a long and painful fall.

Now dressed, Nick pushed silently past me and started across the lawn. Once over the wall, he used a handkerchief to wipe down one of our wet lawn chairs, and then sat in what had to be a great deal of leftover dampness, staring thoughtfully after Elaine and Ophelia. But apparently he didn't feel sociable. Not my problem. I felt much the same.

I started to go through the dining room to use the phone in the living room. My attention was immediately drawn to mud, tracked on the light beige carpeting, opened French doors, and a shattered pane of glass in one of them. Uh-oh. What had we here? Intruders in the night?

My God, had someone decided to rob the place, perhaps not knowing the Brownlees had stored most of their valuables? Or perhaps figured actors were rich and would have cash and jewelry lying around? Had Terese simply gotten hungry and come down to the kitchen at the wrong minute for a snack? Had a burglar, suddenly realizing he was discovered, simply grabbed a chef's knife out of the block on the counter, stabbed her and run for it?

I pulled a pack of cigarettes out of my pocket and then shoved it back. I could hardly light up, much as I could use one, when I'd screamed at everyone else about preserving crime scenes. As I stood there, a movement to my left caught my eye. It was Paul Carlucci, about to come from the Brownlees' bed-sitter, which he was temporarily occupying, into the dining room.

"No! Paul, stop! Don't come in here. It looks like somebody

broke into the house and tracked in mud. It looks like there are shoeprints. Don't mess it up before the cops can make photos."

He did stop. And he stared at me through very red eyes, as if I were a long distance away. He pointed toward the kitchen and croaked, "Is that . . . ?" He cleared his throat and tried again. "Is that Terese in there? Is she hurt? We must get some help, Alex, she's bleeding, and she's probably in pain." He sounded as if she might have cut her finger.

"Oh, Lord, Paul, did you just go into the kitchen?"

"No, I saw her from my other door . . . the one into the kitchen. I was planning to get a cup of coffee, but no one had made any. They never seem to think of the comfort of others around here." He now sounded thoroughly petulant, and I had the strong feeling he was still at least partially drunk and definitely in shock.

"Well, there's coffee at my place." I might be accused of false advertising. I *hoped* there was coffee, I could use some myself. But I had remembered that Cindy was due at work this morning. She must be really pleased to have Carlucci's stunned and frightened group filing into our house and demanding room service, if I judged them rightly.

"However, you're going to have to climb out your window and go get it. You can't use either of your doors until the cops clear them."

Carlucci clutched the doorjamb and leaned his head against it. "Don't be silly. I can't climb out a window. I'm not well."

"Of course you can, Paul," Noel answered over my shoulder. "I'll go around the outside and help you through the window. Put on some clothes and I'll meet you there. We need to get out of the way for the cops to look around."

Noel turned to me and gave a mock salute. "All the passengers are off the ship, Captain, or will be in a minute. You wouldn't believe David Willem. I found him sitting in his room, showered, shaved, fully dressed in a lovely double-breasted Glen plaid suit, shirt, tie and wingtips. I don't know how he managed it in so short a time! He has decided that Terese had a stroke or something, and that, as lead actor, he should be properly dressed when issuing a statement to the press. I think he's dead-ass drunk."

"Jesus, I hope they don't get into our booze. Our cabinet doesn't lock." That would be all Sonny needed. Or Cindy.

"I'll go sit on it." Noel smiled. "See ya!"

Now what was he so cheerful about?

I went on into the living room, noticing that the front door seemed properly closed. A mantel clock told me it was still only six forty. Somehow I thought it was approaching noon. Sonny would not yet be at work. Would he be "home" at Mom's or with Trish? I picked up the living room phone with my shirttail—my bow to possibly interesting fingerprints—and dialed Mom's number. Looking out the window as the phone rang, I noticed Noel and Paul making slow progress. Paul was making frequent stops to throw up. Poor Noel kept trying to look elsewhere. I wondered if he were smiling now?

Mom answered with a sleepy hello. I first told her I was okay, so was Cindy, so was Fargo. Only then did I ask for Sonny.

"Yeah. What's up?" He sounded wide-awake. How did he do it?

"Sonny, we've got what certainly seems to be a homicide at the Brownlees.' Terese Segal has been stabbed, I think more than once, and is definitely dead. No need to send an ambulance with sirens screaming."

"You sound calm enough. I take it nobody is standing over the body with a bloody knife or hatchet." I heard him make sitting up noises.

"Nope, just a bunch of hysterical actors. I sent them all to my house for coffee to get them out of there. They kept wandering around and wanting to rearrange the body more comfortably. A pillow under the head and a little makeup would have been next. I couldn't make them stay put anywhere. The bloody knife is still in her chest. I think it may be part of a set kept in a block on the counter. Looks like someone may have come in through the

French doors in the dining room. They are wide open, with mud tracked in, and a pane of glass is broken by the latch."

I looked thoughtfully at a half-drunk cup of coffee somebody had conveniently left by the phone, God knows when, by the color of it. No, I wasn't that desperate.

"Okay. Good job." Sonny sounded brisk and rested. "We'll be right along. Stay there till the first car arrives, will you? And keep everybody out. When you go home, keep them there until I can talk to them." I could almost hear his mind racing. "Put them all in your dining room. Don't let them get off in corners and get their stories straight, if they haven't already. I'll get a uniform over there as soon as I can."

"Hell, Sonny, we're probably out of coffee and milk by now, and they'll be getting hungry. Cindy is supposed to go to work and is probably going nuts as we speak. I can't stand guard and go shopping, too!" I heard my voice climbing, my cool fading.

Mother had obviously stayed on the line, and now interjected, "Tell Cindy to run along, dear. I'll do the shopping and be there shortly. Don't worry, I'll replenish your stock of food and drink for the Huns."

Sonny intervened. "Hang in, see you soon." He hung up, and apparently Mom did, too. In a second I got a dial tone.

I knew the first car would arrive in two or three minutes. Wondering if there were any obvious clues other than the knife itself, I wandered back into the clear corner of the kitchen. It wasn't exactly neat, but looked reasonable for a kitchen used by five or six people with no real interest in keeping it clean. After all, they knew the maids would be in during the morning.

The maids! Ellie and Betts! We couldn't have them walking in on this scene! They'd faint dead away. I turned back to the living room and got Ellen Hall's number from Information. I started her day with a real bang, and ended our conversation by suggesting she have a disaster-cleaning crew on tap, and call the Brownlees, so they didn't pick it up on the noon news, just in case it merited a national mention. I left her moaning, "Yeah, yeah. Oh, God, why me?"

Indeed, Ellen, why any of us? Most especially, perhaps, why Terese? And by whom?

Provincetown's finest arrived and took over my lonely outpost. I was glad to leave it. Terese and I hadn't had much to say to each other, and I will admit, her presence was beginning to make me shaky.

Cindy was wide-eyed and wild haired and not thrilled by our full house. "I can't even get dressed. People keep coming to the bedroom door and asking where things are! That damned Hamlet first announced he needed a brandy to steady his nerves. I told him we hadn't any liquor. He already smells like a distillery. Then he had to have tea, his sensitive stomach would not tolerate coffee this morning. I told him where it was and two minutes later he was back asking if we didn't have any English breakfast. I was damned if I'd tell him where it was! Let the snooty bastard drink Lipton."

"A perfectly adequate black tea, and certainly good enough for the likes of him and his terminal hangover," I soothed her and gently kissed her cheek. "Keep the good stuff for us. Can you give me ten minutes to shower? Mom is on her way, and we can free you up to get out of this bedlam."

"Bless her. I don't know why I'm even going in. Do they really think I'm going to be able to concentrate on stock options with a murder next door and the killer probably lounging in our dining room?"

Then she had her arms around me. "Darling, is it too awful over there? Are you all right? I remember last summer when you—"

"I'm fine. I may join Snooty in a mug of tea just to coddle my stomach a bit, but I'm all right. She just looks . . . pitiful. All that energy, curiosity, intensity, that inquisitive nose, that tight little mouth . . . just gone, turned into a mannequin doused with red paint." Suddenly I found myself wishing fiercely that Terese were still alive. "You know, she could surely have used a big dose of

150

humility, and maybe some humiliation as well, but not this . . . not this . . ."

Cindy held me long and hard and then said, "Go shower, darling, I'll make you your own little pot of English breakfast tea. No one will ever know it's Twining's best. Then I'll go to work, I guess, at least for a little while."

Showered, shampooed and dressed in fresh clothes, I entered the living room to find Cindy and Mom fending off a mutiny. The merry band had decided they would all return to the Brownlees' to bathe and change clothing, and then go out for a proper breakfast to stabilize them after their ghastly experience. Even Nick had joined them, apparently recovered from whatever had prompted him to sit alone outdoors on a rain-soaked chair.

They were all talking at once and my mild, "Excuse me, everyone," had gotten me nowhere.

"*Shut up, all of you, right now!*" I banged a metal wastebasket down on the coffee table.

That got me their attention. "I spoke with Detective Lieutenant Peres, who has directed that all of you go into the dining room and relax until he can join you. My mom has brought pastries, and we have coffee or tea. Lieutenant Peres says he'll try not to detain you longer than necessary."

Only Noel and Ophelia made any attempt to help Mom and me get stuff out onto the buffet. The others sat in sulky silence, although they had no difficulty in making quick inroads on the pastries.

After asking again about a serving of brandy, Hamlet irritably announced himself ready to leave. He said he needed his morning orange juice, probably with a healthy shot of vodka.

"You can't," I explained for what seemed like the hundredth time. "The police need to learn anything you can tell them about last night and this morning."

"I know nothing," he answered haughtily, "And I can tell them that anytime, anywhere."

The others began to grouse along with him, and I sensed another mutiny in the forecastle.

"Anyone who leaves without police permission will probably have his or her interview held in one of our local cells," I said.

"Oh, that's rich." Hamlet forced a laugh over what doubtless was a pounding headache. "Why would we be in a cell?"

"Because you are all murder suspects."

"Unfortunate but true," Sonny agreed from the kitchen doorway. "Good morning, ladies and gentlemen, sorry to have kept you waiting."

"Good morning, Lieutenant," they chorused, like the good little children they suddenly were.

Chapter 19

Sonny's voice was smooth and pleasant as he took a seat at the dining table, coffee mug in hand, tape recorder tucked under his arm. You'd think he had merely invited us all to breakfast.

"As you all are aware, Ms. Terese Segal was fatally stabbed in the early hours of this morning. We have a tentative time of death between one and five a.m."

He placed the recorder in front of him and took a bite of Danish. "Now we need to establish a time line of events that took place leading up to the death, and immediately following it. We rely on all of you to help us with that." He grinned. "And perhaps one of you will even be kind enough to narrow it down to the exact moment for us."

Then he offered his most sweet boyish smile. "I want to remind you, that while you are not under oath, lying to the police is really foolish. Hiding something you know or think you know is equally unwise. So please be truthful, and please be forthcoming with any information you may have, or even think you have. We'll find out in the long run anyway, and then we wonder just why you lied, and we get a little tense." His smile faded. "And you know how cops can be when they're tense."

Hamlet stood, red-eyed, elegant and condescending to the local cop. "Well, really, Peres, you're treating us like street corner, low-brow suspects in a mom-and-pop-store murder. Yet, it is my understanding that there was definitive evidence of a break-in through the French doors. Obviously poor Terese came down for a late snack and stumbled upon a robbery, or perhaps was deliberately killed by some disgruntled local individual. Unless one of us conceivably saw or heard something related to that, which I did not, I see no reason for us to be detained here. It is clearly a matter for the local police to solve over there . . . or not." He waved in the general direction of the Brownlee place.

"Where was it you wanted to go, Hamlet?" Sonny asked innocently.

"Why, back to my room, since neither you nor Paul has shown the foresight to schedule a press conference. I'll change into something casual and join my colleagues for a suitable breakfast." He smirked, having put the dumb local in his place, along with our pastries and non-gourmet tea and coffee.

"Well, Hammy." Sonny leaned back in his chair. I hated it when he did that, especially when they were *my* chairs. "The Brownlees' entire house plus cellar and garage are being searched inch by inch, inside and out, as we speak. The contents of every closet and drawer will be inspected, shoes will be examined. Drains will be disconnected and checked for blood. It will probably be late afternoon before you may be admitted long enough, and in company of a police officer, to pick up some clothes. By then, we hope the real estate agent, Ellen Hall, will have found you places to stay for a few days. You will not stay—nor would I think you would wish to—at the Brownlees."

❧

154

He began to set up the tape recorder. "Let's start with you, Teri, since you were the first one down this morning. We'll try to make it fast and painless, just like your favorite dentist." His smile was gentle. Teri still looked terrified and an inch away from tears.

I closed the sliding doors between living and dining room, so Sonny and the interviewees would have real privacy in that direction. Then I retired to the kitchen with Mom, and closed the door to the dining room and the shutters to the pass-through. Of course I tilted the shutters so we could see and hear through them with ease.

Everyone except Teri settled uneasily in the living room, a motley looking crew if ever I saw one. Especially Elaine, still barefoot in her rumpled gown with its streak of blood along the hem. Cindy had earlier equipped Teri in a pair of her jeans, a shirt and mocs and had offered Elaine a similar outfit of mine, as being more likely to be a reasonable fit.

According to Cindy, Elaine had sniffed that she would "prefer not to be indebted to Alex" and would wait until she could fetch her own clothing. It looked like a long wait, and I pondered making another proposal. I decided against it. I was not in the mood for temperamental actresses. Perhaps later I'd get Mom to make an offer. Maybe Elaine would be more amenable to that.

As I tuned back in, Sonny was asking Teri where she'd been about eight o'clock last night.

"We were all at the amphitheater. Paul had called for a full cast and crew run-through to check the light cues and music cues, starting at six p.m. It was going along the way they usually do— that means lousy," she said. "We worked until around eight, when it started to rain. Then we all huddled in the dressing rooms, damp and freezing, waiting for it to stop. Finally, about nine, Paul said the hell with it, we'd pick up where we left off this afternoon—I mean today—at two. So we all scattered. Most of us hadn't had any dinner, and that wasn't helping."

Sonny lit a cigarette from a pack I had thought was on the kitchen table. I was strongly tempted to go in and retrieve it.

"So where did *you* scatter to, Teri?"

"Back to the B&B. I was hungry but not very sociable. Nothing about this play has gone well. Some people say that means a good opening, but I guess I'm not that sophisticated yet. It scares me. I was tired and I asked Horatio and a couple of the stagehands to drop me off on their way downtown in one of the vans. They said sure, no trouble. Noel had already asked them to take him home, so they took us both." She cupped her hands around her coffee mug as if she were chilled, leaned down and took a noisy sip.

"Where did Horatio and his friends go after they dropped you and Noel off at the house? Do you know?"

"Yeah, they said they were going to Bocce's for spaghetti and then to the Crown and Anchor for a little mischief. I don't know where they get the energy." She sighed.

"What did you and Noel do when you got home?"

"Like I said, I was exhausted and jumpy." She was sounding irritable now. "Noel found some salami and cheese and asked if I wanted him to slice me some. I told him no and just picked up a pear and a banana and went upstairs. I ate the banana and took one of my panic pills and went to bed and passed out."

"Then what?" Sonny must have felt like he was trying to pull teeth with tweezers.

"Then nothing. I slept. Woke up about six, starving. This sounds crazy, but now I really wanted some of that salami and cheese. I decided to go get some and bring it back to bed. I went down and saw the . . . red stuff near the refrigerator. I thought someone had spilled tomato juice, and not bothered to clean up the mess . . . but then I—I saw her. And I guess I started screaming and then Elaine was there. And then your sister. Then I was over here and Cindy was making me drink coffee."

"Okay, thanks, Lady Ophelia. You've been a help. Just one more question, do you know if any of the people at Brownlees' wear work boots?"

She looked totally lost. "I dunno, I don't think so. Maybe some of the stagehands, you'd have to ask them."

Sonny stood. "Okay, thanks again. Ask Elaine to come in, would you?"

He remained standing until Elaine came in and took a seat. Once again he turned on the Peres personality. "You've had a terrible morning, I know, Elaine. We'll try to move right along here and then get something comfortable of my mother's for you to wear for the time being."

"That would be most kind." She nodded. She sat rigidly erect, face composed, her ramrod-straight spine four inches from the back of the chair, just like royalty. Only her eyes were a giveaway, alert and ever moving like an animal sensing danger from an unknown source.

At Sonny's question, she recounted the rehearsal and the rain. "I guess it was about nine," she continued, "Paul gave it up. He mentioned that he and Terese were going to the Landfall for something to eat. David asked if he and I could come along. I wasn't thrilled to be a member of that foursome." She shrugged. "But I was hungry, so I went along."

"Was there any unpleasantness at dinner?" Sonny asked.

"No. Paul and Hamlet got off onto can-you-top-this tales of funny stage disasters that had happened to them. Terese was cuddling up to Paul. The three of them were drinking quite a bit. I was tired, I just ate." She reached out for a cigarette, and Sonny politely lit it for her, followed by one for himself. I tried to think where I might buy a carton and have them charge it to Sonny.

"When we were finally ready to go, I insisted on driving home," Elaine said. "The others were quite incapable. Paul and Terese were in the backseat doing God knows what. Hamlet was in front with me, dozing, I think. Anyway, when we pulled up, Paul and Terese headed for his room, joined at the hip and drooling." She gave a disgusted little spitting sound.

"Hamlet and I went upstairs to our rooms," she continued. "I took a sleeping pill, and that was all I knew till Ophelia awoke me sometime around six." She took a deep drag and exhaled slowly, finished with her tale.

"Thank you, Elaine. That would seem to be all for now." Sonny extinguished his—my—cigarette. "Oh, by the way, does anyone at the house wear work boots?"

"No-o-o." She pursed her lips. "None of us at the house. The stagehands do. Some safety regulation their union requires, I think. And of course, that nice groundskeeper."

Sonny looked at her as if she had told him the Pope was down at the bookstore signing copies of the Koran. "Nice groundskeeper. You mean Harmon wears construction boots?"

"That's right. Harmon. I recall being in the kitchen a couple of times right after the maids mopped the floor. Harmon came up from the cellar and one of them cautioned him not to track the clean floor with his dirty boots. Will that be all?"

Sonny stood. "Er, yes. Yes, thanks." He looked rattled.

He came into the kitchen to refill his coffee mug, and I quietly eased the new pack of cigarettes I had opened into my pants pocket. He poured his coffee and leaned against the counter. "Did you hear that about Harmon? Where's Mom?"

I answered the second question first. "Mom's gone to get Elaine something to wear and will be right back. Yeah, so what about Harmon? He switches from sneakers to work boots whenever he mows or uses the edger. It makes sense. I guess the boots have steel toes."

"Yes, that makes sense! Much safer." He sounded relieved. "I wonder why he was in the cellar? Getting some yard tools, I guess."

"No." I shook my head. "They're all kept in the garage, over Nick's vociferous objections. Early on he and Harmon almost had a knockdown over that, though I notice they've gotten friendlier lately. I saw them out back having a soda the other day. Seemed quite chummy. I've no idea what's in the cellar . . . oh, yes, I do know one thing. Carla Brownlee told me they locked some silver in a closet down there."

"That's nice," he murmured absently. "Well, back to the grind."

≈≈≈

Entering the dining room, Sonny found Noel already seated at the table.

"Hi, I figured I was next, so I came on in."

"That's fine." Sonny was already sounding tired, and he had a long way to go. "Anything of interest you'd care to share?" He clicked on the recorder.

"Probably nothing that means anything," Noel answered, "But I'll have a shot at it. I guess Ophelia told you we came back to the house together. She took some fruit and went upstairs. I sliced some meat and cheese for a sandwich and grabbed a couple of cans of beer. That will usually put me to sleep, along with TV. At least I hoped it would."

"Why did you hope that?" Sonny's voice was super casual.

"Oh, I was overtired, for one thing, and paradoxically, the more tired I am, the more I can't get to sleep. It had not been a good evening. Our little orchestra had gotten about one cue out of four correct. And that was in the first act. The lights weren't rigged right for a couple of scenes. Everybody was cross, and then the rains came. I was hoping for a good night's sleep and a bright new day." He smiled wryly. "So much for that."

"Yes." Sonny did not return the smile. "By the way, what did you do with the knife after you made your sandwich?"

"Tossed it in the sink." Noel paled. "Oh, God, was it . . . was it the one?"

"Apparently."

"Shit." Noel lifted his coffee mug with a trembling hand.

"It makes no difference," Sonny said. "It would have happened anyway. I was just curious where the killer found his weapon. Anyhow, you made your salami sandwich . . . ?"

"Yeah, and it'll be awhile before I make another! Well, I was getting out the beer when Paul's car pulled up out front. I heard Elaine and David say goodnight to the others and go upstairs. Paul and Terese came through the kitchen, clinging lovingly to each other and bumping into things along the way. They were really blotto. I don't think they even saw me. At any rate, they didn't speak. I scooted out, went to my room and settled down to an old John Wayne oater."

"And dozed right off?" Sonny prompted.

"Well, no." Noel shifted uneasily in his seat. "Look, Sonny, this is embarrassing. You see, my window is right above Paul's, and they weren't exactly quiet. But I think you should ask them about that, if you think it's pertinent."

"I'm asking you. Nothing's private when someone is killed." Sonny loosened his tie and undid the top button of his shirt. He was not having fun.

Noel let out a noisy sigh. "Okay. They were playing a bit of slap and tickle, as the Brits would say, and having another drink from the sound of it. Then they settled down to business." He sighed again.

"Look, Sonny, I tried to concentrate on the movie, but I judged—I can't remember every word of this—I judged from what they both said, Paul was having some major trouble . . . ah, performing. Lord, Paul would kill me if he knew I was telling you this."

"Let's hope not," Sonny laughed. "One's enough. Go ahead."

"Easy for you to say. Well, at first Terese seemed to be understanding and was apparently trying very hard to be of assistance. God, I feel like some sort of Peeping Tom, Sonny! But I guess whatever she was doing wasn't helping, and she got snotty."

Noel paused and seemed to collect himself. "Paul yelled back that he'd been working for sixteen hours and what did she expect. She said she'd expect better than this from a drunken eighty-year-old. He said maybe her toy boys could get it up on demand, but that he needed a little feminine charm. And on and on. Finally she slammed out into the kitchen. I heard cabinets bang and glasses rattle. I think she got a bottle of booze and maybe a glass and stomped up the stairs."

"Did she make it to bed?" Sonny asked.

"Depends on how you look at it." Even Noel was laughing now. "David still had his door open. He's a fresh air freak. Freezes us all half the time. Terese called out, 'Want a drink, sailor? I'm pissed and I'm horny.' He said something like, 'Sure, why not?' She went in and the door closed."

Sonny's eyebrows were rivaling Cindy's in disappearing into his hairline. "My God, what a busy little bee! Well, at least *you* got some sleep."

Noel shook his head. "No rest for the wicked. I was just dozing off when Hamlet's door opened. He was yelling, 'So, I'm sorry. I didn't mean it. So I was a little rushed! We could give it another go.' Then Terese was in the hall, shrieking, 'Why? God knows you're a worse Romeo than you are a Hamlet! You're hung like a Chihuahua and about as romantic as a shar-pei!' Then she stormed into her room, and John Wayne finally kissed the girl."

"Ouch."

Noel nodded. "You bet. I doubt that Hamlet was in any shape for another go after that sweet goodnight. And God knows Terese was striking out all around. Surely she gave up after the second fiasco. I finally went to sleep. But seriously, as I was just going under, I thought I heard somebody go downstairs, and then later I thought I heard somebody come back up. But I could have been dreaming. I don't know. That's it. I guess that's enough."

"Quite a night. Don't worry, I won't use any of this unless it has some bearing on things, and right now I don't know if it does or not. Tell Hamlet I'll be with him in a minute. I need a coffee fix." Sonny stood and came back to the kitchen.

"Actors," I said.

"Reporters," he countered.

We both laughed.

Mom came in then from the driveway with an armload of clothes. "Okay if I give these to Elaine?" she asked.

"Sure. No, wait." Sonny walked to the door and called to the patrolman stringing yellow tape all around the Brownlees' yard. "Ask Jeanine to come here, will you?"

She appeared at the back door momentarily. "Yeah, Sonny, what's up?"

"Come on in." Sonny motioned. "Take Elaine into the bed-

161

room and give her these clothes from Mom. You keep Elaine's nightgown. It's got blood on the hem, so it goes to the lab. See if you spot any blood or stains on any other part of it. Stay with her while she changes. See if you notice any scratches or bruises. If you do, come and get me right away."

"Okay, boss." She took the clothes and turned away.

"Wait." Sonny held up a hand. "After you get through playing lady's maid, put on your waitress cap and offer fresh coffee, especially to Paul Carlucci and David Willem. Bring their used mugs out here and bag them. I want a DNA on both of them. If I'm interviewing Willem, come on in, it's all right."

"Yes, massa, I go now."

"Me too, smartie." He topped off his mug and headed back to the dining room.

"Now, Hamlet, let's get this finished so you can concentrate on your press conference. Am I correct that you were at the amphitheater from about six to nine p.m. last evening?"

"Yes, I was in nearly every scene."

"And that you went to a late dinner at the Landfall with Elaine, Paul and Terese?

"You returned to Brownlees' shortly before eleven? Said good night and retired?"

"Uh, yes, that's all correct." Hamlet sat back silently, as if the interview were over. Sonny waited him out.

Jeanine came in, offering fresh coffee. Hamlet replied that he preferred English breakfast tea, if such were to be had. Jeanine volunteered to look around and find something. She picked up his mug and took it with her. The silence lengthened.

Finally, Hamlet cleared his throat. "Ah-h-h, I suppose I should mention, not that it has any bearing on anything at all, but Ms. Segal stuck her head in my door—oh, nearly midnight, I would guess—and offered me a nightcap. It had been a hectic day, and I felt it might help me sleep, so I agreed. We had a drink, chatted a few minutes and bade each other goodnight."

162

"And Ms. Segal returned to her room at that time . . . after your . . . ah, nightcap? Say, shortly after midnight?" Sonny asked.

"Oh, yes, I heard her door sl . . . close."

"And that was that?"

"Oh, yes." Hamlet's voice was deeply sincere. "Long day, little nip and I went right to Morpheus's arms. Morpheus, as you may have heard," Hamlet added for the poor uneducated cop, "is the famous Greek god of sleep."

"Really?" Sonny replied. "And here all along I thought it was Ovid's name for the Roman god of dreams. Thank you so much for sharing, Hamlet."

My mother snapped her fingers and murmured, "Attaboy! Put that ignorant snob in his place."

Jeanine got Hamlet off the hook by arriving with a cup of tea.

"Ah, here's my favorite brew." He took a deep swallow.

"Yessir." Jeanine smiled. "Luckily I found an old Red Rose teabag in the bottom of my purse."

Hamlet looked greener, if possible, and ran for the powder room.

"Send in Nick Peters," Sonny called after him, with a wink for Jeanine.

While they waited, Jeanine moved closer to Sonny and said softly, "Elaine has a fairly nasty bruise on her right forearm, says she accidentally got caught it in the van door. It looks about right for that. No scratches or cuts I could see." Sonny nodded.

Nick's interview was like the man himself—short with no wasted motions. He confirmed the six to nine routine. He then took one of the vans from the amphitheater to the Bradford Drive-In, ordered some take-out food and went home. He ate while watching *House*, followed by the news, took a sleeping pill and knew nothing until awakened by the loud noises coming from downstairs about six a.m. No, he had not seen or spoken to anyone, although he heard Teri come into her room shortly after he got home.

Sonny asked if anyone could place him at the drive-in.

Nick thought for a moment. "I didn't notice anyone I knew. But the bag the food came in is upstairs in my wastebasket. I imagine the receipt is in there, too. They're usually date and time stamped." He gave a sour grin. "Your people probably got it already."

Sonny nodded. "That's fine. Oh, do you or anyone else in the troupe wear work boots?"

"The stagehands. It's an insurance thing, in case they drop a sofa on their toe or something. I don't have to." His voice sounded bitter. "I'm considered an executive, if you please. I don't move furniture. Anyway, sneakers do it for me. They're quieter backstage and more comfortable. Why?"

"Somebody tracked some mud into the dining room. We just wondered who might have come in wearing boots."

"Sorry, I can't help you."

"No problem." Sonny stretched. "Ask Paul Carlucci to come in, will you? I feel like I've been in this chair since Easter."

"As long as you don't lay an egg." Nick's laugh sounded rather like a rusty cackle itself. I judged it wasn't used much.

Paul came in with an almost shy smile. "Hello, Sonny, I've been trying to decide whether you've saved the best for last, or the worst. I feel just awful about this. That poor woman! I still can't believe it."

"Would you be surprised to learn that you're the only person out of this entire group that has uttered one word of regret that Terese is dead?"

"Oh, I imagine they're just in shock." Paul sipped his coffee, now in a fresh mug. "They don't—didn't know her as I did. She barked worse than she bit."

"I read her article, Paul. It bit. I didn't understand all the nuances about the actors, but I understood she called me gay. I could care less, but in some place other than Ptown, an accusation like that could have a police lieutenant back to patrolling the

164

municipal parking lot. And she made hamburger out of Harmon, one of the nicest guys God ever sent along. And I understood well enough when she hinted that Polonius likes his girls young and virginal. And she didn't care if she hurt Noel's kids. So what was so great about her, Paul?" Sonny's voice was hard.

Paul sighed. "Look, Sonny, somehow Terese liked me. She had it in her head I was some kind of delicate artistic giant that needed protection . . . that I was vulnerable. Maybe I was the child she never had. I don't know. And this doesn't say much for me, but I knew as long as I acted the part she had created for me, I'd keep getting pages of good coverage. Maybe a few cheap shots at some of my people, but not at me. And you can bet, Sonny, even if everybody in this play showed up on Saturday drunk, missing cues, forgetting lines and falling into the orchestra pit, we'd get rave reviews, even the people she sniped at last week. She thinks being with me gives her a touch of class. She told that to her editor, and he told me. You think I was going to risk losing that? I played right along with her . . . in every way."

"That side of her is hard to see," Sonny said.

"I can understand that. But go back and look at her past reviews. It's the way they play her game at the *A-List*. They love to get everybody upset and wondering what she's going to say next, but believe me, they always back off in the end. Their editor admits it openly. They love to have people *threatening* to sue, but not actually filing suit. Hell, in the end Terese even praised *The Tanqueray Tragedy*, calling it a sensitive insight into the problems of today's alternative lifestyles. Frankly, Sonny, it stank. But she made it into a gay cult piece that still gets performed hither and yon. And I've been approached regarding a TV movie. Nothing definite, but who knows?"

"Un-huh." Sonny sounded disbelieving, but to me it all sounded crazy enough to be true.

Sonny fiddled with the tape recorder volume. "Now you went out to dinner with Terese, Elaine Edgewood and David Willem, right? Were there any arguments over dinner?"

"Yes, we four went to dinner. No, there were no arguments that

I can recall. David and I got to telling old war stories about plays we'd been in. Frankly, I don't remember much after that. We were all a little high except for Elaine. She was exceptionally quiet, I think."

"Who drove home?"

Carlucci looked confused. "Why, we were in my car. I would assume I did. You mean all this third degree is because I dinged some guy's fender in the parking lot and forgot to leave my name or something?"

"It's about what you remember."

"All right, so I drove home and pulled in the driveway as usual, and we all went inside and went to our respective beds. That do it for you?"

"No. In point of fact, Elaine drove home, and parked on the street so as not to block either of the vans, I presume. She and Willem went upstairs. You and Ms. Segal retired to your room off the kitchen."

"Oh, well, I said I was a little drunk." He blinked his eyes hard. "Are you saying Terese heard that glass door break and went to see what happened and the burglar stabbed her?"

"No, she left your room—at least the first time—before we think the door was broken."

"The first time?"

"Yeah, apparently Ms. Segal was quite amorous, but you were quite drunk and couldn't—shall we be frank?—you couldn't get it up. Remember that? Or did you manage to forget that part of the evening, too?"

Carlucci actually blushed. "No, I don't remember that at all. But, hell, it happens to us all sometimes. Surely you have had times when things just didn't work well, haven't you?"

Obviously Sonny was not about to swap tales of any malfunctions he might ever have suffered. "Ms. Segal got angry at your inability. The two of you had loud, unfriendly words. She left in a huff and went upstairs, where she had drinks with David Willem."

166

"Willem?" Carlucci sounded incredulous. "Are you sure? They didn't much like each other."

"Maybe he was the least of the evils left awake." Sonny accepted a thin, expensive looking cigar from Carlucci's gold case. Well, I wasn't going to take up cigars so Sonny could swipe *them*. "Or maybe she was just getting even with you."

He looked at Paul quizzically, but got no answer and continued. "Everybody else in the house seems to have been drunk and passed out or sober and took a pill and passed out. I've never seen people so concerned about sleep."

"Now, my question is this." He nudged the tape recorder nearer to Paul. "We know Terese later went back downstairs for a drink or something to eat. Did you hear her or did she come to your door? Did she come into your room? Did she start taunting you again? Had you had enough of it, enough of her ridicule, enough of Lady Dominatrix? Enough of playing sad little boy to promote your shaky career? Had *she* had enough of your saccharine yes-man behavior and threatened to reveal your sexual nonprowess in her column? Did you stab her several times and then smash the French doors and make it look as if some unknown burglar had broken in?" He ground out the cigar and stood up. "Paul Carlucci, did you murder Terese Segal?"

Carlucci jumped up and huffily threw his cigar at Sonny, who managed to deflect it into the ashtray.

"Well?" Sonny asked.

"Well, shit, Sonny. To be honest with you, I don't remember a damn thing after I ordered dinner last night until I woke up this morning. But I would never kill anybody. I'm not that kind of person. I wouldn't lower myself. And I certainly wouldn't have thought to throw dirt all over the floor. You're just being mean, Sonny, downright *mean*!"

He ran his hand through his already unruly hair. "You know I'm worried sick about this play. I don't have time to go around killing people. And I'm not the one who hates her. The whole cast does."

He blew his nose. "So do half the people in town. Don't pick on me, Sonny. I'm not well."

He buried his face in the handkerchief and sobbed.

Sonny sighed and clicked off the recorder.

"I'll take that as a definite maybe not."

Chapter 20

Sonny came out and slumped at the kitchen table. "Is it too early for a drink?"

"Not if you need one." I smiled. "But I can't very well go into the living room to get it with that flock of vultures roosting there. Settle for a beer?"

"I better not. Too many people would love to say they smelled it."

"Yeah, probably. Sonny, can you get these people out of here soon? I've about had it with them and their pills and lies and messes and demands and complaints." My voice sounded shrill to me, and I saw Mom look up sharply from the morning paper.

She turned to Sonny. "Why don't you see if Ellen Hall has come up with any place for them to stay? Otherwise, send them out to their precious theater. This really is not Alex's problem." He looked at me and nodded.

The wall phone was beside me. "I'll call," I said, checking a small address book on top of the phone.

Ellen picked up on the first ring. As I announced myself, she interrupted. "I was just looking up your number. We lucked out. The Chambered Nautilus had a cancellation. Somebody got sick. Your two women will have to share a room and bath, but it has two double beds. I found four rooms on the ground floor of the Marshes, so your men can go there."

I thought of the group sprawled in my living room. "Oh, God, Elaine and Teri will scream at having to share. And the men, especially Hamlet and Carlucci, will take one look at those third-rate rooms at the Marshes, opening onto a parking lot, and toss a fit."

"Alex, this weekend is Labor Day. I booked those rooms and considered all of us fortunate I found them. If they don't like them, their only other choice is going to be a sleeping bag in their vans. Who told them to go and stage a murder, anyway?"

Mother took the phone out of my hand. "Ellen, it's Jeanne Peres. They'll take the rooms, wherever they are, and owe you a bottle of Moet for them! They don't know how lucky they are." She paused and listened. "Thank you, my dear. Ladies at The Chambered Nautilus and men at the Marshes. We'll get them there shortly." She hung up.

"Sonny, these people are now leaving. I will deliver Elaine, Teri and Noel in my car. The other three, for all I care, can be sent in the paddy wagon. It might be good training."

Sonny and I looked at each other and chorused, "Yes, Mommy Dearest."

The house felt strangely empty and silent. Yet somehow vague aromas of cologne and cigars and coffee and the occasional whiff of sweaty fear made it seem still eerily populated. I went around opening windows while Fargo plodded, whuffling, beside me.

I picked up mugs and cups and plates and dumped ashtrays and loaded the dishwasher. I moved tables and chairs back where they belonged. I even vacuumed and used some of that spray stuff that makes smells go away without leaving its own sickening perfume behind.

I finished by actually changing the sheets on our bed. I didn't know why I did it. Certainly no one had lain in it except us. Then I had to smile at myself. My next move would probably be to call Peter and the Wolf and ask if they knew a good exorcist. I gave Fargo fresh water and a belated breakfast and myself a beer. As of now, I was off duty. My ankle was aching. I'd try an Ace bandage as soon as I felt like looking for it.

But that didn't mean I was able to put another matter aside. There was something I had to tell Sonny, something I had quite seriously promised I would never tell another soul.

It seemed like yesterday to me that Cindy and I had been comforting Elaine in our backyard. She had broken down and recounted the story of her father's ghastly death, her mother's lifetime in a hospital for the insane and the adoption of her and her brother, and her brother also ending up as one of Carlucci's group. And I had sworn that Cindy, Fargo and I would maintain her secret.

And now, of course, I could not. Sonny had to know.

And worse, yet, I supposed I had to tell Elaine I could no longer keep her confidence. I imagine she had guessed it. I could think of no other reason for her coldness to me. Maybe she figured I had already told him. I wouldn't dream of doing that without informing her first. But she didn't know me well enough to know I'm funny about things like promises.

I'd take a chance she was at her new B&B. I took a jacket from the hooks in the pantry. The rain had quit, but it was gray and chill. Fargo didn't care, he was already at the back door. "Dog of dogs, let's get out of here. I promise you a late lunch of your very own hamburger, okay? Just let me get this Elaine thing over with."

We pulled into the Chambered Nautilus parking area, and Lexus strolled off the porch to greet us. Fargo pounced out of the car, damn near landing on top of the irate cat, and they were off. They circled the house twice at top speed, with Lexus finally leaping for the mimosa tree and gaining the first branch, where he sat hissing and spitting. Fargo sat beneath him, looking up, with the first happy expression I had seen on his face all day.

We found Martha in the kitchen, making out next week's breakfast menus and consulting cookbooks. According to her, Ophelia had gone to a rehearsal. Elaine wasn't needed till later and was in their room.

Reluctantly leaving the wonderful kitchen smells, I went up the back stairs, Fargo equally reluctant at my heels. I knocked lightly on the door of their room.

"Come in," Elaine called pleasantly.

She sat in a comfortable chair, feet propped on the bed, reading a book. Immediately upon our entrance, the feet came down, the book snapped closed, the smile faded and she drew herself slightly away from Fargo.

"Could you please leave the animal outside? I have allergies."

She also apparently had memory problems. She had always known "the animal's" name before, and she had not hesitated to pet him, with no noticeable discomfort. Obviously this scene would be played to the hilt.

I walked back to the hall and called down the back stairs. "Martha, could you guard my ferocious animal for five minutes? Ms. Edgewood has developed acute allergies. She thinks it is the dog. I rather imagine it is I."

Martha looked up the stairs, grinning. Clearly she had understood my tone if not the words. "Sure. C'mon down, Fargo, you can help me plan tomorrow's breakfast. Good boy."

Turning back into the room, I sat uninvited in the other chair. "This won't take much of your time," I began mildly.

"It needn't take any of it," she said. "You have either told, or are about to tell your detective brother all that I imparted to you in complete confidence, thereby casting unnecessary suspicion on my brother and me around this unfortunate incident involving Terese. Good-bye."

"Let's just say I am about to provide Detective Lieutenant Peres with information I can neither legally nor morally withhold from him in his efforts to solve a vicious, brutal murder. It bothers me more than you apparently can understand to break a promise of confidentiality, especially one of such a personal nature. You have my deepest apologies. You also have my assurance that Lt. Peres will never make any of this information public unless it proves to have direct bearing on the case. But he has to know it. You can believe none or all of that as you please. Good day."

We found Sonny in his office, surrounded by blackboards holding lists and notes. This was the way he always studied a confusing case. He said it let him see everything at once without shuffling through piles of paper or dragging stuff around on a computer. It also let him prop his feet on the desk, lean precariously back in his chair and allow his thoughts to roam. It was a system that worked well for him. He usually came up with the answers.

His first list held the names of those he felt the most likely suspects and their alibis, if any. Carlucci was head of the pack, with no alibi. Hamlet was a close second, also with no alibi. Polonius was apparently clear. He had been at the all-night diner with the lighting crew. Nick's garbage had yielded up a receipt showing he picked up his takeout order at nine fifty-two, which proved nothing except that at some point, he brought the bag back to his room.

Horatio had been with two of the stagehands, out drinking. Noel seemed to have the least motive, and had been extremely cooperative. Too much so? Elaine and Ophelia were possibilities, but Sonny had marked them "Unlikely." Well, one of those was about to change.

At the bottom of the board was "Unknown burglar," with the added notation of "Unlikely" crossed out. I wondered why that had changed.

Beneath it had been added the name "Harmon!" A joke, to tease him? Surely not serious.

One board showed that the hours in which Terese was presumed to have died had been narrowed to today—Wednesday—between one and three a.m.

A note followed saying "Seminal fluid and clear liquid sent to lab for DNA checks." I wondered exactly what that meant.

There were other cryptic notes. "Check boots with Sears." "Dumpsters?" "Raincoat & hat?" "Zilch computer."

I grinned and asked, "Is Zilch a new brand of computer?"

"Zilch is what is left on Terese's laptop. Not a word. The whole hard drive is clean as a whistle. And something tells me it wasn't Terese housecleaning. Although maybe it was. We didn't find any faxes either." Sonny sounded disgusted.

"No. I can't believe she dumped everything. I doubt she knew she was going to be killed. But for one thing, I don't get the idea that bunch of *artistes* is very big on today's technology, for one thing. For another, who would have time to do it? We cleared the place out pretty quickly."

"Alex, almost anybody today can turn on a computer and start hitting the delete key. It doesn't take long. I'm just hoping Nacho can retrieve something of interest from the hard drive. The faxes are my fault. We did not personally search the suspects before they had a chance to dump them. Hell, they may have gone out in your garbage." We looked at each other and shrugged.

Finishing up Sonny's blackboard display was a smaller board with a rough, amateur sketch of a woman's torso with red chalk marks where the six stab wounds had been. Somehow the very unprofessionalism of the drawing made it seem more personal and the red marks somehow more invasive and cruel.

Sonny pulled a pack of cigarettes from his shirt pocket and actually offered me one. I clutched at my heart and let him light it. He nodded at the boards. "Any additions? Disagreements? Questions?"

I nodded at him. "Unfortunately, all of the above." I filled him in on the gory history of the Leonard family and ended by explaining that Terese had told Elaine's brother she had dug up an old school chum of his. He and Elaine were both afraid that would lead to the entire ghastly story surfacing and appearing in the *A-List* next week.

"And you're saying that David Willem—Hamlet—is actually the grown up Leonard boy, Bobby? How many names does he have, for God's sake? You're sure about all this?" Sonny made a note.

"Oh, no doubt about it when you recall them as children," I assured him. "If you can get an old copy of *The Tell-All* that had the original story in it and photos of the kids, they look then just like they do now. His adoptive family changed his first name, which Elaine's didn't. She says she still has trouble not calling him Bobby. Also, I have some vague memory of that bio-drama saying that Papa Leonard was stabbed six times. Not sure. But it could be significant in some ritualistic way."

"I'll get Nacho on *The Tell-All* right away," he said. "She could get the original of the Magna Carta in an hour if we needed it. Okay, what else?"

"Have you had lunch? I'm starving and I promised Fargo a hamburger."

"No, I haven't. You buying?"

"After what you did to my house this morning?" I snorted. "You owe Cindy and Fargo and me a six-course dinner starting with Beluga caviar and a magnum of Krug!"

"Please!" He sounded insulted. "The town of Provincetown will gladly reimburse you for any expenses up to fifty-nine cents. Just file seventeen copies of each receipt and have two men of the cloth attest to your honesty."

"I'll settle for my usual and a Bud, plus an extra rare hamburger, plain."

Without discussion we started walking toward the Wharf Rat Bar. I brought up the questions Sonny's blackboards had raised in my mind.

"Hey, Sonny, why was that Unknown Burglar crossed out and Harmon's name put in? Are you just pulling his leg?" I turned to look at my brother and was surprised to see deep lines of worry appear around his nose and eyes.

"God, I wish I were, Sis! I wouldn't blame him if he did kill Terese, after that article she wrote, and then threatening to tell the world that Rob, the brother he worshipped so much, was yellow, shot in the back while running away, saying the whole medal thing was a cover-up! He's right. Nobody *should* be allowed to tell those kinds of lies! Did you hear about it?" Sonny slammed one fist into the other, and an elderly lady skipped briskly into the gutter to give him way.

I nodded and recalled Harmon's words to me, "I shall take action." I should have paid more attention at the time. I decided not to mention that statement right now. Right now I would concentrate on not limping.

"We've got a real problem with Harmon, Alex. There is a work boot print that's quite clear in the mud on the dining room rug. It does not match any of the boots worn by any of the Hamlet crew. And none of them are sporting brand new boots today. Harmon readily admits to wearing that type of boot for protection when he does heavy yard work. He says he kept them in the garage next to the mower. We can't find them."

"Oh, God." My stomach was now feeling emptier than ever.

Sonny went on, his voice harsh with anxiety. "He says he bought them last winter at Sears. Hatcher has gone down to the store with the dining room photos to see if they match up with the style Harmon bought. Alex, I'm scared to death they will." He wasn't alone.

"Then," Sonny continued, and I wondered how much more disaster he had to relate. "When Mitch went over the cellar, he found the padlock on the storage closet forced, and what looks like two cartons of whatever the Brownlees had stored in there are missing. Harmon took one look and said it was two cartons of their silver. He said Bob Brownlee gave him a key and asked him to keep an eye on it. We haven't found any trace of the cartons."

I felt a little brighter. "Well, if Harmon meant to steal, which I will never believe, he didn't have to break the lock. He had a key, and he might as well have taken it all."

Sonny shook his head. "I think it was a ruse. I think someone—I fear Harmon—broke in through the dining room doors, went down to the cellar, and forced the lock. Harmon would be too smart to use his key, I think. Then he took two cartons, apparently the smallest and easiest to carry, which will turn up in one of the vans or a dumpster or somewhere. Then I think he waited outside for Terese to come out of Paul's room. But she came out earlier than he had figured on, and Paul was still awake then and might have seen him. So he waited some more, and finally Terese came back down, and he killed her."

We were almost at the Rat and I was glad. My ankle was beginning to throb. Why had I never managed to get a bandage on it? Fargo was glad, too, whuffling noisily, wondering what goodies were in store.

I turned to Sonny. "That seems like taking a chance—hanging around at that hour just hoping Terese would show up. What if someone woke up and saw him? And if Harmon was smart enough not to use his key, why wasn't he smart enough to scuff out his footprints?"

He shrugged. "Nobody is smart all the time. Maybe he heard a noise. And he had to have been under a lot of stress. Stress means mistakes."

"Well, he seems to have made some, skipped some. How did he know Terese would come back downstairs at all? If he didn't realize he left footprints, how come he made his boots disappear? And why did he have them on in the first place, in the middle of the night? Was he going to mow the lawn at three a.m.? In the rain?"

"We don't have all the answers yet," he answered stiffly. "But Dr. Gloetzner raised an interesting point. You see that torso on my blackboard? It shows the approximate locations of the six wounds. Five of them were not deep and would not have been fatal if she'd gotten help. Gloetzner thinks they were done immediately after she died, though. The first, where the knife was apparently replaced in her chest, was deep. In fact, it nicked the heart. That accounts for nearly all the blood, and the swift, quiet death. But back to the other five, they were small, almost decorative. That's a total of six wounds, if you figure the knife was placed back in the first, fatal wound. Not counting Terese, six people live in the house. You don't suppose it's one of those things where everyone stabs her so no one can squeal on the person who actually killed her, do you?"

I slowed down as if I were thinking. "I could possibly believe it of everyone except Hamlet. He'd be too scared to prick her with a pin if anyone else was going to know about it. He'd be afraid someone would somehow blame it on him. I can see him losing his temper and killing her, but not as part of a ritual."

"Okay," he said. "I can buy that. Then consider this, if you connect the dots, as it were, the wounds could be said to form a rough letter 'R.'"

I tried to think of where he could be going with this. Finally, I tried, "R for revenge? R for rage? For retribution?"

"Or for Rob."

"Sonny, are you *trying* to put this onto Harmon?"

He left me tying Fargo to the big anchor in front of the Rat and stormed through the door. Inside, I stopped at the bar to order Fargo's burger. The Blues Brothers were out in full force at the front table, minus Harmon. They all watched Sonny move across the room toward a table for us. Their eyes were not friendly.

I waited at the bar for the burger and took it and some water out to my patient pooch. By the time I got back inside, Sonny had us a beer and had ordered lunch.

Just getting off the ankle made me feel better. A large swallow of Bud helped even more. I broke the silence. "I'm sorry, Sonny. I shouldn't have said that about you and Harmon. I didn't mean it. You must be terribly upset."

"Yeah. And there's one more thing. Dr. Gloetzner has confirmed sperm in Terese's vagina. The sperm's gone off to the lab, along with a clear liquid, which is not seminal fluid, but a fluid which some men 'leak' when they have sex. Before they ejaculate, or even if they don't. We are pretty sure the sperm is Hamlet's. We're going to be real interested in the leaker. We'll have DNA on both in a few days."

"Well, maybe Carlucci wasn't as impotent as everyone thought, unless it is Hamlet's." They seemed the most obvious. "Hell, that only leaves Nick and Noel in the Brownlee building."

"Uh-huh," Sonny gave me a weary smile. "Or Harmon."

"Sonny, just hush!" I chewed a bite of my sandwich viciously. "Oh, all right. I might as well tell you."

"Tell me what?"

I told him of Harmon's practically wrecking my backyard, and of his final statement, "I shall take action."

Sonny looked puzzled. "Now that isn't like Harmon. That sounds like something out of a book or a movie. Harmon would say he'd get her for this, or she'd pay for this, not 'I shall take action.'"

"Look, Sonny, he didn't necessarily mean he'd kill her. Maybe he meant to get a lawyer and sue the *A-List*. Or get Carlucci to throw her out. Hell, maybe he meant to put a dead bluefish in her bed."

"Now that sounds like fun! Can I play, too?" I looked up to see Noel smiling above us.

"Hey, Noel, sit down," Sonny said. "We could use a little cheer."

"Did you say beer?"

"That, too." Sonny stood up and waved for Joe's attention. "Hey, Joe, three Buds please. And a pastrami and fries for Noel." He turned and asked belatedly, "That okay?"

"Absolutely. I apologize for interrupting your lunch, but your office said you would probably be here, Sonny. I have a couple of things to tell you. They may not be important, but . . ."

I picked up my sandwich and beer. "I'll finish eating at the bar so you two can have some privacy."

"Not for my sake," Noel said. "They aren't anything secret as far as I'm concerned."

179

Sonny waved me back to my chair. "Stay here. You've been making brilliant comments all morning. I can't wait for more."

Noel looked as if he wished he'd picked another time, but began bravely. "I called my ex-wife when we got to the motel. I like her to know exactly where I am, because of the kids. She has my cell number, but I'm just overcautious, I guess. Karen, my ex, is a good friend of our wardrobe mistress, Diane Hoskins. They had been speaking on the phone yesterday. Do you know Diane?"

I shook my head, Sonny nodded. "Slightly."

Noel smiled his thanks as his lunch and beer arrived. "When Terese first got involved with Paul and being *embedded* up here, she wrote a sidebar on the duties of the wardrobe mistress and how important she and her assistants are to any stage production. Keeping costumes fresh and clean, mending, getting the right costumes to the right dressing room for every performance, etc. It was a well-done article."

Noel dragged a french fry through some ketchup and chewed for a moment. "Diane wanted to do something to thank Terese. Diane and her husband George own a farm just over the border into Connecticut. One of those farms where you can go and pick your own tomatoes or pumpkins and whatever. It's a great place. I've had the kids there. Well, Diane called George and asked him to bring up a bunch of produce for Terese, enough for all of us, actually. George and the three kids came up yesterday morning."

"What did Terese do?" I asked. "I know it was something awful."

"Yes, worse than you can imagine, and I'll bet you'd never guess. As George was unloading the stuff from the truck, Terese asked if he didn't get lonesome with Diane away so much. He said he did, but that the kids kept him company. Terese said they were certainly beautiful children, but wasn't it strange not one of them looked like him, or with Diane traveling, was that to be expected? Then she laughed and walked away."

"She never missed a chance, did she?" Sonny shook his head in disbelief.

"It may not all have been her fault," Noel said. "Terese had a single mother, father unknown. As a kid, she interfered with mom's 'social' life, so mom farmed her out to a grandmother, whose coat of arms was, *Do unto others before they can do unto you.*

"Terese thought any sign of kindness was a sign of weakness that would be used against her later."

I lit a cigarette and left the pack on the table. It would save Sonny asking. "That's sad. She did goof once, though. At the cemetery the other day she told Harmon she was sorry about his brother. Of course, she made up for it later." I was curious. "How did you know all this?"

"Karen worked with her years ago at *Variety* before Terese got so thoroughly nasty. But that's not the finish. Yesterday morning, when she made that crack, George got more and more pissed, finally threw all the produce back in the truck, left the kids with Diane and went looking for Terese. He said he was going to drive her to Hyannis and put her on a bus for New York, and she'd damn well better not show up anywhere near him again. And one of the kids says he thinks there's some kind of gun in the glove compartment."

Sonny had a notebook and pencil out before I even thought of it. "His full name? Do you know the make and color of the truck? Connecticut plates, I guess. Where was he staying?"

"George Hoskins. Otherwise, I don't know. I think he was just going to make a round trip. Oh, the truck was blue, I think."

Sonny was already muttering into his cell phone. "Pick up Diane Hoskins . . . . Wardrobe mistress for Hamlet . . . husband, too. George . . . careful . . . may be carrying. Make sure his kids are with their mother. ASAP. Let me know."

"This gets worse and worse," Noel said. "It never occurred to me the kids might be a problem. You think he just hung around and came back and killed her? But wouldn't he have shot her? You think he would use his own kids to help him get away?"

Sonny grimaced. "Probably none of the above, but I don't want some hostage situation arising out of this. He was most likely just in a snit and is home or off drunk somewhere. I hope. Look, sorry to run, but I'd better get back. Noel, can you walk back with me? Alex left her car at the police station and she's hobbling on a bad ankle. Could you play chauffeur? I don't want my mother accusing me of police brutality."

Sometimes he bordered *so closely* on being nice.

Chapter 21

After dropping Noel off at the Marshes, I pulled in our driveway to find Cindy backing out of it.

"Whither goest?" I got out of the car, did my Quasimodo hobble over and kissed her through the open window of her car.

"If you can't guess, you really need help. Where would I go if I couldn't concentrate at work, couldn't find you, couldn't stand the sight of a police car and plan to write a whole new song about yellow ribbons?"

I rested my forefinger delicately on my chin and pretended to think.

"If you're really stuck, there's a note on the kitchen table."

"Aha! Could it be that lovely little cottage by a homey little pond?"

"Your adjectives are reversed, but yes. I really want peace and quiet. If you've been running around all day, you must be ready to go hide, too. Why are you limping?"

I was embarrassed to mention it. "Oh, when I was playing Superman this morning, I tripped on my cape and turned my ankle. I'll get an Ace bandage at some point."

"Like now. It can't be good to walk or drive with it not supported."

"I don't—"

"In that little cabinet in the half bath. Go get it."

The thing that amazed me was not so much that Cindy could tape an ankle as well as Lainey, but that she knew exactly where the bandage had been. Honest, could you walk right to a certain spot and lay your hand on a bandage you use maybe once every two years?

Anyway, I then drove to the cottage while Cindy went off on a spree to Evans's Market where delicious things awaited—all ready, or very nearly ready, to eat. Later, we sat on the deck, where Aunt Mae had joined us, the three of us nibbling a smooth Stilton and sipping a smooth bourbon, tea for Aunt Mae, and at least two of us listening to our nerves loosen up with almost audible twangs.

I was working slowly up to a nap, when a car came to a noisy halt in the gravel in front of the cottage. Two doors opened and closed, one normally, one in a manner that made me listen to see if it dropped to the ground.

My brother stomped onto the deck, followed by an anxious-looking Trish. Leaning against the railing, he spread his arms like an evangelist in full swing. "Sing hallelujah, everybody. The murder is solved! Solved by none other than our own genius, Captain Anders."

"Aha!" I laughed. "Let me guess. It was a transient who broke through the French doors to get out of the rain. He just happened to fall down the basement stairs and into the closet where the silver was stored. Coming back to the kitchen, he spied Terese, didn't want her to give him a bad write-up, stabbed her and ran away with the loot, wearing Harmon's boots because his own were wet."

"You're closer than you think," Sonny snarled. "The only big difference being he kept stabbing Terese until she told him where the valuables were kept. And the entire household slept right through it."

Captain Anders had an IQ almost up there with the speed limit, and blamed every crime in town on an unknown and therefore virtually uncatchable transient. There were many of us who could tell you his age right to the day. His retirement party would be a crowded affair.

"Well, that could be good in a way," Aunt Mae teased Sonny gently. "Now you can just relax and refer everyone to the clever Captain."

I saw Trish wince, as Sonny slammed his fist down on the railing. "You got it, Aunt Mae. You fu . . . darn well got it. Thanks to Anders, I'm relieved of the Segal case. *Relieved!*"

"Why?" I managed to ask.

"Because Anders went to Chief Franks with very good reasons I should recuse myself," he said. "Could I please have a drink? Yours looks good."

"I'll get it," Cindy said and stood. "What about you, Aunt Mae? Trish?"

Trish asked for iced tea, Aunt Mae said she'd stand pat and Cindy returned moments later with two drinks, both about the same color. Sonny had some hefty comfort in his glass.

He took a swallow and his eyes watered slightly. Clearing his throat he explained, "Aunt Mae, if you recall, you gave Ophelia a plant which Terese destroyed. That angered you, so if you had any information about her, you might not report it. Doubtless you will be rigorously interrogated shortly. Mom has been out with Noel a few times. In case it isn't our transient, it is one of the actors—perhaps Noel—and Mom is protecting him. Alex is friendly with the whole bunch, plus Harmon, and was one of the first on the scene, possibly changing various evidence to shield them all. I kid you not."

Aunt Mae set down her glass. "I don't know whether to laugh or go slap the old fool silly."

"He ought to be retired as being mentally impaired," Trish

snapped. "This is the dumbest thing I ever heard of. Why did Chief Franks go along with it?"

Sonny was now calm enough to snake a cigarette off the table. "Well, he did and he didn't. Anders would have been quite capable of stirring up the Board of Selectmen, although I doubt they would have done anything. But he could have caused some talk that might possibly affect a later trial. This way, Mitch is publicly running the investigation, but he reports quietly to me, and I report quietly to Franks. Probably no real harm done."

"But there will be talk." Aunt Mae sighed.

"Oh, yes, some," Sonny said. "But everyone will know who started it. I guess I shouldn't have been so upset. Chief Franks is the guy who fills out my efficiency reports, not Anders. Now, who's this?" Another car door slammed.

It was Mom. "If it's a family reunion, shouldn't I have been invited? Oh, what gorgeous cheese! Sonny, you're bright red. Have you a got a fever?"

We finally got her updated and provided with some white wine, and then we were all suddenly quiet.

Finally, Mom set her glass down firmly. "Well, I think we are all as smart as Anders and Mitch. So who's the killer? What about Harmon, first? I think we can cross him off. The thought of Harmon stabbing and robbing is beyond comprehension."

"Mother," Sonny said, "People can snap, even for only a few minutes, and do things they would never ordinarily do. You know better than I how he adored Rob. The older brother, the hero, the medals, the big military funeral. And now, even though he knows it's just another Terese lie, he has this tiny little doubt. Was Rob a coward? Was it all a sham?"

He took a cautious sip of his drink. "So he flips. He kills her then covers up as best he can. It's even possible he doesn't remember what he did."

We all began to speak at once. Aunt Mae rattled her ice cubes loudly for attention. "I know all you say is correct, Sonny. People may indeed slip out of character under stress, but not usually in the small things."

"What do you mean?" Trish asked.

"I've known Harmon all my life," Aunt Mae said. "I never knew him to enjoy discomfort or have much patience, except with animals. It's hard to think of him standing in the cold rain for at least an hour, hoping Terese *might* come back downstairs, and then going through all that brouhaha of broken glass and tracked-in mud and broken locks. He'd have forgotten why he was there. If he were going to stab her, it is likely to have been in the middle of Commercial Street at high noon, after three beers."

I laughed. "And don't forget the missing boots. Harmon would never throw away boots less than a year old. Hell, some of his overalls are older than I am! If Harmon had worn those boots, you'd have found them under his bed. And the Brownlees' silver. If you assume Harmon hasn't gone truly crazy and really stolen it, that's under his bed, too. He would never just toss it where a passerby might find it and keep it. If he was using it for a ruse, it's somewhere safe and close to him, till he can return it."

Sonny nodded reluctantly. "You may have something. I hope so. If it's Harmon, let Anders arrest him. I don't think I could do it."

"You won't have to, darling. He's as innocent as a lamb!" Mom gave him that motherly assurance that means absolutely nothing and yet somehow makes you absolutely sure everything will be okay. "How about Nick Peters? He certainly loses no love on Terese." She looked coyly at her empty glass. I started to get up, Cindy pushed me back and took the glass, and Mom continued.

"I went over to the Marshes to give Noel a ride out to the amphitheater. We were waiting for Hamlet to get dressed so he could ride with us. Nick was explaining Terese to me. I thought it was quite insightful."

"In what way?" Sonny asked. "He never seemed the philosophical type to me."

187

"It's amazing what I bring out in people." She grinned. Actually that was true, but I don't think she knew it.

"Yeah?"

"*Yeah*," she mimicked. "Nick was saying that no matter who took the silver or why, Terese was the real thief in the bunch. I first though he meant she literally stole things, but his interpretation was quite different. He said she liked to steal things of no intrinsic value, but that people loved. Oh, look!" She pointed to the pond where a pair of rare saddleback ducks had just landed in their migration trip. "Fargo, don't you dare chase them!"

"Nick mentioned Diane and George Hoskins," she added. "After Terese's crack about George's kids not resembling him, every time he looked at one of them in the future, he'd have just the tiniest doubt it was his child. Terese had stolen a little piece of George's trust in Diane. And Harmon. Wouldn't Harmon always have the tiniest doubt that army medal he's so proud of displaying means nothing? Nick mentioned some other incidents, like Ophelia's little plant, destroyed because it was a thoughtful gift to a girl not used to receiving presents with no strings attached. He said he had suffered a similar loss as a boy, and he knew the hurt never went away. I was really quite touched."

Sonny and I swapped a fast quizzical look. Had Nick known Terese before Ptown? I quickly interjected, "Well, you never know what sensitivity lurks in people, do you? I mean, take me, right now I'm getting very sensitive on the subject of food."

"Try not to cry." Cindy patted the top of my head. "Trish and I just ordered a bunch of goodies from the Chinese place. We are on our way to go and fetch it, if it will all fit in the car."

While they were gone, Aunt Mae and Mom went inside to arrange plates and flatware. Sonny took this opportunity to tell me that two apparent untruths had turned up in Elaine's story. I wasn't surprised. Her nervousness and her unwarranted anger at me indicated she was afraid of something or someone. I wondered what she didn't want known.

"First," he said, "Was her comment about the maids warning Harmon not to track up the kitchen with his boots. Remember, Elaine made a point of calling attention to it? Well, I asked Ellie and Betts about it. They both deny ever yelling at him about his boots, said he was always super careful about wiping his feet. How does that grab you?"

"Like Elaine wanted you to remember it. But why?"

"I don't know." He shrugged. "By the way, do you know for sure where Harmon kept his boots over there?"

"Absolutely, by the mower in the garage. He always brought them out and sat on the back porch to change from sneakers." I sucked on an ice cube. "Everybody knew," I said.

"Great. And there was another thing. Remember Elaine said she took a sleeping pill and was aware of nothing till Ophelia started screaming yesterday morning?"

God, was it only yesterday? It seemed like a month ago. I nodded and he continued. "Ellie and Betts are like maids the world over, I guess . . . curious. They say that except for Noel and Elaine, all the people in the house have regular pharmacies stocked in their bathrooms. You name it, they got it. Carlucci in particular. But Noel only has some acid reflux stuff and some allergy pills and Tylenol, and Elaine has an antidepressant and something for urinary tract infections. No sleeping pills, not even nonprescription ones. Yet she said she took one."

"Maybe she got one from someone else."

"Maybe. I will—pardon me—*Mitch* will check that out."

"Little cracks are beginning to show here and there. They'll lead to big ones at some point." I sipped my drink. "I liked Elaine so much. Now, I'm afraid she may have done something silly, trying to protect Bobby, and she certainly has got it in for me all of a sudden."

"Hmm. Wouldn't you think she'd be intelligent enough to know you couldn't keep that family tale quiet once Terese was killed? In a way, it doesn't matter. Hamlet and Paul are the front-runners, so far, anyway."

"I think she's hoping you'll blame it on Paul, assuming Hamlet doesn't crack and confess." I heard the car in the drive. "The caterers are here!"

"Good. I just realized I'm running on empty. One quick thing." He looked around to see that we were still alone. "When we were walking down to get your car this afternoon, Noel told me something. He had said nothing in front of you, because he thought it might lead to something dangerous, and he didn't want you to know it."

That irritated me. "Who is this guy, Sir Lancelot, the white knight?"

"Could be. Or Merlin, who's manipulating this whole scenario to go the way he wants. Anyway, he said he was lying down resting this afternoon, sort of dozing, and seemed to recall a voice from last night. Terese's he thought. Apparently after she went downstairs, he thinks she laughed and said to someone, 'What are you doing in that crazy getup?' And then she may have said something like 'Oh, God, no! Don't! No!' And then silence. Or, he said, he could have dreamed it."

"Oh, hell, he dreamed it, Sonny. Or it was something on TV he halfway heard in his sleep. What does he think she saw, somebody dressed up like Henry VIII, carrying an executioner's axe, chasing Terese—made up like Anne Boleyn—around the kitchen?"

"My thoughts exactly." He kindly offered me a cigarette from my pack. "Except for one thing. Back to Ellie and Betts. They noticed right after the Brownlees departed that they had left one of those cheap, see-through plastic raincoats and hats hanging in the hall closet. Probably left it there on purpose for anyone to use in a pinch. The maids say almost everyone in the house *has* borrowed it at one time or another. Either one of those tall male suspects would have looked pretty silly all zipped and hatted up in it, maybe naked underneath, wouldn't they? And it would have worked wonders protecting a killer from Terese's blood, wouldn't it?"

He paused and smiled. "And it's gone."

"Oh, shit."

Chapter 22

I don't think I had ever been aware of *time* in quite the same manner I was during the days that followed Terese's murder. Heretofore, I guess my idea of time had pretty much been: Christmas comes slowly when you are a kid, quickly when you are an adult and haven't done your shopping. Or, you need to keep an eye on the clock because you have to pick your mother up at two thirty. It moves slowly until you get busy doing something. Then suddenly it's quarter of three.

As I drank my eleven o'clock coffee, I recalled the old Einstein anecdote explaining relativity. An hour, he said, felt like a minute when you were leaning against the garden wall talking with a pretty girl. A minute felt like an hour when you accidentally backed up against a hot wood stove.

At the moment, time seemed to be racing and standing still simultaneously. The players were going full tilt toward Sunday, when they would present their murderous drama. The town was making ready for an influx of playgoers. We all wondered just who the killer might really be. And was he or she dangerous in any way that would further affect any of us? Did one killing end it, or were others in danger?

The actors all seemed as sane as they ever had, which wasn't saying much. But one of them just about had to be guilty. Which one of them would be out there on stage secretly giggling, "I got away with it! She's dead and they haven't the foggiest idea that I'm the one! And even if they do, they can't prove it." Sunday seemed to loom closer by the minute.

It seemed to be taking an ice age to put together any kind of viable case.

Where was the silver? Where were the boots, the raincoat and hat? Why was there no blood in any of the drains at the Brownlees'? The killer *had* to have needed a serious washup after his/her attack.

How could the entire group have slept so well on that particular night? They'd certainly gone out of their ways to explain why they all slept so deeply! Were their stories preplanned? Could Dr. Gloetzner be right? If they hadn't all participated in Terese's death, had they all at least agreed to it and selected one of their braver number actually to do the deed? And who would that be? Blustering Hamlet? Quiet, chubby Nick? Big, strong, good-natured Noel? Tense and jangled Paul? Hotheaded Teri? Deeply angry Elaine? The ubiquitous transient? And there were other questions.

Who had deleted all the data on Terese's laptop computer? Had she done it herself for some reason? Had the murderer done it? And when? And would Nacho ever be able to salvage anything from the hard drive? Her faxes—all gone. Had she scrapped them? Hidden them somewhere?

My bet was Elaine. Her room was next to Terese's. She would have known when Terese was in or out. The locks were flimsy. A screwdriver would have easily popped any of them. She could have taken the faxes and tossed them in a trashcan almost anywhere.

Only one fax was available. It had come in early Wednesday afternoon, long after Terese had ceased to care, from her assistant, reading, "Got it pretty well nailed here. Going north now. (signed) Willie." The number traced back to a motel outside Philadelphia, where no one named Willie or William or Bill or whatever, had been registered.

I knew that one of Sonny's unofficial chores today was to chase down the editor of the *A-List*, who had been unavailable yesterday. Among Sonny's many questions would be: who and where was Willie?

And when would Sonny have the DNA data from the semen from the state lab? He wanted definitive information in hand before he confronted Carlucci and/or Hamlet.

But one thing Sonny had accomplished last night was pure genius. Word was out that the media had lost one of its own, no matter how obnoxious, and the vultures were circling. Sonny had convinced Chief Franks to appoint Captain Anders Press Officer for the duration of the case. He had persuaded the chief that Anders would keep the nosy reporters so busy and confused, they'd be glad to leave the cops alone to do their jobs.

I was still smiling over various imaginary Anders vs. Media scenarios, when Fargo ran to the back door, barking. Looking up, I saw Marvin Goldstein peering in the back door, with someone standing behind him. Marvin was the forensics guru, a slight man always nattily dressed and looking more like an affable CPA than a man who reveled in drops of blood, fibers in strange places and fingerprints at odd angles. Behind him was a woman with a lovely not-quite-young face, a gorgeous cap of curly hair and a build that told me she'd have trouble getting into tight corners before too long.

As I shushed Fargo, the two came into the kitchen. "Hi, Alex, beautiful day out there! Meet my assistant, Arlene."

"Hello, Arlene, nice to meet you. How's it going, Marvin? What can I do for you? You two out bumming coffee and I'm the closest place to invade? You're in luck. I just made some."

"Well, maybe later." Marvin looked slightly ill at ease. "Right now we need to check the drains plus your rugs and upholstered items and clothing."

"*What?*" I was on my feet, rather towering over the two technicians, who might have been shrinking slightly under my roar. "You think Cindy or I killed Terese? Maybe it was a neighborhood effort. Maybe we all got together. Have you checked every house on the damn block? You better have, or they'll be taking *your* bodies out of here in a small shopping bag!"

"Now, Alex." Marvin spread his hands placatingly. "It's just routine. You did know her and had reason to dislike her. And that whole acting crew was here right afterward."

"Aha! Do you figure one of them came in covered in blood and asked to use the shower and the washing machine? Don't you think Cindy or I might have considered that a little odd?"

"Actually, Alex, we think it's pretty silly, too," Arlene added, "But Captain Anders ordered it, and we really don't have much choice."

I smiled at her sweetly. "May I see your warrant, please?"

Arlene studied the floor, the table, the ceiling as if wondering just where she had placed that pesky warrant. "Well, to tell the truth . . . well, Captain Anders said you'd understand."

"Oh, I do, completely." I set my mug down. "I understand that Anders is the biggest fool this town can claim. You have entered my home and attempted a search without a proper warrant. Go back and tell Captain Asshole I am suing the Ptown PD for illegal entry, harassment, false accusation, threatening an illegal search and frightening my dog." Fargo, sensing danger—or at least agitation—was now in my chair, nudging me furiously to get rid of these people. "Good-bye, Marvin. Nice to have met you, Arlene. Next time we'll have the coffee."

They sidled out, and then Arlene stuck her head back in. "I'm a tea drinker."

"Good, me too." I grinned.

She winked and was gone. I knew I was going to like her.

194

I couldn't stay mad at Marvin or Arlene. Anders was a captain. He gave an order. They went. But I could sure lay him out in spades, and loudly, the next time I saw him.

In my imagination, I had him backed up against a file cabinet in his office . . . "You featherbrained moron, sending people into my house with no consent to search and no warrant. When my lawyer gets through with you I'll own your house and all those stocks you're always buying! My lawyer will—" The phone rang.

"Hello."

Sonny's voice sounded almost lyrical as he sang, "Oh, what a loverly morning. Oh, what a perfect new da-a-ay!"

"You solved the case!" I squealed.

"Not quite. But God's in His Heaven! It's looking better for Harmon. Meet me at the park by the bank, and bring Cindy, she'll love this! See you in fifteen." As he banged the phone down, I heard him murmuring to himself, "Sometimes it is so *good!*"

I couldn't wait. It was about time something good happened! I called Cindy and told her to meet us in the park. She was as happy as I. This murder was getting us all down.

I freshened up by tossing some water at my face and a brush at my hair. On the way out of the yard I broke off two rather overblown roses and took them along.

At the park, Fargo, Cindy and I waited for Sonny. When he came from the parking area, we ran up to him. We then went backward along in front of him, bent over, tossing rose petals in front of where he walked. Fargo helped by barking and jumping at him. Sonny smiled, nodded from side to side and made gracious little bows, hands outstretched. Most people grinned at our antics. The lone killjoy snapped, "Are you all crazy in this town?"

"Yes!" We laughed all the harder.

We found an empty bench. Cindy and Sonny sat on that, while Fargo and I settled for the grass . . . well, we didn't have to go back to work. "Speak, genius," I directed Sonny.

195

"Oh, I did nothing special. But here's what happened. I heard the whole thing. My office door just happened to be open." He gave me a syrupy smile. "This morning a fellow came in the front and asked to speak to the detective handling the Segal case. Mitch was out, Anders was in, so the lucky man was turned over to him."

Sonny took a generous swallow of a soda he had with him. "He said his name was Webster Dermott, from Meriden, Connecticut, where his wife and he own a real estate business. She was at a realtor's seminar in Boston and would join him here tomorrow. Average looking man, well dressed, around fifty, I'd say. He was staying at the Voyager Motel. Anders had been giving him bored, polite nods, until Mr. Dermott began to hem and haw a little bit. Finally, even Anders realized he was holding something back and closed in on him."

I pointed a finger at Sonny. "Don't tell me. Anders finally has his transient!"

"His transient *plus* Ptown's most unlikely local!" He laughed. "Mr. Dermott backed and filled and eventually got it out that he had literally run into a lady while making a purchase in a liquor store last night. Apologies and conversation ensued, and she came back to his room for a drink. And whatever. About three a.m. he was looking out the window of their darkened room, waiting for her to finish dressing so he could drive her home, when he saw a car with no lights pull into the parking area and go up to the dumpster parked back behind the restaurant."

He lit a cigarette and graciously offered one to me. Did that one count? Was it one of the five I allowed myself daily, if I didn't initiate the smoke? I thought not!

"Next Dermott saw someone tall and, he thinks, rather slim, get out of the car, reach in the backseat and pull out two cardboard cartons, which he put in the dumpster, and then drove away. The person, by the way, had on a regular tan raincoat, some kind of hat or cap, and may have been barefoot."

"Carlucci, Hamlet or Elaine," Cindy breathed.

"That would be my guess." He nodded. "Anyway, Dermott

took the lady home and came back to the motel. He said the car- tons bothered him. Of course, we all know people put things in dumpsters that aren't theirs, mostly harmless junk that won't fit in their own garbage cans, but Dermott said these got to him for some reason. He kept worrying there might be a baby in one of the boxes. Maybe even alive. He couldn't bear the thought that it might survive if only he would do something about it."

"Decent man," I said.

"Yes. He sneaks out to the dumpster, climbs up and manages to wrestle the cartons out. Seeing they do not hold a child, but vari- ous silver items—and apparently he knows enough to realize they are expensive pieces—he takes them to his room, catches a little sleep and brings them to the station this morning."

"Did he ID the car?"

"No, he's not into cars. It was a dark color, period. So, at this point, I badly wanted to look at that dumpster, while poor Dermott was stuck with an increasingly suspicious Anders. So I drove over there, and my timing was perfect! Pulling into the Voyager right in front of me was the truck bringing in an empty dumpster to replace the full one! And guess what was lying right on top, ready to be carted away?"

"What?"

"Harmon's boots. At least I assume they're his." Sonny looked happier than I had seen him in days. But he wasn't finished. "Harmon's boots stuffed with torn up faxes!

"And since whoever put them there was tall and slender, that eliminates our five-foot-nine, rotund Harmon. Thank God! I take it Marvin and Arlene are deep in the odiferous dumpster and the smelly boots, looking for prints."

"Yeah, why?" He looked confused.

I told him of their visit and he laughed. Nothing was going to bother him today.

We sat in silent satisfaction, until I remembered a question I'd been meaning to ask. "Oh, Sonny, any news on George Hoskins, or the kids?"

He shrugged irritably. "All a lot of nothing. The kids are with their mother having a ball. We had a local police car check Hoskins's house in Connecticut. He was at the kitchen table, curled around a bottle of Seagram's, so hammered he couldn't even talk. They took his car keys and put him to bed."

"What about a gun?"

"Big artillery." He grinned. "An air pistol with rock salt to discourage rabbits and squirrels and hedgehogs from his crops."

"Are you going to tell Harmon?" I asked.

"I shouldn't. It's evidence and it's still not my case."

"Sonny, I think he's literally dying. He looks ten years older than he did last week."

"He's in the bank," Cindy said. "Painting one of the file rooms. Shall I go get him?"

"No," I said. "Sonny, you go bring him outside by the fountain and call Fargo over when you get him there."

"Why?" He stood up.

"He's going to cry. He'll need to hug Fargo so you won't see."

As we sat that late afternoon, having iced tea in a yard that was still warmed by a summery afternoon sun, Cindy was as happy as I about Harmon. Theoretically, Harmon could still have stabbed Terese, but his odds had dropped dramatically. Even Carlucci was not the semi-favorite he had been on the killer tote board. Cindy and I agreed that Hamlet was the killer—Bobby gone berserk—and Elaine his accomplice. Perhaps not accomplice in the usual sense. Maybe misguided protector was a better phrase.

Our pleasant silence was broken by the sound of a car, followed by the arrival of Sonny. I was surprised to see him again today. He seemed much in evidence lately, and I was doubly surprised at the way he looked. My usually well-groomed brother was wearing no jacket. The top button of his shirt was undone, and I could see sweat stains under his arms. His tie was askew and his chinos wilted and baggy. And, horror of horrors, the shiny black boots had a sizeable smudge on the left toe! Something serious had happened.

He looked so longingly at the pitcher of iced tea, I thought he was going to pick it up and drink it. I hurriedly filled my glass and gave it to him. He nodded thanks and downed about half of it before he even sat.

"Would you like a real drink? Or some food?" Cindy was eying him with concern.

"No, thanks. I'm going home to shower and collapse but"—he turned to me—"I thought you would want to hear the rest of the day."

"Sure." I gave him a cigarette and took number four for myself. From the way he looked, number five might not be far behind.

"I got back to the police station after lunch to discover that Anders had decided Mr. Dermott was our transient killer/robber. Anders said Dermott had turned in the silver, which he had stolen from the Brownlee B&B, because he feared someone had later seen *him* taking it out of the dumpster, where he had temporarily left it, to give to the woman with him who was really his local accomplice in the robbery, if not the murder. So he arrested Mr. Dermott and demanded to know who the woman was."

"Probably the town manager's wife." Cindy giggled.

"Damn near as good!" Sonny took another swig of my tea, and I snuck a sip of Cindy's. Cindy stared at the empty pitcher. Soon, I guessed we'd all be into Fargo's water bowl. "When Dermott finally got browbeaten enough to admit who he was with, he said he only knew her name was Cleo and she lived on Alerton Street."

"*Cleo McKinley Smith!*" Cindy and I shrieked together and burst into laughter. Cleo Smith was a not very attractive woman in her late forties with a stiff hairdo, a tight mouth and pale blue eyes that didn't miss a trick. She left no stone uncriticized and had been my personal candidate for Provincetown's last living virgin over twelve. Oh, yes, she was Choate Ellis's personal secretary at the bank.

The fact that she had been in a liquor store and then in a motel with a strange—and married—man struck me as about as likely as my Aunt Mae opening a massage parlor complete with handcuffs and whips. Sometimes my record in judging people really worried me. Would I have considered Attila the Hun the Teddy Roosevelt of the Dark Ages?

Even Sonny managed a weak grin. "Our beloved Cleo in the flesh. All ninety bony pounds of it. And by the time I got there, Anders had already sent a car with Hatcher and Jeanine to the bank to arrest her and bring her in."

By this time Cindy and I had collapsed halfway out of our chairs and into each other's arms in complete hysteria.

"They brought Cleo in, weeping, with Choate Ellis and the bank attorney sputtering right behind them, demanding to speak to Chief Franks, who was up in Hyannis testifying at a trial. Dermott was alternately screaming for a lawyer and begging us not to tell his wife about Cleo. That seemed to bother him a lot more than being arrested for murder. Cleo took up the cry, saying she had never done anything like this in her life. Whether she meant killing Terese, robbing the Applebee's or getting picked up for a roll in the hay, I don't know."

He ground out his cigarette. "And Anders had already called a press conference for four o'clock."

"Lord, help us," Cindy managed to gasp. "Was he going to put those poor people in little cages and show them as trophies?"

"Just about, I guess. We finally got Franks pulled out of the courtroom and on some phone. You have to turn your cell phones off in court. I told him what happened and that we now had less than an hour to face the press. I suggested releasing the two prisoners and putting Anders in a cell. I think Franks actually considered it. There was a long silence. Then Franks said he couldn't make it back in an hour. Of course he could have but, well, you know how he hates the media people."

"Like you like 'em." I grinned.

"Not always, but they can be helpful. Anyway, Franks chews out Anders, right on the speakerphone, and tells him he's on unpaid leave. Then he tells me to straighten things out and go play meet the press and hangs up."

"What on earth did you do?"

"Told Cleo it was all a terrible mistake, that Anders got the

200

wrong name, and then sent her off with Choate patting her shoulder, saying, 'There, there, my dear. We all knew it could never be you shacked up in a motel with some picked-up John from a liquor store.' I thought that was a nice delicate way to comfort her. Oh, and I had Nacho send her two dozen roses with apologies from Anders."

He stretched, the fatigue showing. "Dermott was a little trickier. I told him Anders wasn't well and apparently forgot his pills. I gave Dermott my two tickets to *Hamlet* and told him he and his wife could have a lovely pre-theater luncheon at the Inn, courtesy of the Ptown PD."

"Not bad for a rush job," Cindy said. "Did he buy it?"

"Yes, especially after I asked him to be with me at the press conference. I introduced him and announced that he couldn't sleep last night and happened to look out his motel window and saw the dumpster caper. Then I really expounded on how he worried about a baby being alive in one of the cartons, and then how honest and what a help he was in turning in the silver. He was grinning and bowing by that time."

"What did you tell the media about the boots?" I was right. Cigarette number five met its match.

"Nothing. I just said that finding the silver and other items had put us much closer to a solution, and we'd keep them posted."

"Are you going to talk to any of the cast about this discovery? Especially the boots?"

Sonny yawned. "I'm not sure. Maybe Elaine. I'd almost bet she's the one who staged the whole robbery thing, footprints and all, to lead us away from baby brother, but it doesn't make much sense to accuse her of that when we've yet to accuse Bobby of anything."

"Be nice to find the plastic raincoat and to get the DNA results on the semen. Not to mention finding Willie, wherever—whoever—he is."

My answer was a light snore. Diplomat Peres was asleep.

Chapter 23

Some people thrive on a certain amount of stress. I know I do my best work when there's some amount of pressure. Cindy does well when she's got several balls in the air at once. Cassie and Lainey both do well when a nice neat schedule starts falling apart here and there. Sonny usually wallows in stress like a pig in mud, the worse it gets, the wider he grins.

But not this time. I think the whole situation was somewhat foreign to him. God knows it was to the rest of us.

While any of us might occasionally read a scandal sheet like the *A-List*, we simply took the stories as gospel if we were naïve, or as so much scurrilous amusement if we were not. The real threats it could impose on the subjects being pilloried throughout its pages had probably never occurred to any of us before now.

And the sheer, gleefully malicious investigators and writers who turned out the smoking pages were a breed completely alien to most of us.

It seemed that no one in the cast of Carlucci's play was left untouched. From Hamlet on down there was a little something for everyone. Even the young man who played Laertes apparently had a juvenile record—a record which is *supposed* to be sealed—for assault and robbery. And one of the electricians had an entire bed-room in his home turned into a Katharine Hepburn shrine of photos and artifacts, including a threadbare terry robe stolen from the set of *Adam's Rib*, which he used as a bath towel.

These appetizing tidbits were Terese's current notes and had come to Sonny via the *A-List's* editor, whom Sonny had at last reached Saturday morning, at his Long Island home. The editor had solemnly declared that the public "had the right to know." And when Sonny had asked "Why?" had seemed genuinely confused.

Fortunately, the publisher either had better sense or had come under some pressure from high places, however, for after speaking with Sonny, he had ordered the editor to dump all the Hamlet printed files plus any other of Terese's files or notes already trans-ferred to the main office computer, right down to any stray grocery lists. The editor was then to write a brief, but praise filled and fact sparse obituary of that dedicated journalist for next week's issue. When Terese's body was released, *A-List* would provide a private funeral. Terese was being gently erased.

Willie, he added, was on extended vacation in the South Pacific and could not be reached. And whoever had blanked out Terese's laptop was still unknown. My bet was still Elaine. Before or after the murder, she still was the one with the best opportunities before the murder. After the murder, quite possibly, she was awake early, found Terese's body, went back upstairs and erased the hard drive, made her trip to the dumpster and then waited patiently for some-one else to "find" the body. She would have taken the risk in a heartbeat to protect Bobby and, perforce, herself from Terese's account of their lives.

While Sonny, like the rest of us who knew of his conversation with the publisher, was relieved that next week's published *A-List* would contain no spurious anecdotes for Ptown, its citizens or vis-iting players, the editor's information simply broadened the field of those with reason to kill Terese.

Sonny was keeping this information quiet and urged us to say nothing. He was hoping the worry of what they feared might be published the following week would cause one of the players to reveal information. Either accidentally or to incriminate someone else.

We agreed not to tell anyone, whomever that might be, but personally, I thought he was being overcautious. The players were now concerned about presenting a play to a large audience, hoping for good reviews and eager for a reasonable run in New York. Murder came second.

Still, they were a nervous group. I estimated, among actors, chorus, technicians, stagehands and musicians, they had at least thirty-five people who were totally innocent of murder and had the usual reasons for wishing the show to be a success. They had one, and probably two, people involved in Terese's death, who had an extra reason for hoping for a triumphal presentation. They wanted to look innocent.

After all, if they dressed and acted their parts to perfection, who would *dream* of thinking them capable of bloody murder only a few days prior? If they were relaxed, handled their lines and songs or other activities with obvious competence and ease, who would ever think they carried the weight of a brutal killing on their conscience?

There's an old superstition among theater people that a bad dress rehearsal means a good opening show, and vice versa. Paul had scheduled the final dress rehearsal for Saturday afternoon.

Mom drove Noel and a couple of the other men out to the amphitheater for the rehearsal and, at Paul's invitation, stayed to watch. According to her, if the old fallacy were correct, Sunday's version of *Hamlet* should be the greatest success ever produced, up to and including the original opening night at the Globe Theater some four hundred years earlier!

Rehearsal was a disaster. Lines were forgotten, music cues were missed, the mike for Ophelia's swan song didn't work at all, and her voice carried to about the second row. Noel and Elaine messed up their love song. Again. The pistol with which Hamlet was to kill

Polonius was not in the table drawer, so Hamlet casually pointed his finger and said *Bang!* which broke up Polonius, causing him to forget his dying lines. Elaine came on stage for a formal soiree in tennis shorts meant for the next scene, and finally everyone was draped in sudden darkness as the electrician skipped a cue and cut the lights before the end of the act.

And that was what Mom remembered offhand. We ran into her and Noel at the Ocean's Bounty having dinner, and joined them for a drink. At least Mom was having dinner. Noel seemed to be pouring down drinks, pushing an appetizer around his plate and trying not to scream. Finally, he could stand no more of our light, bantering conversation meant to make him feel better, and announced that he was going back to the Marshes. No, thank you, he did not need a ride, the walk would do him good.

He stood and gave us all a wobbly little bow. "Good night, dear ladies. Enjoy your evening."

"Good night, dear Duke," Cindy said. "Break a leg." He turned deadly white and walked unsteadily away.

Cindy looked stricken. "What did I do? I thought that meant 'Good luck' in theater talk."

"Perhaps it isn't used when someone is upset about their play and about to take a long walk in the dark and has had several drinks," I replied gently.

"He's just got a bad case of nerves," Mom said. "He'll be fine tomorrow when it's the real thing. They're all an inch away from hysteria right now. Ophelia is still screaming about the mike. She won't have a voice left if she doesn't quit. Elaine says if Noel screws up tomorrow on that song, she's walking off the stage. Nick says Hamlet reached in the wrong drawer for the gun. Hamlet just laughed and said to put a gun in each drawer to avoid problems. He's about the only one just going with the flow." Mom finished her clams casino.

"He's probably guzzling Xanax."

"Quite possibly," Mom said. "Everyone else is. Won't you two join me for dinner? I've already ordered, and I hate to eat alone in a restaurant for some reason."

We looked at each other and nodded. "Love to," Cindy said. "We're meeting Walter and Billy at the A-House later, but we've loads of time."

We enjoyed our threesome dinner and appreciated Mom's treat as well. When we parted outside the restaurant, I thanked my mother and then asked. "Mom, do you think Noel is all right? Should we check on him?"

"I think he will be perfectly fine. He's probably on my answering machine as we speak, apologizing. Remember, he's an actor. I think he feels he must *over*react or he's not doing his part for the team. They'll all get together and weep and moan and drink too much and blame everyone but themselves. And tomorrow they will be gorgeous and letter-perfect. And I don't need to spend a boring evening being part of the chorus. Worry not, darling. He's not about to put his head in the oven. See you tomorrow for the big event."

We kissed goodnight, and as Cindy and I walked out of earshot, I said. "Well, you heard that little speech. I must say, my romantic one, that didn't sound to me like anyone who is *dating*. Don't you agree?"

"Absolutely, I agree. Sounded much more like a wife to me."

I hadn't had enough sleep, and what I had was laced with strange dreams, but what did Fargo care? He wanted out. My mouth was dry, my head slightly achy, my humor unhelped by my bedmate sleeping soundly at my side. But what did Fargo care? He wanted the beach, and he knew who took him there. It wasn't Cindy he was nudging with a cold nose and begging with those big brown eyes.

I made the mistake of meeting his look. He grinned and the tail wagged faster.

"Oh, all right."

I let him out, got dressed and picked up his leash. When I went out the back door, I found him sitting by the garage door looking angelic. How could you stay grumpy?

The cool, salty air helped. Finding the beach virtually deserted at this early hour helped. Watching Fargo chase imaginary foes in and out of the surf helped most of all.

By seven o'clock the beach began to fill with people. Well, it was the last big summer weekend. In a few days children would be back in school. There would be slowly diminishing crowds for another month or so, but then the Atlantic would begin to show its stern autumn face, and nights would replace their soft caress with a harsh nip. The days would still be pleasant, but even their warmth would be tentative. So people were going to enjoy every minute available to them. And why not?

Fargo and I headed toward home via the newsstand. In the backyard we found the omnipresent Sonny, with three containers of Costa Rican coffee on the table, plus a bag that obviously contained pastries.

He walked over to the car and spoke softly. "I think Cindy is still asleep, the house is quiet."

"Probably." I yawned. "Only idiots are up at this hour. And dogs."

"And cops bearing good news. And naughty actresses."

"Oh? Tell all. Especially about naughty actresses."

"I think the boots have told us who took them, or more to the point, who wore them to the dumpster." He took the newspapers and we walked back to the table.

I popped the lid on one of the coffees. "Like who?"

"Arlene found a drop or two of fresh blood in the heel of one boot. She also noticed that the laces were pulled out of the top two holes of both boot tops. She made a quantum leap and decided that someone with considerably smaller feet than Harmon had worn the boots and kept them from slipping off by tying the laces tight around their lower legs. The boots had evidently moved up and down some and caused a blister on the left heel. The blister broke, and a little blood is in the boot, along with a small piece of skin. Clever, what? All buried under the pieces of fax paper, which the whole office is now trying to fit back together."

"Very clever." I tried the coffee and approved. "Can you get a match on the blood?"

"Not sure there's enough, but the skin looks good," Sonny said. "But I've been busy spreading the joy. I called Paul and Hamlet. You can't imagine how happy they were to hear from me. Hamlet wears the same size shoe as the boots. Carlucci wears one size smaller. Not enough to make any difference in the short run. Get that, the short run? Neither of them would have had to tie the boots on. That left Elaine."

I groaned at the pun, Sonny's were invariably awful. Then I informed him, "I can assure you, Elaine does not have feet the size of Harmon's."

"No," he said and sipped his coffee. "I went by the Chambered Nautilus and got her up. She was simply thrilled to see me and flatly refused to lend me or even show me any of her shoes so I could look for a size, not that I would know how to compare them with a man's without just placing them side by side."

"So get a warrant and let Arlene handle it," I said.

"I will." He grinned. "But since Elaine was barefoot this morning, I saw the big Band-Aid on the back of her heel. I asked her how she got the wound. She said Noel accidentally kicked her while they were dancing on stage."

"Well, it's possible, I suppose, but I doubt it. Noel can't sing worth a damn, but he isn't clumsy."

Sonny's cell phone played a couple of bars of "Me and My Shadow" as he pulled it from his shirt pocket.

"Peres." Big wolfish grin. "Great, Nacho, read it to me." Silence. Grin faded. "Read it again." Pause. "Shit. Balls! *Fuckit!*"

He threw the phone violently to the ground, where it hit a stepping stone and bounced impressively skyward before falling back to earth in three pieces. Cindy flew through the back door nightgown-clad, eyes wide, hair wild.

"What's wrong? What happened? What's all the noise?"

Sonny gave a logical answer to three illogical questions. "I just got the report. The semen is Hamlet's, all right, but the clear fluid is Paul Carlucci's. So Terese was *not* attacked during or after her death. She just had sex with two drunks. One couldn't pull the trigger and the other couldn't wait. Dammit all to hell! From what Noel said, and what Carlucci himself implied, I assumed Paul had good old can't-get-it-up problems and didn't have sex with Terese at all. It seems he did, in some manner or other."

Cindy looked at him long and unbelievingly. Finally she spoke. "You made all that racket and demolished a perfectly good phone over somebody's semen? *Men.*"

She walked back inside.

"Maybe you could arrest Elaine for obstruction," I said. "Maybe then she'll tell you what she really knows about all this."

"Yeah."

"Maybe by now Paul has remembered more of what happened between them. Maybe he really is the killer . . . or maybe even Hamlet, later that night."

"Maybe." He was trying to fit the pieces of his phone back together. "Dammit! I was sure the leaker was the killer!"

"Just relax for awhile, you'll work it out." I pulled the *Sunday Times* closer and found the Book Review section. I reached in the paper bag and settled down with a French cruller. But it was not to be.

"Good morning, children! I do hope there's an extra donut. I walked over and I've worked up an appetite. Ah, well, I burned some calories walking. I guess I can just put them back and no harm done. Oh, is that an extra cup of coffee? Could I?" My mother was being noisily, obnoxiously and very falsely cheerful. And what was she doing here at this hour, anyway?

"Hi, Mom," Sonny and I chorused. "Help yourself to whatever," Sonny added.

"Thank you. I'm glad I happened to catch you both together. Save me explaining twice." She sipped the coffee and didn't even seem to realize that it *had* to be stone cold.

"Explain what?" I asked. "Is anything wrong?"

"Far from it," she said. "As you know, Paul Carlucci plans to send everyone back to New York Wednesday for a few days rest, and then go into a couple of weeks rehearsal for the Broadway version of *Hamlet*. It's just slightly different, being an indoor and smaller stage adaptation. And, of course, there are always a few script revisions after the first performance." She was beginning to sound like a pro herself.

"Well, Noel has asked me to come down to New York and let him show me his native's-eye view of the city during the time he's off, and then stay for the opening night performance. I've accepted his invitation, and to top it off, Cassie will fly us down Wednesday morning, along with Paul and Elaine. I'm so excited! I can't wait!"

I was suddenly and deeply in shock. I looked at Sonny, whose mouth was literally open. I saw Cindy in the doorway again, this time with her face screwed up and eyes tightly closed. Pain? Prayer? Anticipating an explosion? And I knew I could never, ever ask my mother the question that had been forming on my tongue. I managed somehow to make a seamless transition by leaning across the table and bringing her hand lightly to my lips.

"Mom, how wonderful! I'm absolutely envious. Seeing New York with a real New Yorker for your guide. You'll see all the great little nooks and crannies the rest of us miss. You lucky dog, you!"

Mom smiled, and I saw her whole body relax. Out of the corner of my eye I saw Cindy slump against the doorjamb and blow me a kiss. I kicked my brother under the table and he pulled together a smile.

"Great, Mom! Aren't you turning into the cosmopolite! Chartered planes, Broadway openings. Gee, Alex, think she'll give us her autograph when she gets back?"

Cindy appeared with a bottle of champagne and glasses. "It's a little early, but you look like a champagne-for-breakfast-lady! Here's to a divine vacation, Jeanne, you deserve it."

And indeed she did.

But with an actor?

Chapter 24

The entire area surrounding the amphitheater sported a festive atmosphere, if a confusing one. Bright flags flew in a circle around the parking lot, as they had flown around the Globe, and Paul had provided groups of costumed strolling minstrels playing Elizabethan airs, while some people enjoyed folk dances and others tailgated and made the rest of us hungry. There were booths with free soft drinks and non-alcoholic punch. I think there were many beers tucked away in coolers and harder stuff concealed in numerous pocket flasks.

Cassie and I taught one group of minstrels what we considered an appropriate addition to their repertoire. It was a sardonic take-off on a Medieval ditty about Mayday and the dance around the maypole, welcoming summer.

The minstrels quickly set it to some catchy rhythm and Cassie and I did our own little folk dance until Cindy and Lainey suggested we sit down and have some black coffee. So much for carefully concealed flasks.

Then a flag with a giant comedy/tragedy mask fluttered up the high center pole, and three musicians blew a stirring fanfaronade on those long, gorgeous silver trumpets to announce play time.

And we filed down to our seats. Fortunately, Cindy and Lainey—along with most other playgoers—had remembered to bring cushions to soften the unforgiving concrete construction, and we comfortably awaited . . . what? A triumph? A mess? A sleep-inducing drone?

The conductor brought the orchestra to life with a heart-lifting crescendo, and the overture was underway. What is it about overtures to musicals that rouse one so?

I'm the audience any cast would love to have, doubtless an inheritance from my mother. I'm up, I'm trembly, I'm excited. I'm with them all the way. I expect great things from them. Sometimes I'm disappointed, but not because I started with a blasé attitude. I was always entirely ready to be entertained and pleased. Despite all the things I knew about these players and this play itself, that first orchestral chord had still invoked its familiar magic.

And I was entertained and pleased. I've seen better shows, but God knows I've seen worse. If mistakes were made, they were not obvious. Queenie and the Duke were dutifully married and their reception party was lively with dancers and romantic with their wedding waltz and touching duet. Both perfectly done.

Tension grew as Hamlet's suspicions around his father's death deepened and his indecision grew more debilitating. Laertes duly outed Horatio and Hamlet, effectively ending Hamlet's "romance" with Ophelia. Ophelia's final song—perfectly miked—was a sweetly sad ballad about a tree which fell in the forest, mourned by the birds and wildlife that had enjoyed its fruit and shelter, but leading her to ask: *Will I fall alone and ungrieved ? Will anyone cry when they say goodbye to me? Will a sparrow weep on the day I die?* And she, having swallowed her lethal potion, fell gracefully dead, alone on the stage, to long and loud applause.

Laertes wasn't too popular at this point, and Polonius figured he'd better get his kid out of town for a while, so he sent him to the

Caribbean with a bunch of stolen KustomerKing money, ripe for the laundry. Polonius showed a surprisingly subtle comedic talent as he answered his son's questions of what to expect on his first trip as an illicit courier:

Son, you can sell shares in companies that will never be
Just don't come to the attention of the SEC
As long as you have a million or two
Anything that you do
Will be quite all right

You'll find ladies and gents all quite fond
When they see your sheaf of bearer bonds
When you've got a million or four
Any way you care to score
Will be utterly all right

The IRS? Don't give them a worry!
Just fuel your Gulfstream in a hurry
When you've got a billion or so
You can be happy wherever you go!
And any little thing you do
Will be positively . . . perfectly . . . superbly all right!

Made me kind of sorry the old fraud went and got himself killed.

I thought the cast was doing a helluva job, considering the various stresses they must be under. Much as I hated to admit it, I was most impressed by Hamlet. He must have simply coasted through the few rehearsals I had heard or seen, saving himself for the performance itself. And if he were indeed our killer, you'd never know it.

His timing was perfect. He neither trampled other actors' lines nor lagged. He seemed young and vigorous and vacillated between uncertainty and arrogance, as so many of us do in young adulthood. He managed to come across as both a know-it-all and a boy/man confused and devastated by his father's death and his mother's behavior. I could easily visualize him charming his way right past a jury and into an acquittal.

Queenie was playing well, too. Elaine managed to be sexy and conniving and a respectable southern lady, all at the same time. And doubtless with big personal worries and an aching foot.

We had reached the final scene, where Paul Carlucci's direction would revert to pure Shakespearean tradition, carried out by a bunch of vengeful people littering the stage with corpses, with only Horatio left standing for his "Goodnight, Sweet Prince" soliloquy, which he would deliver as written by the original playwright.

Gathered on stage in the living room for the final scene were Hamlet, his mother, Duke and Horatio. The CFO of Big Mart was expected in half an hour for a final answer: Would KustomerKing sell or not? And still the family could not reach a unanimous decision.

Duke and Queenie were a definite "Sell." The absent Laertes, everyone knew, would wish to keep the shares he had inherited from Polonius.

Hamlet still worried about how Big Mart would treat the KustomerKing employees they would inherit, and whether they would effectively put the small stores in various towns out of business. On the other hand, a summer in France with Horatio and a permanent escape from small town Georgia beckoned enticingly.

As they hashed and rehashed, the screen door flew open and Laertes—just back from his offshore trip—crashed in, drunk and waving a pistol. He screamed at Hamlet, "You murdering bastard! You killed my father, and you might as well have shot my sister! You think your family owns this county, but you won't get away with this!" He fired.

A squib went off under Hamlet's shirt, and apparent blood soaked through the cloth. Hamlet grabbed his chest and staggered back. "Maybe not, Larry, but there's blame to go around. Your father was complicit in the death of mine, and stole millions from him to boot. After all my father did for him!"

Hamlet reached into the end table drawer and pulled out the pistol, this time in its proper drawer, and shot Laertes.

And then strange things began to happen.

The front of Laertes's shirt spouted some blood as programmed. But instead of lurching around and spewing out all the crimes and faults of the Hamlet family, Laertes grabbed his shoulder, sat down abruptly on the floor and screamed, "You shot me, you stupid son of a bitch!" And I could have sworn I saw something red oozing between his fingers.

Hamlet rallied. Laertes had obviously forgotten his lines, but Hamlet would cover for him. "I know you think no one in our family should survive, and you may have a point."

I looked at Noel, seated beside Queenie on the couch. He was staring with deep interest at Laertes who was staring with equal interest at his shoulder. Noel took a clean white handkerchief from his breast pocket and tossed it to Laertes, who pressed it against his shoulder, where it began to streak with red.

Horatio, making a move I was pretty sure was not in the script, crawled behind the dubious shelter of a little coffee table and curled up in a smaller bundle than one would think he could make, with his eyes tightly closed. He reminded me of Fargo going to the vet.

Hamlet's meandering fill-in speech wobbled to a close. And he turned, pointing the gun at Duke, and bawling something about Duke murdering old King Hamlet. As he raised the pistol, Noel made a surprisingly agile leap for a guy his age and disappeared over the back of the sofa.

From behind it came his voice in a desperate bellow. "David, don't shoot, man! You've got real bullets!"

Finally, it dawned on me that indeed he had. David/Bobby/Hamlet had gone entirely round the bend and intended to strew the stage with *real* corpses!

I fought my way to the end of the aisle and ran down the slanting ramp toward the stage. The ramp was fairly steep and I was running out of control as I crashed through a frightened and cursing orchestra and up the small access steps to the stage.

I tripped over a footlight and skidded to a stop on a knee and an elbow in front of Hamlet. Meantime, Noel was trying to wrestle Elaine over the back of the couch into some kind of safety, but she wouldn't move. She seemed as stiff and unemotional as a cigarstore Indian, but I had no time to help Noel.

Managing to stand and briefly to wonder why skinned knees hurt so much and garnered so little sympathy, I grabbed at Hamlet's pistol.

"Give it here, you idiot, before you kill somebody! Those are *not* blanks!"

"Of course they're blanks," he hissed. "Get off the stage. You're ruining the finale! Look, I'll show you." He yanked the pistol away and fired in Elaine's general direction. Noel dived back behind the couch again, and an enormous pillow burst to send a seemingly endless cloud of feathers wafting across the stage in the light afternoon breeze.

The audience had become understandably bewildered. Was this all part of the play? Or had some crazy woman in the audience decided to run up on stage and save the potential victims?

When the pillow exploded there was laughter and cheering and applause. Someone called out, "Run for it, Duke." Someone else yelled, "Get 'im, Hamlet!"

Finally, a movement in the corner of stage left told me I was not alone in realizing something was terribly wrong. Sonny had come onto the stage from that side and was running toward us. Jeanine had come through the screen door in center stage—in uniform—and was trying to sidle around to the other side of Hamlet. Some people were still laughing and cheering as the cavalry entered. A few were beginning to leave.

216

I looked at Hamlet and am sure my expression turned to one of horror. He now had the pistol pointing toward his own eye, staring down the barrel as if trying to spot the problem.

"Hamlet . . . David . . . Bobby . . . Whoever," I almost whispered. "Take your finger away from that trigger. If that thing goes off, you're hamburger."

Did Bobby plan to kill himself, too? Could well be.

Hamlet did his foot stomping routine and shrieked, "Oh, you silly dyke, you've ruined the whole last act. There's nothing wrong with the gun!"

He threw the gun from him. It hit the concrete floor and went off. Sonny grabbed his leg and went down, screaming, "O-oh, shit!" Since he landed right beside one of the floor mikes, his shout seemed to echo round and round the theater. There was heavy applause, mingled with a few catcalls.

A nanosecond later a woman's voice screamed from the audience. "Harry, I'm hit in the behind. I tell you I'm fucking *shot!*" That earned her cheers and loud clapping, plus several scatological suggestions.

A woman nearby in the audience squealed, "Did you hear that, Frank? Did you? I swear that was Mama. Mama says she's *shot!*"

"She can't be shot too bad, making all that noise. Just sit down! I want to see the end of this thing. For the life of me, I can't figure what they're at."

He wasn't alone.

I was quite anxious to get to the end of this maelstrom also, before we were all dead. I lunged for the gun and got it before Hamlet could change his mind and pick it up again.

I noticed that Nick, the stage manager, had come out of the wings onto the stage, speaking sternly and calmly to Hamlet, apparently unaware that *I* now had the gun.

"Give me that gun, David. Somehow you got the wrong kind of bullets in there! I swear you can't get anything right. You used real cartridges!" He shook his head in exasperation.

"No, I didn't!" Hamlet was practically spitting with petulance.

I thought he was going to stamp his foot again. "I loaded it with the ones from the new box, just like you told me." I couldn't believe this conversation, casually taking place in front of a thousand people, a few of them bleeding badly.

"I didn't say the *new* box." Nick shook his head again impatiently. "I said the *blue* box . . . *blue!* You're shooting all the wrong people." He smiled ironically. "Now give me the gun before we have somebody accidentally dead." He extended his left hand.

At this point, I became aware of two things. Nick was holding a thirty-eight revolver in his right hand, and I knew there was no question what kind of ammunition its cylinder held. I knew because suddenly, finally, I saw him. I grasped that I was actually looking at Bobby.

Not Hamlet. Nick. Nick Peters, stage manager with revolver, was Bobby Leonard, grown up little boy.

His child's skinny body had not grown tall and willowy like his mother's, but had stayed short and become thickset like his father's. The tight blond curls had darkened to light brown waves, and only the beautiful blue eyes and full mouth had remained the same.

Jeanine was still angling here and there on stage, trying now for a clear shot at Bobby, and not having any luck there, either, because everyone seemed to keep moving. I now had Hamlet's gun. Should I try a shot? My path was clear. If I missed, I wouldn't hit anyone in the audience. I hated to shoot. He wasn't really threatening anyone. At least, not at the moment.

"Bobby . . . Nick," I tried to speak calmly. "How about giving me that gun you're holding? We've got way too many people with guns out here. As you indicated, it's getting dangerous."

"Stay out of this, Alex. I like you. Anyway, this is strictly a family affair. None of your business. Remember Hamlet's line . . . she doesn't deserve to live? Keep it in mind."

Bobby was now turned toward Elaine. "Well, Elaine, nothing to say? I thought you'd have a lovely soliloquy for us, telling everyone how good and noble you were and how awful everyone else was."

He leaned nonchalantly against the back of a chair and continued. "And I really should thank you for that dramatic red herring you dragged all over town to make Terese's demise look like a robbery gone bad. I assume it was to make people think you were protecting your crazy little brother. You had to know the cops would figure out it was phony. Didn't you? They aren't morons." He paused and leaned forward slightly, obviously expecting a reply.

But Elaine had no words. She was staring stolidly into space, seeing . . . what? A little boy? A young girl? A crazed woman and a dismembered man? She looked like someone waiting for . . . for the lights to go off.

"Silence, Elaine? Well, you know you never deserved to live after all the lives you ruined. So I guess it's time."

I saw his arm start to straighten and I fired. I was rewarded by the click of an empty chamber. Hamlet hadn't been playing with a full clip.

That figured.

But at least the sound threw Bobby's aim off. When he shot, Elaine hardly moved. She lifted her lower left arm across her breast and looked disinterestedly at the fleshy part of her upper arm as a thin stream of blood began to trickle.

Jeanine had finally worked her way around to a clear shot, and she called out, "Okay, you, drop the gun or I shoot! Drop it *now!*"

Bobby smiled almost sweetly, shook his head and raised his arm again toward Elaine.

Jeanine fired.

At first I thought she had somehow managed to hit Hamlet, as he collapsed at my feet, but then I saw that he had simply fainted.

At the same time, Bobby's white T-shirt blossomed into an obscene red rose. He took a slow step back . . . and fell.

If there was a hero in the following chaos, it was the conductor of the orchestra. People now realized that actual shooting was going on, and that real blood was being shed all over the stage and even into the audience. They were pushing to get up the aisles and out.

Pandemonium was seconds away, with all the injuries and even fatalities that could cause. Maestro got his people out of their terrified crouch, and seconds later, his first trumpet sounded the high, sweet notes of "The Star Spangled Banner."

It worked. As other instruments joined in, some people stopped running, faced the flag flying above the theater and placed hands over hearts, or came to attention and saluted. Some began to sing. Most continued their exit, but in march-time and without panic.

When the anthem finished, "Colonel Bogey" followed. The large oval emptied, briskly and safely, of an audience which would doubtless claim to have seen the strangest *Hamlet* produced in four centuries.

Chapter 25

The waiting room at the clinic strongly resembled Grand Central Station at five p.m. on Christmas Eve.

We were all gathered nervously there to receive medical bulletins and, hopefully, eventually to see those we loved who had fallen in the Battle of the Amphitheater. From the number of people milling about, the casualty list would seem to be right up there with Gettysburg.

Mother, Aunt Mae, Trish, Cindy, Noel and I were waiting for news of Sonny.

Two stagehands and the electrician were waiting for Horatio, who, they said, should be released shortly. He had simply cut his head diving under the coffee table and needed a few stitches.

Another man waited quietly for information on Laertes, whose name, I had discovered from consulting Cindy's *Playbill*, was Michael Novak.

☙❧

And all of us, I was sure, were wondering at Bobby's fate. From where I had stood on the stage, it did not look hopeful.

Carlucci paced the floor, genuinely concerned for all, I thought. He was a basically decent man with big dreams and an amazing facility to drum up the money to finance them. He was blessed with an imagination that made them somehow work, and had even more talent at not knowing when to shut up.

I heard him a few moments earlier, expounding to Mother that this whole event, while desperately tragic for the injured and their loved ones, was manna from heaven for the future of the play to a New York audience.

Mom and all the rest of us in earshot, looked bewildered, and he explained. The New York theater would be SRO for at least a year with people from all over the country who would want to attend the play where attempted murder for real had occurred right on stage, and to see the actors who had so bravely performed, even as the people around them had been cold-bloodedly shot down. The play would stand on its own, of course, but the publicity around it now was priceless and could be kept timely with occasional updates, such as ongoing physical recoveries, recurring nightmares, claims to have seen Bobby's ghost, should he have passed on, etc.

Mom favored him with a dazzling smile and said she hoped Sonny and the others currently lying on operating tables would be as pleased at their contribution to the play's success as Paul. Personally, she would be thrilled to trade her son's leg to sell an extra block of tickets to *Hamlet*.

Carlucci turned beet red, muttered something about going out for a smoke and practically ran to the exit.

He caromed off Dr. Gloetzner, who was coming in from the parking lot, where he had just informed the ever-increasing number of media people that under no circumstances would any of them be allowed inside the hospital. If they caused any further disturbance outside, they would have to leave the premises entirely and that he, personally, would make only one statement: The staff were busy doing what hospital people do. Treating patients.

He looked at me and made a follow me motion. We went

through the ER, which was busy with its ordinary nightly casualties of bar fights, falls, migraines, women going into labor and chest pains. In his small office, he motioned me to a chair.

"Well, Ms. Peres, again and again we meet under arcane circumstances. Have you ever consulted a spiritualist? Do you perhaps have some special wiring that places you here on evenings like this?" Before I could answer, he picked up a buzzing phone and asked, "Anything new?" He listened and looked strangely at me. Then he said, "Okay, she's right here. We'll be there shortly."

Hanging up, he turned to me. "Lt. Peres is just now coming out of surgery. We've been like a MASH unit here tonight. Had to practice some triage, you know. As you are aware, our facilities are neither large nor heavily staffed. Sonny was in no danger and could wait a little while. The bullet ricocheted off the concrete floor and lost a lot of pizzazz. It hit the fleshy part of his calf, with no bone damage. There is minor muscle damage, and he may need a little therapy, but one hundred percent recovery is probable. He'll be our guest for a day or so." He made a little tick on the notebook he held.

I breathed deep in relief. "Mom will be glad to hear that. Has anyone told her?"

"As we speak." He nodded. "The surgeon is entering the waiting room. I'm glad it's good news." He made a thumbs-up sign.

"Mrs. Fields, a member of the audience," he continued, "Caught the piece of concrete that Sonny's bullet dislodged, and it penetrated her . . . ah, sizeable *gluteus maximus*. Not seriously. She is already on her way home, counting up the numbers of people she can call to tell of her great adventure." He took a drink of some coffee that was frighteningly black and thick.

"Also released is that young man who played Horatio. In an attempt to occupy a space much smaller than himself, he cut the top of his head, four stitches worth. Three of his raucous friends have rescued him and were last known headed for the Crown and Anchor. Not wise, but perhaps they celebrate life."

"I'm glad he's okay," I said. "So he'll have a headache. He would anyway."

"Good thinking. Now, Ms. Edgewood has a slight flesh wound on the inside of her upper arm and can leave tonight if she wishes. That's a tender spot and it's going to hurt, but we can give her something to help that. She's lucky it missed her breast. She must have been sitting crooked." He checked his little book again.

"Mr. Novak's shoulder is a mess. We are doing all we can, but at some future date, he will probably require additional surgery. He also lost quite a bit of blood, but we expect him to recover without incident."

"By the way, Ms. Peres, what say we give that knee and elbow of yours a little wash up and some ointment and bandages?"

I sighed. "Wonderful! With everything that's going on, I didn't have the nerve to ask anybody. But the damn things hurt!"

"Oh, there's nothing like a good scrape to hurt. I sometimes wonder how children survive so many of them. Come over here."

I managed not to scream when he doused my knee and elbow with some solution I swear was Clorox. Then he put some soothing antibiotic ointment on them both and applied bandages. "Better?"

"Yes, much, thanks."

"Change those bandages tomorrow, then the next day, leave them off to let it dry up. Do you have antibiotic ointment at home or do you need some?"

"No problem, I've got some Panalog," I replied.

"A wonderful medicine. Is your dog injured? Here." He handed me the partly used tube.

"Oh, God." I laughed. "I'm so dicey I don't know what I'm saying. Thanks." I shoved the tube in my pocket. "Doctor, you haven't said anything about Bobby—Nick Peters."

"Because you are on the way to see him. He regained consciousness several minutes ago and has asked for you. That was the phone call."

"*Me!* I hardly know him. His sister is Elaine Edgewood. Isn't she well enough to go to him?"

"Yes," Gloetzner said, "But he told Lainey specifically to keep her away from him. He wants you, and frankly, I don't know how long we have with him. He might make it, or he could go any second. So let's go."

As we went down the corridor to an intensive care room the doctor explained, "The bullet hit the sternum and fragmented. The largest portion of it has rough edges and is resting right against the abdominal aorta. That kind of surgery is beyond the experience of any doctor here. We've called in Dr. Weeks from Hyannis, who will arrive shortly, although he doesn't sound too optimistic after my description of the wound. Maybe we can get him stabilized sufficiently to transfer to Boston. I just don't know yet."

He shrugged. "Meanwhile. If Bobby—Nicky?—moves wrong or gets agitated, the bullet could puncture the artery and I doubt we could control the bleeding. So try to keep it calm."

"Christ. You don't want much, Miss Scarlett. I don't know nothin' 'bout birthin' babies or keeping aortas at peace. Are you sure this is wise? Surely there is someone else!" I was feeling shakier by the second.

"It could be the last request of a dying man. We try to honor those," he answered simply.

I felt my palms grow sweatier and my throat tighten. Suddenly we made a sharp turn into a room draped with cables and framed with various TV-type screens, one of them quietly beeping as small lightning strikes marched across its face. A seemingly shrunken Bobby lay on the bed, head slightly raised, with tubes going here and there about his body. I hated the smell of hospitals. The antiseptics, sickness, pain, fear. They all had a combined odor that made me want nothing more than to run outdoors, look at a live tree and breathe deeply.

"Hiya, Nick, it's Alex. Is there anything I can do for you? They're taking real good care of you, my friend. But if I can help . . ."

He looked up at me for several seconds, as if remembering who I was. He spoke softly. "Wanted to say . . . knew you would believe me . . . sorry about the mess on stage. It really *was* David's screw-up. I had no intention of anyone getting hurt, except Elaine. But I should've checked. Elaine was the one. My plan was . . . when Hamlet shot her with a blank, I would fire live from offstage. Lots of confusion later when they discovered she was really dead. Had a good place to hide the gun . . . didn't much care, as long as she got hers. She sold me out to Terese. I'm thirsty."

I turned to a nurse. She held a glass with a straw to his mouth, "Easy, pull easy on that, young man, don't be greedy." After two sips she took it away.

"More," he said irritably. "More!"

"More in a minute or so," I said placatingly. "Nick, don't worry about David and the bullets. We all know that was truly an accident. And everyone is going to be okay. But what do you mean Elaine sold you out?"

"Told Terese all about *me*. But the article would say they never could locate Elaine. Water, dammit! I heard 'em talking . . . Terese's room. Water now!"

The nurse gave him another carefully monitored sip while I steadied the straw. I wondered what we were all trying to save him for, a lifetime in a mental hospital? In prison? I felt a deep stab of sorrow for a rough-tongued, gentle man who could understand a young girl who mourned a dill plant.

He cleared his throat and stared at a space where no one stood. When he spoke, his voice was strangely childish.

" . . . said you bled down there sometimes and it was gross . . . said he loved me, loved me best, man to man . . . If you hadn't told, she wouldn't have . . . now she's gone, too . . . gone . . ." Tears filled his eyes and started slowly down his cheeks.

Then he looked back at me with recognition. He was still crying quietly, but his voice was his own.

"It's funny, now she'll get away . . ." He gave a soft laugh. "They will all think that I . . ." Suddenly he choked and a gush of blood shot from his mouth.

I backed away and ran from the room. I found my way back to Gloetzner's office and lit a cigarette. Screw hospitals, there was no oxygen in here. I was shaky and cold and pulled my jacket around me. I felt something hard against my chest and tugged a flask from an inner pocket. That's how Gloetzner found me, on my second cigarette and nursing an almost empty flask of bourbon.

He ignored my various infractions and said gently. "He's gone. We couldn't help him."

"Well, I sure didn't help much."

"You reassured him about the bullets and the wounded. That had to help. What else was he trying to say? Did you know?"

"Not really," I lied. I polished off the contents of the flask and stowed it in its pocket. "Something about his mother and father, I think. A family feud."

"Well." The good doctor took my arm to steer me out. "Let's go give everybody the happy news and the sad." At that, his phone rang again. He listened, smiled tiredly, and once again just hung up.

"Sorry, I got waylaid. Ms. Edgewood is checking out. She seems to be alone. I hope she'll be all right."

"She's staying at the Chambered Nautilus. I'm sure they'll look in on her and give her dinner. They're nice people."

He nodded with relief. "Good. Glad there are a few left. They won't need to feed her. She had dinner here."

I laughed. "Then they'll definitely need to feed her. Have you eaten here?"

"Rarely," he admitted. "We also got a phone call from Mrs. Willem in New York. She and a nurse will be up in the Willem's private plane to pick up Hamlet in the morning if he stops crying and thrashing around and yelling that none of it was his fault. We've given him enough medication to knock out a bull. But he keeps telling us how sensitive he is. He'd better desensitize by morning. I've had about enough of his hysterics."

"It's his big scene, how can you deny him? He missed the one on stage."

"A-ah. Okay. Let's go tell the visitors to go home. No one who's had surgery will be awake before morning. Wish I could say the same."

I huddled with our little group with the good news about

227

Sonny, the unhappy news about Bobby and the news about Hamlet.

I turned to Noel. "Is that for real? He has a private plane? Then why was David so worried about Terese's article? I thought his family lived in a tenement on the Bowery or something."

Noel laughed. "Not hardly! The family has been here since the Bowery was an uptown street, however, and they own very large chunks of Manhattan and Long Island. Now there was a rumor—a rumor, I say—that when David went to the RADA, he met this English stripper, fell madly in love, got her pregnant and married her. His family had a fit, but he wouldn't give her up, so while he went to one acting school, she went to another."

"To be a real actress, you mean?" Aunt Mae asked.

"No, to be a real aristocrat instead of a Cockney stripper. And she learned well. She eats, speaks, walks, dresses and probably dreams *high falutin'*. She really is a great gal, though. I like her. But obviously, none of the Willems wanted her youthful career publicized by the *A-List*. That's what was worrying David."

He got a good laugh, and we separated for the night. Mom was chauffeuring Aunt Mae home. Cindy and I took Noel back to the Marshes.

Poor Fargo thought we'd all fallen off the planet. He pushed past us out the door and to the closest shrub. And then to another. And finally to a third. Only then did he come to us and whine his sad tale of abandonment. Wells disappeared into a dark, far corner and stayed a while.

The four of us had had no dinner. It was only a little after nine, but it felt like next week. I fed His Nibs and Her Majesty and then started making my famous grilled cheese sandwiches while Cindy changed to pajamas.

Dinner was neither gourmet nor festive, but served to make us all sleepy. So after another outing for the dog and cat, we packed it in.

Chapter 26

Fargo was snoring lightly within seconds. Cindy was breathing deeply within minutes. Wells was a silent dark blob on the windowsill. I was abruptly wide-awake and apparently going to stay that way. I tried my left side and then my right. I tried counting backward from a hundred. I tried naming all the states alphabetically. I got up, slipped into some sweats and mocs for the cool night and headed back to the kitchen. Looking at me in sad reproach, Fargo sighed and padded down the hall behind me, whuffling irritably.

I made myself a bourbon highball, gave him a biscuit and sat down at the kitchen table with a cigarette. Thoughts were circling in my brain in some sort of jumble that I couldn't turn off. They were bothering me badly. I was sure some of them were wrong, felt that some of them were backward, and others were escaping me entirely. An example? I wasn't sure I even *had* an example. I wished I had Sonny's blackboards.

Lacking them, I went into the office and brought back two fairly large pieces of cardboard I used in matting my photographs. I propped them on the kitchen table.

On one I wrote: *Elaine, relatively famous leading lady. Charming and warm as long as things go her way. Threatened by Terese.*

On the other I wrote: *Bobby, failed actor, excellent stage manager, not famous at all. Growly but appealing. Lonely? Afraid of being hurt by Terese?*

Funny, how I had changed the wording. Then I remembered something Elaine had said the evening she told us her whole sad tale in the backyard. She told us Bobby had sworn his father abused him, had touched him intimately and made him feel uncomfortable, had done things that had hurt. Yet Elaine was adamant her father had never abused either her or Bobby.

If true, how would a seven-year-old boy know certain kinds of sex with a grown man could hurt? And how come the shrink hadn't managed to get him to admit he had lied? Surely the shrink could get the truth out of a seven-year-old! What if it was not Bobby who lied, but Elaine?

I remembered a book of Sonny's on child abuse that I had read once, when we had a man on the prowl for kids here in town. I had been quite surprised to learn that over time, abused children could be quite flattered by the attention and feeling of importance and adulthood, even though they knew it was wrong, even though it might be painful. They could even be jealous of other children the abuser paid attention to, if they knew about it.

Recalling the book further, I remembered that abusers usually grew tired of their male or female victims when they reached certain ages, usually puberty, when they lost the cuteness and sweet softness of the young child. In a girl, perhaps when "she began to bleed down there" and the abuser found it "gross." Then perhaps a father might turn his sights to his young son and explain to him the special "man-to-man love" they could share.

Then I mentally finished off another sentence that Bobby had tried to utter a few hours back, and wrote it on my cardboard. "If

230

you—Elaine?—hadn't told . . . she—mother?—wouldn't have . . ."
I ended it for him: *"wouldn't have taken Daddy away, and then they took her away, too."* Maybe it was not Bobby who squealed to his mother that Daddy was abusive, but a jealous Elaine who decided to get even with both fickle father and the new love object son.

Obviously, she wouldn't have counted on her mother killing her father, but Elaine's hatred may have been deep enough to make the act seem justified when she did. And being unsaddled from an unstable mother after the murder would have been okay, too. Young Elaine was already a pretty good actress! She was just a sweet young girl who finally convinced the authorities nothing had happened, because, batting her big dark eyes, nothing could possibly have happened with her loving, *normal* father.

And Bobby, poor little brother, was imagining things, mentally unhinged like his mother.

Then Elaine had charmed her way into a nice adoptive family and never looked back.

When she visited Bobby once in Pennsylvania, she did him in again, purposely or accidentally. When she bragged of being an actress, he immediately sought her approval by saying he would be an actor. And when his adoptive parents couldn't afford tuitions, Bobby took it as one more abandonment episode in his rocky life and filed his silly, but hurt-filled lawsuit. Failing at that, he went to New York to seek out the one person still standing from those few years when he had had his own family, and when they had all loved each other.

I drained my highball and put on a pot of coffee. I needed to stretch my legs, so Fargo and I took a turn of the yard, which we found safe from two- or four-legged intruders. Back inside, coffee was done, and we shared a pastry left from breakfast. With an apologetic lick, Fargo left my side and retreated across the kitchen to the cozy warmth of his bed, and I was left with my jigsaw puzzle.

But the pieces were becoming easier to fit now, and I could see a definite picture.

My cardboards were becoming filled with abbreviated notes.

Elaine could have subtly sabotaged what acting jobs Bobby did get, and this could have triggered the antagonism he displayed if at all threatened or opposed. I had seen examples of that in the last few weeks. His personality was not geared to smoothing troubled waters. But eventually he gave up acting and became a capable stage manager. So he no longer comprised competition for Elaine. She had once again gotten him out of her way, and further away from the possibility anyone might tie them together and dig up the woodchopper scandal.

Then up pops nosy Terese Segal, far from an imaginary menace! Bobby, I thought was mainly scared of being back in a lurid spotlight. He seemed a retiring soul who liked his work and simply wanted to be left alone with whatever life he had managed to cobble together for himself. He may have had a few friends but probably was fairly content just being quietly alone most of the time. Now the whole thing might well surface again, with him in the painful heat of the limelight.

But Elaine had more to lose than privacy. She was pretty much a household name. A good actress with feature roles on stage and on TV. Perhaps not the brightest star on the marquee, but definitely up there and shining. And her lover was a teacher. Scandal was a no-no for teachers. Now Terese was threatening to revive the whole disgraceful event, from child abuse to a dismembered father and a lunatic mother, to a lesbian affair, with the two lesbians raising a child, and one of them a teacher. A plum, a big juicy plum for the star reporter of the *A-List*.

That couldn't appear in type. They simply couldn't let it. To paraphrase Harmon, action had to be taken.

That night in our backyard, I think Elaine's tears, while very well done, were all of the crocodile variety. Maybe our alligator gave acting classes. I think she told that tale with the full knowledge that she was prepared to kill Terese, knowing I would have to tell Sonny the entire screed at some point. And of course, it would be slanted just the right amount in her favor. Because that's the way

I had heard it, that was the way I would remember it. I would inadvertently put Sonny firmly on Elaine's side.

According to Noel, Elaine tried several times the next day to talk with Terese, unsuccessfully and almost certainly growing more freaked out with each refusal. And the events of Tuesday offered one good opportunity after another. The messed up rehearsal had the entire company irritated, frustrated and tired. The heavy rains added to their misery.

The two people Elaine most needed not to be thinking clearly—Terese and Paul—were drunk. The others staying at the Brownlees' had either had several drinks or taken a pill to help them sleep.

After two frustrating bouts of unsuccessful sex, Terese was in a drunken rage. In all probability she went downstairs to scrounge a final nightcap. Possibly, having had little dinner, she went for a snack. Either way, when Elaine heard her go down the front stairs, Elaine went down the back, stripped, donned the plastic raincoat and hat, and stabbed Terese.

Elaine's first red herring was the six stab wounds—implicating Harmon, Bobby, the household members or the ever-handy transient robber. The Hicktown cops could take their choice.

Her second was the entire robbery scene, complete to suggesting that even the maids knew Harmon was careless of boot tracks. Although, the police could still have thought it was our visiting robber, after the silver, which Elaine carefully "stole."

The third was Carlucci's car. Elaine had doubtless stayed sober and appointed herself designated driver so that she could keep the car keys after driving home from the restaurant. She could easily deny keeping the keys, since the next morning they were on the hook by the back door with all the van keys, as usual.

At some point, she had to discard the raincoat and hat and redress in her own clothing. She could most safely have done that outdoors, perhaps behind the garage, letting the rain wash both the coat and her body and hair. If the police ever found the plastic raincoat and hat, it would certainly help . . . but much less so if they were washed clean by the downpour.

Right now, *I* needed help, and something told me Sonny would not be answering his phone. Fortunately, Mitch was, after a number of rings, and not happily. Following a lengthy conversation, he agreed to meet me at Elaine's room at the Chambered Nautilus at eight thirty.

I went back to bed, certain I would be unable to sleep. I'd be happy just to get horizontal and try to relax for a few hours. Fargo had no such problems. He simply came back into the bedroom, flopped on the floor and was gone.

I set the clock and steeled myself for the sleepless hours. That was my last thought for the remainder of the night.

Chapter 27

The next morning the clock sounded at six thirty. Fargo leaped eagerly onto the bed, ever hopeful of a beach run. Wells mewed and nestled deeper between Cindy's shoulder blades. Cindy emitted a bear-like growl and burrowed deeper into the pillow.

I nobly headed for the shower. In the kitchen later, I took a look at the clock and decided to nuke the coffee left from last night. Well, it certainly woke me up.

But then, I wanted to be wide-awake when I spoke with Elaine. I was hoping for a confession, naturally, or at least an informative slip or two.

I thought my chances of getting either were better if I could be alone with Elaine, and I hoped to arrive at her room before Mitch and his backup did. I figured Elaine would tend to have more of a relaxed conversation with a woman she knew, even one she disliked, than a police detective and a uniformed officer she did not. And maybe I could lead her down the primrose path to telling me more than she realized.

I got to the Chambered Nautilus at eight sharp, using the back door as a concession to any guests that might be around this early, and went upstairs. I left Fargo in the kitchen, assuming Martha or Bill would be there soon and wouldn't mind.

Knocking on Elaine's door—Ophelia had obligingly taken a room at the Marshes to give Elaine some privacy—I got Elaine's musical, "Come in." Obviously she didn't know who it was yet.

I entered.

"Get out!" Now she knew. No musical tones in that request!

"I'm afraid that won't be possible," I answered, making my voice as cold as hers. "We have a number of things to talk about. Is Ophelia at the Marshes?"

"Yes. She, at least, was courteous enough to know I might wish to be alone after Bobby's death. I have much to adjust to. I still cannot believe he would have killed me."

"Oh, I can. A lifetime of lies, subtle undermining of his already difficult life. Telling Terese his deepest secrets in order to protect your own." I gave a small but dramatic Queen Elizabeth hand wave. "I can think of several very good reasons for killing you, myself."

"Alex, I spent a bad night. I am in no mood for you and your silly gracious lady character or your tough detective act. Now, if you must say something, say it and *get out!*"

I lit cigarette two and blew out a cool Humphrey Bogart puff. "Doesn't much matter. Do you want to tell *me* how you killed Terese, or do you want me to tell *you?*"

"You can't smoke in here. The Meyers don't allow it."

"I'll send them an exhaust fan."

There was a knock at the door I had left half open behind me, and Mitch stepped into the room, followed by Officer Mendes. Officer Oliver Mendes was Provincetown's newest rookie cop and looked about twelve. He also looked unhappy to be in a lady's bedroom at this early hour, especially with the lady clad only in a filmy nightgown and favoring him with an ominous glare. Poor laddie, he broke all too easily in the daunting presence of a pro.

"Good morning, ma'am." He actually gave a short bow. "I'm

236

Officer Mendes, of the Provincetown Police. We hate to intrude upon your privacy in this manner, but there are certain questions we must ask in the line of duty. You see, Ms. Peres thinks you offed the Segal broad—"

"Jesus Christ, Oliver! Talk about subtlety!" I barked.

"Mendes, for God's sake, stop babbling like an idiot!" Mitch looked unhappy at Mendes's taking over the opening statement he had probably spent the early morning rehearsing.

Mendes looked unhappier still, at the public reprimand.

If anyone had cared to notice, I almost certainly looked the unhappiest of all.

While Mitch, Mendes and I had had our little family squabble, Elaine had stepped over to the bed, reached in her purse and pulled out a tiny little derringer-like pistol. Said pistol was at the moment pointed about two feet from my stomach. Even Elaine couldn't miss from that distance.

The fancily engraved pistol looked like something ridiculous and for show that an actress would have. On the other hand, I recalled, one very much like it had worked quite well for actor John Wilkes Booth.

Of course, unless she fired it, we now had a hostage situation, where I was the costar. It was a billing I would gladly have relinquished.

I cleared my throat. "Elaine, you really don't want—"

"Don't tell me what I don't want. I'd as soon shoot you as not. Things can't get a helluva lot worse." She waved the pistol in the general direction of my face.

"You." She pointed at Mitch. "You're a sergeant or something. Listen to me. You will fly Alex and me to Boston. You will have a plane waiting to fly us to Belize. When we reach there, I will let Alex go and we will forget all this silliness ever happened."

Gosh! Vacation time at last! I wondered if the IRS knew Elaine must have some big bucks squirreled away there?

"Ms. Edgewood, this is not *Law and Order!* We don't have hel-

237

icopters in the parking lot. And this 'silliness' of yours is murder."
Mitch was coming on tough.

"It'll be more than that if you—"

"Why Belize?" I asked. "Not that it doesn't sound lovely."

"No extradition treaty, I think," Mitch answered. "But it *is* great. My mom was there last . . ."

God knows what travelogue we would have been treated to, but at that moment Lexus tore into the room with Fargo in hot pursuit. Lexus bounced off a chair, onto Elaine's shoulder and then to the top of an armoire, where he crouched, growling and hissing. Elaine stood screaming and waving the gun. "Get him out of here. Get him away from me! I hate cats!"

Fargo made a furious attempt to run through Elaine's legs to get to Lexus, got tangled in her nightgown, and took them both down in a heap. Terrified she would shoot him or Lexus, I fell on top of her and managed to anchor to the floor the hand holding the gun, at least for the moment. She was moaning something about her bad arm, but I didn't care.

"Mendes! Cuff her!" I yelled.

Martha raced into the room. "What the *hell* is going on? It sounds like mating time at the zoo in here. Be quiet, all of you. We have guests *sleeping*!"

I doubted it. Then she yelled, "What are you doing? You can't do this! Take your hands off me, you little prick!" Now I really doubted it.

I looked over my shoulder to see Mendes putting handcuffs on Martha.

"Not her! *Her!*"

"Oh, sorry."

Throughout most of this segment of our Keystone Kops movie, I had heard a soft thud—thud—thud in the background. I wondered if it were poor Bill, beating his head against the refrigerator. But no! It had been Sonny making his slow and doubtless painful way up the stairs on crutches.

He came through the door, blessing us with the full wattage of the Peres smile.

"Good morrow, gracious people! My, what an interesting scene."

And in ten seconds he was in charge.

"Ms. Edgewood, you are under arrest for the murder of Terese Segal. Mendes, cuff Ms. Edgewood to yourself by her right arm to your left and show her your dramatic ability in reciting the Miranda warning. Have Sgt. Mitchell drop you both at the clinic. That left arm is bleeding slightly, and we want no mistreatment."

Elaine saw a slight opening and leaped at it. "Police brutality. I shall sue you for police brutality."

"The cat knocked you off balance, and Fargo got tangled in your gown as you fell. Alex held you to the floor. None of them are police officers. There was no police brutality. You, on the other hand, were waving a gun around and yelling threats. And you've already killed one person. Now run along.

"Martha perhaps if you could coax Lexus down, Fargo would quit hurtling himself against your antique armoire and stop barking. Wouldn't that be loverly?"

"Indeed it would." Martha kissed Sonny's cheek and finally laughed. She got the cat down. I got Fargo's collar. Peace reigned.

"Sonny," Martha said, "Are you supposed to be out and around yet?"

"No. Have you ever seen a hospital breakfast?"

"Ah. I understand. That gives me a thought. Why don't I make a big luscious breakfast for the two heroes? I'll just bet they've worked up a gigantic appetite by now."

Sonny and I tried to look modest and hungry, and succeeded at least in the latter.

We all went down the back stairs into the kitchen. Martha said with some embarrassment, "Would it be okay to stay out here to eat? We'll have guests coming into the dining room any minute. Poor Bill."

"Of course, the kitchen is fine. But why *poor* Bill?" I asked.

"He'll be out there trying to pretend nothing happened. He's convinced De Nile is a river in Egypt. Now, you two just sit here at the table and excuse me while I go to work." She set glasses of

239

fresh, cold juice and mugs of hot, wonderful smelling coffee in front of us, and moved to the business end of the kitchen.

As we addressed our juice and coffee, Sonny said, "Let me update you, my little sleuth. You were the first one of us to get it right. Sometimes you amaze me. You get into unbelievable mix-ups, and you do everything ass-backward, but somehow you turn up with the right person in the end."

"Aw, shucks."

"Yeah, well, first things first, strictly personal. Remember Harmon's problem with Terese saying his brother was a coward?"

"Sure." I laughed. "Has he taken action yet?"

"Yes, he called the President."

"Of what?"

"Of the United States. He figured he was commander in chief and ought to know if Rob deserved those medals or not." He leaned back in his chair and then came forward quickly as he forgot and put weight on his wounded leg. I smothered a smile. It served him right.

"He really talked to the President? I can't believe it." I took a sip of coffee. It tasted like heaven after my sleep deprived night.

"No, he got shuffled around to about six people. Finally, some colonel said she would look into it and get back to him. She actually did. Surprise, surprise! It seems all Rob's medals are in order. He was indeed a hero. Confirming letter follows, and Harmon is dancing on air. He is also drunk."

Sounded good to me. "Can you blame him? That's splendid! The President, who would think to call the President?"

"Harmon would. He said it was an army matter, so he called the commander of the army. Makes perfect sense, doesn't it? If you're Harmon."

"I guess it does. What else is new?"

"Marvin found the hat from the plastic raincoat set, pushed down in the corner of the dumpster. No blood on it, but lots of prints, including Elaine's. Also, two of Elaine's hairs." He sniffed, and closed his eyes in rapture. "Smell that, Alex? That's sautéed kippers. Oh, gracious Fate!"

I wasn't crazy about kippers, but somewhere in the olio of delicious aromas floating around, I caught a whiff of a broiling breakfast steak, doubtless reaching a perfect medium rare just for me. I decided against a cigarette, breakfast obviously being near. "Anything on Terese's computer?"

"No. We figure that when Elaine got back from her tour around town, she deleted everything on the hard drive. I'm sure any of the cast would have been happy to do it, but she'd be about the only one who had opportunity. We took charge of it pretty quickly."

"What about the plastic rain coat?" I asked.

"Nothing yet. Hatcher is talking to the Voyager kitchen staff. Maybe they'll help.

"And one of Elaine's prints is on a piece of silver. She must have taken it out to admire it and forgot to put her gloves on."

"Yeah." I wasn't happy. "You think the DA will go for murder? Everything is circumstantial."

Sonny polished off his orange juice to the sound of beaten eggs being poured into a hot iron skillet. "Maybe. Plenty of cases are won on circumstantial evidence. And at least we have her nailed on obstructing justice and abetting a crime."

"Yes, at least we have that," I said. "I just hate to see poor Bobby's last sentence come true. I think he was trying to say, 'It's funny. Now she'll get away with it, and everyone will think I killed Terese.' That's an injustice in itself."

"I know one thing, Alex, Elaine may not be *convicted* of murder, but nobody's going to think she's innocent." He straightened in his chair and looked down the kitchen, smiling broadly. "Here it comes!"

Martha approached us, carrying two bowls. "For my heroes, my two brave heroes! Come here, my darlings!"

She walked right past us and set the smaller bowl on the kitchen

241

counter, where Lexus immediately jumped up and began eating his kippers and scrambled eggs, delicately, but quickly.

She set the larger bowl on the floor, where Fargo already waited. "Your steak and eggs, big boy." Delicacy wasn't in Fargo's vocabulary, but speed was. He was demolishing that food even faster than I think I could have.

Martha stroked one and then the other. "Aren't they sweet? *Bon appetit!* Dig in, my heroes."

Sonny and I smiled at each other sourly and managed a weak duet.

"*Bon appetit!*"

Afterward

In the wee hours of the Thursday after Labor Day, a throbbing molar ended Betty Atwood's sleep for the night. Finally, after feeling it with a finger and pushing at it with her tongue for a while, she could lie still no longer, and got out of bed so as not to disturb her husband. When he arose at seven, she was at the kitchen table, on her second cup of steaming hot coffee and deep into the Tylenol bottle, anxiously awaiting the time when she could call her dentist's office in Orleans.

Betty dialed her dentist promptly at eight and was told they could "fit her in at eleven." Her husband, Alan, called his office to say he would not be in until after lunch. Then he called Billy Madeiros, a fourteen-year-old boy who often babysat for them, and was a favorite of their eighteen-month-old daughter, Tina. Could Billy oblige them from ten this morning to around one o'clock in the afternoon? Billy could.

Betty bathed and dressed Tina for the day. While Alan straightened the house, she set out some junior foods and other tidbits Billy might feed Tina for lunch, and left him a note telling him to help himself to whatever was in the fridge. Finally, it was time to go. Alan brought their car out of the garage just as Billy's mother dropped him at the end of the rather long driveway, which curved prettily up the small hill from a brackish pond across the road.

Tina was fussing about her parents' departure, and Billy took her for a little toddle around the yard, pointing out different flowers and letting her pick one for herself. The sun was hot, so at the end of their walk, he placed her in her shaded outdoor playpen, and went into the house to get them both something cool to drink and to check what Mrs. Atwood had left for Tina's lunch.

He poured some juice and a little water into a bottle for Tina and popped a soda for himself. Then he glanced out the kitchen window onto a scene so horrifying he knew it could not be true, even as he realized that it was.

A large alligator was waddling up the driveway toward the playpen where Tina awaited her bottle.

Whom could he call? Where could he run to get help? All of a sudden, Billy grasped the truth that it all came down to him. There was no time for explanatory phone calls or running to the neighbors and convincing them to grab some sort of weapon and run back with him. So he did a most courageous thing.

He scooped up everything in the kitchen he could carry. A couple of pans, a skillet, the toaster, the coffee carafe, surprisingly heavy jars of baby food, a bowl, two plates, the blender jar. He took them all in his arms and burst through the back screen door, yelling and running down the driveway toward the ever-nearing alligator.

Billy had a pretty good throwing arm. Most of his homegrown artillery shells were landing on or quite near the alligator, and they were making a lot of noise. They crashed, they shattered, they rattled and rolled. They weren't doing the gator any serious injury, but they distracted him. The hefty *whomp!* of the blender jar on his nose stopped him for a moment to reassess his approach. And that gave Billy just enough time to grab Tina and sprint for the house.

They made it inside and he dropped the baby unceremoniously to the floor, howling. He ran around the house, closing and locking all the doors and windows. Then he shut himself and Tina in the bathroom and dialed 911 on the walk-around phone he had snatched from the hall.

He was terribly frightened and shocked and winded, and by then almost totally incoherent. The 911 operator couldn't be sure just who he was and who, or what, was about to kill the baby she could hear screaming in the background, but she managed to get the name Atwood and the address out of him. In seconds, patrol cars were on their way, followed by a fire truck and an ambulance, just in case.

Either the bop on the nose or the approaching sirens sent the reptile back to the temporary safety of the pond, for there was no sign of him when police finally coaxed a white and shaking Billy and a red-faced, hiccupping toddler from the bathroom. But the cops didn't doubt his story. They didn't think anyone could have made this up. There was stuff thrown all over the driveway, and the boy was a wreck. And, they soon recalled, there had been that naked lady up in that tree, and Harmon's rabbits, and the old tomcat . . .

The Atwoods arrived home to this nerve-shattering scene and were told what had happened, and what would doubtless have happened except for a very brave fourteen-year-old. They found themselves crying and laughing and trying to hug Tina, and each other and Billy, all at once.

And Provincetown had a new hero.

By afternoon the media had arrived. The Atwoods were cooperative at first, posing with the pretty little girl, telling and retelling the event, praising Billy's courage. But by a little after four, with Betty's tooth beating like a drum, they got the police to give them an escort out of town and went down to Betty's mother's place in Sandwich for a few days.

The Madeiros family soon found their yard surrounded by a myriad of TV and newspaper cameras and reporters, calling out a battery of questions. Billy had a hard time of it, still shaken, losing his composure, trying not to cry. Finally, his father had enough and ordered everyone off his property. He then latched the gate and let out the family Rottweiler, an aging and docile old lady who snuffled and grumbled all around the fence line, in ever-fading hopes someone would offer a treat. But the media didn't know that, retired, and left the Madeiroses to a peaceful evening.

The alligator was also getting considerable attention. Provincetown Police sent out a call for help with their voracious visitor, and people eventually arrived from the Mystic Aquarium in Connecticut and, less helpfully, the state's Department of Environmental Protection, on hand to guard the alligator's rights. The local Coast Guard station sent over some hefty young men and women who were good-humored and willing and quite adept with ropes. Well-meaning volunteers and not so well-meaning rifle toting hunters were restrained with difficulty.

The pond was baited with large chunks of raw, slightly smelly meat, and the alligator's would-be captors retired a fair distance back from the pond, where they waited silently. Around midnight, the gator finally came forth to dine and was, after a great scramble, many misses with various nooses and many suggestions by the DEP, successfully roped onto, of all things, a surfboard. He was then placed in a temperature and humidity-controlled box truck for his ride to Mystic, where he would be carefully tended until a Florida home was found for him.

Unofficially, he measured five feet, four inches in length. Mrs. Withers's guess hadn't been so far off, after all.

The person or persons who brought the reptile to Provincetown, their reasons for doing so and how they accomplished the feat, have never been discovered.

Unless, of course, Harmon was right.

Publications from
BELLA BOOKS, INC.
The best in contemporary lesbian fiction

P.O. Box 10543, Tallahassee, FL 32302
Phone: 800-729-4992
www.bellabooks.com

OUT OF THE FIRE by Beth Moore. Author Ann Covington feels at the top of the world when told her book is being made into a movie. Then in walks Casey Duncan the actress who is playing the lead in her movie. Will Casey turn Ann's world upside down?
1-59493-088-0 $13.95

STAKE THROUGH THE HEART: NEW EXPLOITS OF TWILIGHT LESBIANS by Karin Kallmaker, Julia Watts, Barbara Johnson and Therese Szymanski. The playful quartet that penned the acclaimed *Once Upon A Dyke* are dimming the lights for journeys into worlds of breathless seduction.
1-59493-071-6 $15.95

THE HOUSE ON SANDSTONE by KG MacGregor. Carly Griffin returns home to Leland and finds that her old high school friend Justine is awakening more than just old memories.
1-59493-076-7 $13.95

WILD NIGHTS: MOSTLY TRUE STORIES OF WOMEN LOVING WOMEN edited by Therese Szymanski. 264 pp. 23 new stories from today's hottest erotic writers are sure to give you your wildest night ever!
1-59493-069-4 $15.95

COYOTE SKY by Gerri Hill. 248 pp. Sheriff Lee Foxx is trying to cope with the realization that she has fallen in love for the first time. And fallen for author Kate Winters, who is technically unavailable. Will Lee fight to keep Kate in Coyote?
1-59493-065-1 $13.95

VOICES OF THE HEART by Frankie J. Jones. 264 pp. A series of events force Erin to swear off love as she tries to break away from the woman of her dreams. Will Erin ever find the key to her future happiness?
1-59493-068-6 $13.95

SHELTER FROM THE STORM by Peggy J. Herring. 296 pp. A story about family and getting reacquainted with one's past that shows that sometimes you don't appreciate what you have until you almost lose it.
1-59493-064-3 $13.95

WRITING MY LOVE by Claire McNab. 192 pp. Romance writer Vonny Smith believes she will be able to woo her editor Diana through her writing . . .
1-59493-063-5 $13.95

PAID IN FULL by Ann Roberts. 200 pp. Ari Adams will need to choose between the debts of the past and the promise of a happy future.
1-59493-059-7 $13.95

ROMANCING THE ZONE by Kenna White. 272 pp. Liz's world begins to crumble when a secret from her past returns to Ashton . . .
1-59493-060-0 $13.95

SIGN ON THE LINE by Jaime Clevenger. 204 pp. Alexis Getty, a flirtatious delivery driver is committed to finding the rightful owner of a mysterious package.
1-59493-052-X $13.95

END OF WATCH by Clare Baxter. 256 pp. LAPD Lieutenant L.A Franco Frank follows the lone clue down the unlit steps of memory to a final, unthinkable resolution.
1-59493-064-4 $13.95

BEHIND THE PINE CURTAIN by Gerri Hill. 280 pp. Jacqueline returns home after her father's death and comes face-to-face with her first crush.   1-59493-057-0 $13.95

PIPELINE by Brenda Adcock. 240 pp. Joanna faces a lost love returning and pulling her into a seamy underground corporation that kills for money.   1-59493-062-7 $13.95

18TH & CASTRO by Karin Kallmaker. 200 pp. First-time couplings and couples who know how to mix lust and love make 18th & Castro the hottest address in the city by the bay.
1-59493-066-X $13.95

JUST THIS ONCE by KG MacGregor. 200 pp. Mindful of the obligations back home that she must honor, Wynne Connelly struggles to resist the fascination and allure that a particular woman she meets on her business trip represents.   1-59493-087-2 $13.95

ANTICIPATION by Terri Breneman. 240 pp. Two women struggle to remain professional as they work together to find a serial killer.   1-59493-055-4 $13.95

OBSESSION by Jackie Calhoun. 240 pp. Lindsey's life is turned upside down when Sarah comes into the family nursery in search of perennials.   1-59493-058-9 $13.95

BENEATH THE WILLOW by Kenna White. 240 pp. A torch that still burns brightly even after twenty-five years threatens to consume two childhood friends.
1-59493-053-8 $13.95

SISTER LOST, SISTER FOUND by Jeanne G'fellers. 224 pp. The highly anticipated sequel to No Sister of Mine.   1-59493-056-2 $13.95

THE WEEKEND VISITOR by Jessica Thomas. 240 pp. In this latest Alex Peres mystery, Alex is asked to investigate an assault on a local woman but finds that her client may have more secrets than she lets on.   1-59493-054-6 $13.95

THE KILLING ROOM by Gerri Hill. 392 pp. How can two women forget and go their separate ways?   1-59493-050-3 $12.95

PASSIONATE KISSES by Megan Carter. 240 pp. Will two old friends run from love?
1-59493-051-1 $12.95

ALWAYS AND FOREVER by Lyn Denison. 224 pp. The girl next door turns Shannon's world upside down.   1-59493-049-X $12.95

BACK TALK by Saxon Bennett. 200 pp. Can a talk show host find love after heartbreak?
1-59493-028-7 $12.95

THE PERFECT VALENTINE: EROTIC LESBIAN VALENTINE STORIES edited by Barbara Johnson and Therese Szymanski—from Bella After Dark. 328 pp. Stories from the hottest writers around.   1-59493-061-9 $14.95

MURDER AT RANDOM by Claire McNab. 200 pp. The Sixth Denise Cleever Thriller. Denise realizes the fate of thousands is in her hands.   1-59493-047-3 $12.95

THE TIDES OF PASSION by Diana Tremain Braund. 240 pp. Will Susan be able to hold it all together and find the one woman who touches her soul?   1-59493-048-1 $12.95

JUST LIKE THAT by Karin Kallmaker. 240 pp. Disliking each other—and everything they stand for—even before they meet, Toni and Syrah find feelings can change, just like that.
1-59493-025-2 $12.95

WHEN FIRST WE PRACTICE by Therese Szymanski. 200 pp. Brett and Allie are once again caught in the middle of murder and intrigue.   1-59493-045-7 $12.95

REUNION by Jane Frances. 240 pp. Cathy Braithwaite seems to have it all: good looks, money and a thriving accounting practice . . .   1-59493-046-5 $12.95

BELL, BOOK & DYKE: NEW EXPLOITS OF MAGICAL LESBIANS by Kallmaker, Watts, Johnson and Szymanski. 360 pp. Reluctant witches, tempting spells and skyclad beauties—delve into the mysteries of love, lust and power in this quartet of novellas.   1-59493-023-6 $14.95

ARTIST'S DREAM by Gerri Hill. 320 pp. When Cassie meets Luke Winston, she can no longer deny her attraction to women . . .   1-59493-042-2 $12.95

NO EVIDENCE by Nancy Sanra. 240 pp. Private Investigator Tally McGinnis once again returns to the horror-filled world of a serial killer.   1-59493-043-04 $12.95

WHEN LOVE FINDS A HOME by Megan Carter. 280 pp. What will it take for Anna and Rona to find their way back to each other again?   1-59493-041-4 $12.95

MEMORIES TO DIE FOR by Adrian Gold. 240 pp. Rachel attempts to avoid her attraction to the charms of Anna Sigurdson . . .   1-59493-038-4 $12.95

SILENT HEART by Claire McNab. 280 pp. Exotic lesbian romance.
1-59493-011-9 $12.95

MIDNIGHT RAIN by Peggy J. Herring. 240 pp. Bridget McBee is determined to find the woman who saved her life.   1-59493-021-X $12.95

THE MISSING PAGE A Brenda Strange Mystery by Patty G. Henderson. 240 pp. Brenda investigates her client's murder . . .   1-59493-004-X $12.95

WHISPERS ON THE WIND by Frankie J. Jones. 240 pp. Dixon thinks she and her best friend, Elizabeth Colter, would make the perfect couple . . .   1-59493-037-6 $12.95

CALL OF THE DARK: EROTIC LESBIAN TALES OF THE SUPERNATURAL, edited by Therese Szymanski—from Bella After Dark. 320 pp.   1-59493-040-6 $14.95

A TIME TO CAST AWAY A Helen Black Mystery by Pat Welch. 240 pp. Helen stops by Alice's apartment—only to find the woman dead . . .   1-59493-036-8 $12.95

DESERT OF THE HEART by Jane Rule. 224 pp. The book that launched the most popular lesbian movie of all time is back.   1-1-59493-035-X $12.95

THE NEXT WORLD by Ursula Steck. 240 pp. Anna's friend Mido is threatened and eventually disappears . . .   1-59493-024-4 $12.95

CALL SHOTGUN by Jaime Clevenger. 240 pp. Kelly gets pulled back into the world of private investigation . . .   1-59493-016-3 $12.95

52 PICKUP by Bonnie J. Morris and E.B. Casey. 240 pp. 52 hot, romantic tales—one for every Saturday night of the year.   1-59493-026-0 $12.95

GOLD FEVER by Lyn Denison. 240 pp. Kate's first love, Ashley, returns to their home town, where Kate now lives . . .   1-1-59493-039-2 $12.95

RISKY INVESTMENT by Beth Moore. 240 pp. Lynn's best friend and roommate needs her to pretend Chris is his fiancé. But nothing is ever easy.   1-59493-019-8 $12.95

HUNTER'S WAY by Gerri Hill. 240 pp. Homicide detective Tori Hunter is forced to team up with the hot-tempered Samantha Kennedy.   1-59493-018-X $12.95

CAR POOL by Karin Kallmaker. 240 pp. Soft shoulders, merging traffic and slippery when wet . . . Anthea and Shay find love in the car pool.   1-59493-013-9 $12.95

NO SISTER OF MINE by Jeanne G'Fellers. 240 pp. Telepathic women fight to coexist with a patriarchal society that wishes their eradication.   ISBN 1-59493-017-1 $12.95

ON THE WINGS OF LOVE by Megan Carter. 240 pp. Stacie's reporting career is on the rocks. She has to interview bestselling author Cheryl, or else! ISBN 1-59493-027-9 $12.95

WICKED GOOD TIME by Diana Tremain Braund. 224 pp. Does Christina need Miki as a protector . . . or want her as a lover?   ISBN 1-59493-031-7 $12.95

THOSE WHO WAIT by Peggy J. Herring. 240 pp. Two brilliant sisters—in love with the same woman!   ISBN 1-59493-032-5 $12.95

ABBY'S PASSION by Jackie Calhoun. 240 pp. Abby's bipolar sister helps turn her world upside down, so she must decide what's most important.   ISBN 1-59493-014-7 $12.95

PICTURE PERFECT by Jane Vollbrecht. 240 pp. Kate is reintroduced to Casey, the daughter of an old friend. Can they withstand Kate's career?   ISBN 1-59493-015-5 $12.95

PAPERBACK ROMANCE by Karin Kallmaker. 240 pp. Carolyn falls for tall, dark and . . . female . . . in this classic lesbian romance.   ISBN 1-59493-033-3 $12.95

DAWN OF CHANGE by Gerri Hill. 240 pp. Susan ran away to find peace in remote Kings Canyon—then she met Shawn . . .   ISBN 1-59493-011-2 $12.95

DOWN THE RABBIT HOLE by Lynne Jamneck. 240 pp. Is a killer holding a grudge against FBI Agent Samantha Skellar?   ISBN 1-59493-012-0 $12.95

SEASONS OF THE HEART by Jackie Calhoun. 240 pp. Overwhelmed, Sara saw only one way out—leaving . . .   ISBN 1-59493-030-9 $12.95

TURNING THE TABLES by Jessica Thomas. 240 pp. The 2nd Alex Peres Mystery. *From ghosties and ghoulies and long leggity beasties* . . .   ISBN 1-59493-009-0 $12.95

FOR EVERY SEASON by Frankie Jones. 240 pp. Andi, who is investigating a 65-year-old murder, meets Janice, a charming district attorney . . .   ISBN 1-59493-010-4 $12.95

LOVE ON THE LINE by Laura DeHart Young. 240 pp. Kay leaves a younger woman behind to go on a mission to Alaska . . . will she regret it?   ISBN 1-59493-008-2 $12.95

UNDER THE SOUTHERN CROSS by Claire McNab. 200 pp. Lee, an American travel agent, goes down under and meets Australian Alex, and the sparks fly under the Southern Cross.   ISBN 1-59493-029-5 $12.95

SUGAR by Karin Kallmaker. 240 pp. Three women want sugar from Sugar, who can't make up her mind.   ISBN 1-59493-001-5 $12.95

FALL GUY by Claire McNab. 200 pp. 16th Detective Inspector Carol Ashton Mystery.   ISBN 1-59493-000-7 $12.95

ONE SUMMER NIGHT by Gerri Hill. 232 pp. Johanna swore to never fall in love again— but then she met the charming Kelly . . .   ISBN 1-59493-007-4 $12.95

TALK OF THE TOWN TOO by Saxon Bennett. 181 pp. Second in the series about wild and fun loving friends.   ISBN 1-931513-77-5 $12.95

LOVE SPEAKS HER NAME by Laura DeHart Young. 170 pp. Love and friendship, desire and intrigue, spark this exciting sequel to *Forever and the Night*.

ISBN 1-59493-002-3 $12.95